Lovers in the Demagogue's Shadow

BACHELOR BUTTON PUBLISHING

2538 N. 80th Street

Wauwatosa, WI 53213

www.bachelorbuttonpublishing.com

Copyright ©2022 by **Bob Young**

ISBN: 9798353841234

Names, characters, and incidents depicted in this book are products of the author's imagination or are used fictitiously. Any resemblance to actual events, locales, organizations, or persons, living or dead is entirely coincidental and beyond the intent of the author or publisher.

No part of this book may be reproduced or transmitted in any form or by any means, electronic or mechanical, including photocopying, recording, or by any information storage and retrieval system, without permission in writing from the publisher.

Credits:

Cover Design: James Robinson

Cover Artist: James Robinson

Cover Talent provided by Spotmatik through Dreamstime.com

"The persons in the cover images are models and there is no connection between the models and the characters in the book."

Printed in the United States of America

Dedication

"With three simple words: we, the people; we, the people… These two documents [the Declaration of Independence and the Constitution] and their ideas they embody – equality and democracy – are the rock upon which this nation is built. They are how we became the greatest nation on earth. They are why, for more than two centuries, America has been a beacon to the world."

President Joseph R. Biden, Jr.,

September 1, 2022

To Nathan, Will, Evy, Dean, and Sebastian, our grandchildren, who inspire us to leave them a better world by using our intellect and aging energies to do our bit for The Constitution.

Lovers in the Demagogue's Shadow

By
Bob Young

I was late for the start of the hearing. My saving grace was Owen Townsend, an emeritus attorney from Watkins and Townsend, another firm defending persons of interest before the House Un-American Activities Committee. He always saved me a seat about four rows from the witness chair. The room was packed and the cameras whirred, rolling film. Burl Ives was testifying before the committee that day in 1952.

As I mouthed my apologies slipping past half a row of onlookers, I flashed a big smile to Owen breathlessly sitting down. He reached over and squeezed my gloved hand as I exhaled.

"Hello, Ella," he whispered softly.

"Then no action upon such a request would have been taken by you?" a Republican investigator to the committee asked.

"No, sir. From 1944 or 1945 on, I was so busy that I practically had no time to sleep. And all of those things, the mail I got used to pile up in piles, and I wouldn't get to half of it, because it was all mixed with fan mail and requests for this, that, and the other," Ives offered in response.

"I ask you to comment upon the fact that in a leaflet of the Citizens Committee of the Upper West Side in 1946, your name was listed as a sponsor of this organization."

"This one has been a mystery to me. I had read it in the Red Channels book. Now I can give you some information on it. Mrs. Ives, my wife, went to a party, and it was there that there was some political candidate's party of some kind, and she gave a donation in my name, and that must be the answer to that, because the organization I do not know."

Owen and I would attend McCarthy's hearings noting the committee's strategy and grading the witnesses' performances. I could see enough of Mr. Ives' face to assess his discomfort. His well-trained voice was harder to read. In my first year practicing law, I was the least expensive attorney to be away from my desk to assess HUAC's strategy.

Our client was on the calendar to be gathered into their Communist net. While some young attorneys might grouse about such secretarial duty, I couldn't have been more excited to make the quick trip from my office to the Congressional Office Building.

"According to the New York Times of November 3, 1947, page 19, the name of Burl Ives was listed as a participant in the broadcast Hollywood Fights Back. This broadcast on November 2, 1947 was sponsored by the Committee for the First Amendment. Can you comment on that, if you please?"

"Yes, sir. I appeared on the second broadcast. I had heard the first broadcast, and there were so many names, a great many names which were obviously very good Americans, and not left wing, that I concluded that it would be a proper thing for me to do. And I did appear and, as a matter of fact, I read on the air part of a column written by Drew Pearson. That was my speech."

"In connection with the Committee for the First Amendment, are you aware that the California Committee on Un-American Activities, in its 1948 report, stated that the CFA is 'a recently created Communist front in the defense of Communists and Communist fellow travelers?' Its immediate purpose is to create favorable public opinion for the Communists who refuse to testify before the House Committee on Un-American Activities in Washington, D.C.?"

"No, sir; I am not aware of that, or was not."

"Were you aware of the implication or the possibility that the organization might have been a Communist front organization at the time of your affiliation with it?"

"No, sir; I did it because it seemed to me the proper thing other citizens of repute who were on the program, the first one as well as the second one. There seemed to be an attack on the film industry and writers and at that time it appeared to me that it was against a man's civil rights, this investigation, and I felt it was wrong."

"May I ask a question?" Investigator Connors asked. I observed Owen and his face was as grim as I felt. Owen Townsend was one of the original partners of his firm and had stepped back from most duties. But he was doing what I was charged with doing. The embarrassingly untried youngster and the obviously ancient septuagenarian willingly took on our important task. We kept an eye on the hearings because our clients would be before it soon. I only recently graduated from the law school at Howard University. "Do you re-call who indicated to you that it was against the civil rights of these people questioned before congressional committees?"

"Yes, I got that idea from the first broadcast." Ives replied.

"I know but what individuals convinced you that that was the proper action?" Connors pressed.

"I listened to the whole show. There must have been 20 people on it. That was my conclusion at the end," Ives responded.

"Mr. Ives," Connors continued, "did you have any independent conversations with people aside and apart from the broadcast in connection with that?"

"I went over to Don Bernard's home, and from there Peter and I went to some comedian's home, and there was a meeting there about it, and it was when they called up and asked me to appear on the program."

Ives makes a first amendment defense and in the next gives up Bernard, a friend, who discussed civil rights, constitutionally protected speech. This guy is liable to say anything, I thought. *I wondered how Dr. Edward Barsky, my client, would choose to present himself. He was a surgeon not used to performing verbally in front of large audiences. I was already practiced operating in court. I had been trained to perform dispassionately, to script out every possible encounter. Personally, I was not so bold.*

"Do you recall who called you and asked you?"

"I believe it was Norman Corwin's secretary."

"Speaking on behalf of Norman Corwin?"

"Yes. He directed the program."

"Where was this meeting?" Mr. Duffy interjected.

"It was at one of the very well-known comedians, but I don't know which one. I just remember it was one of those very well-known comedians, who was not a Communist at all. At the party, I would say, were not Communists, people like Bogart."

'Very well-known comedian but I don't know which one? C'mon. There was a murmur in the hearing room as Owen stifled a laugh. *What Mr. Ives' plan in this hearing? He was being, alternatively, evasive, and compliant. He seemed to be attempting to prevent as much reputational damage as he could. But this hearing was the lion's den.*

"Was Edward G. Robinson there?" Connors asked.

"I don't recall him being there."

"I state as a fact," Duffy asserted, "and ask you to confirm or deny that according to the Independent dated June of 1945, that you attended a Division Midwest meeting sponsored by the Independent Citizens Committee of the Arts, Sciences and Professions."

"Yes, this is true, at the Stevens Hotel. This was to pay tribute to the memory of the late President Franklin D. Roosevelt. It was the Independent Citizens Committee of Arts, Sciences and Professions. There were many people there. I know we had a picture taken, and I sang and they took up a collection. I remember that. That is about all I remember about it."

"Did you contribute to the collection?"

"Oh, I must have. Yes."

"What was the purpose of the collection?"

"I don't remember. This Arts and Sciences Committee at this time was also an organization that had a great number of people involved were not Communists, and it was, so far as I know, just a progressive organization, in the position slightly left of center."

"Did you know at the time that the Independent Citizens Committee of Arts, Sciences and Professions was the Communist-front organization that grew out of the Independent Voters Committee of the Arts and Sciences?"

"No; I didn't know that it was."

"Are you now aware of the fact that the ICCASP has been cited by governmental agencies as a subversive organization?"

"Yes, sir."

"I give to you as a fact and ask you to affirm or deny that on Sept.11, 1948, between the hours of 4 and 7p.m., Mr. and Mrs. Burl Ives of Van Nuys, CA., held a party at their home for the purpose of introduceing a congressional candidate, William B. Esterman, running on the Independent Progressive Party ticket. Invitations for the were distributed on behalf of the Independent Progressive Party. The entertainment at the meeting was to be furnished by Earl Robinson and John Howard Lawson, and the latter was to give a talk on civil rights, racial discrimination, and free speech. Earl Robinson, William B. Esterman, and John Howard Lawson have been identified as members of the Communist Party. Can you comment on this, Mr. Ives, if syou please?"

It was not surprising Esterman was mentioned. He publicly promised to prevent the House Un-American Activities Committee members' reelection even if it impoverished him.

"I remember that there had been a party at my house, but I was away at the time on a concert tour or something. According to my wife, two young fellows came and asked for some money for the Wallace campaign and she refused. They looked around and asked if they might not have a party and she said that she felt that she should do this, so they had a party for them. They asked her if our names could be used, and she said that she refused them permission, because we were not members of the Progressive Party. She didn't know who attended, and this is the first time, to this moment, that I have heard of the guests who appeared. I did know that Earl Robinson was there, but I didn't know of anybody else concerned, and I don't even know the names of that man who was running for something. So far as I am concerned, I knew nothing of this. I have to wash my hands of it. My wife says she was not at the party. This information that I have just now received from you, Mr. Duffy, I mean about those people that were there, these people who were there, I didn't know that."

"Very well," Duffy replied.

"That this party was held at my house, and the people who attended it, I was not aware of that at all. This probably accounts for an incident which occurred some time ago, where some publicity man, whose name I cannot tell you because I don't know it, told the girl who was doing the hiring at a club in Palm Springs, called the Chi Chi Club, and recommended that I not be hired there because he had attended a Communist meeting at my house in California. This made me very angry because I knew there had been no such meeting, and I thought, well, I'll just give the old boy a chance to prove this one, but I was persuaded not to do that, because the publicity in it would be more detrimental than to have the man just say it. At the time I had no idea of it. So, this clears that point up, of what this man meant. He must have been to this party. As a result of this, I didn't get the booking in Palm Springs, and I didn't get a booking in Las Vegas that I was slated for, because this man had made this statement to the girl and she was afraid to take the chance."

"According to the Daily Worker of March 1, 1942, it was reported that in connection with a photograph published of Burl Ives that Burl Ives would perform Monday evening at the Village Vanguard in a show and dance to aid the Emergency Joint Anti-Fascist Refugee Committee Fund. Do you have any comment to make on that?"

At the mention of Joint Anti-Fascist Refugee Committee, Owen and I lifted our heads. We both were defending clients with ties to this organization. It was a benevolent organization started by Dr. Edward K. Barsky and others assisting Spanish immigrants fleeing the fascist regime of Francisco Franco. Many of the supporters of JAFRC were surviving members of the Abraham Lincoln Brigade. This military unit was made up of Americans who volunteered to fight against the fascist insurgents in Spain backed by Germany and Italy from 1936 to 1939.

To pass the hours I sat in the hearing room, I would sketch the participants. My pad also was useful when Owen and I needed to communicate. In this moment, Owen took the pad and wrote:

'Ives performed at JAFRC benefits?'

'News to me.'

'What could he say?'

'Let's see.'

"Would you excuse me? What was the date of that, sir?"

"March 1, 1942."

"I was at this affair. I remember this thing."

"You are making reference to a program of this performance, Mr. Ives, that you are now holding in your hand?"

"Yes, sir. I have this in my scrapbook and brought it here. As a matter of fact, I brought all of the things that I could find in this regard, to present to you. I remember being at this party, I remember singing there."

"Were you aware at that time the Joint Anti-Fascist Refugee Committee was a well-known Communist-front organization engaged in collecting moneys which ultimately found their way into the coffers of the Communist Party in this country?"

"No, sir. I wasn't aware of that. To me it was another good cause, so-called. At that time we were engaged or about to be engaged, in a conflict with the Fascists, and anything that was anti-Fascist seemed like a proper thing to do, to be affiliated with."

I sometimes wondered how House Un-American Activities Committee members and staff could forget about Hitler and World War II as they sat in judgement.

"According to the Chicago Daily News dated April 17, 1945, Burl Ives, the ballad singer, then currently appearing on the stage in Chicago, was to be the guest artist at the Spanish Refugee Appeal Party for the Joint Anti-Fascist Refugee Committee to be held on April 21, 1945 in Chicago. Do you wish to comment on that, Mr. Ives?"

"Does it say where it was?"

"At 5012 Woodlawn Avenue, Chicago."

"I don't recall having been to this party; however, it is possible that I did, because I had entertained at such parties during that time. I don't recall it, however, it's a long time ago. I remember the name and that I did appear for them, but I cannot remember any specific place. It is very possible that I did appear there, too."

"Were these appearances at meetings sponsored by this organization made by you at any time with the knowledge that this organization was a notorious and well-known Communist-front organization?"

"No, sir. As a matter of fact, that term was not known to me at that time, and it was only later when the Attorney General published this list of Un-American organizations, that I realized that they were Communist-front organizations. Before that they were liberal, do-good organizations, so far as I was concerned."

"I put it to you as a fact, and ask you to affirm or deny that the Daily Worker on June 11, 1941 in connection with its report on the League of American Writers Fourth American Writers Congress stated that Burl Ives was included on the 'Poets, Songwriters and Folksingers Panel.' I ask you to comment on this in any regard you see fit."

'Whew. He made our case for us,' I wrote.

'Fascists are still bad, right? Hitler types?' Owen wrote smiling. I smiled back and wrote,

'The domestic versions, too, I suppose…'

'Whatever do you mean, child…'

I fought off a laugh. My business jacket, skirt, and blouse with string tie marked me as an attorney on the job as I entered the Senate Office Building that morning, but I ran into a Capitol Hill police officer who was a cracker. Usually, the Capital officers were so used to the diverse humanity trying to get time with senators and representatives, a Negro girl with a brief case got a pass. Not the guy I ran into. I was asked to produce my business card and a registration document from my firm indicating I could represent witnesses on Capitol Hill.

Born in Holly Springs, North Carolina, I knew the drill. There were almost a dozen daily reminders, though the allies had won World War II against nationalist oppression, the American brand of regional nationalism was alive and well. It wasn't lost on me Washington, D.C. was a southern city.

D.C. had its comfortable, bustling Negro community. Having done undergraduate and law school at Howard, I traversed Washington as comfortably as I had Holly Springs. My current world featured great restaurants, every kind of shop I needed and a lively jazz scene. My girlfriends and I socialized freely in the Anacostia section of D.C.

I had dated another Third Year at Howard but he relocated to L.A. after graduation. He invited me to come with him but I wanted to pursue the law where the framers created it. I surprised myself when I ended up grieving the loss of the old boyfriend. I charged forward with a heavy heart, suddenly alone after graduation. I was thrilled to be working for Cedric, Brown, & Jacobs but those bus rides home were frequently weepy missing my transplanted boyfriend.

I wasn't sure where I wanted to end up professionally but hanging out with Owen had planted the seed making partner and helping to run our firm someday was on my to do list.

My Aunt Flora, with whom I lived, had been coaxing me to date a businessman who belonged to our church who was a widower with two grade school children. He and his parents owned three highly successful grocery stores in our neighborhood. I was hesitant. Earnest was warm and gentle but an instant family, his fifteen years difference in age, and the likelihood he would pressure me to leave the law behind felt like negatives. Besides, Owen had been deftly sharing little stories about a guy named Marion Forman from his firm who had been defending a former Abe Lincoln Brigade officer. The Commonwealth of Pennsylvania had its own sedition act. Owen tried to tell the stories from the legal angle. But the only lawyer he talked about was the young, dashing Mr. Forman. When the conversation shifted this way, I gave Owen, my 'I ain't buying what you're sellin' face,' and he would chuckle and change the subject for a while.

"I have no recollection of this organization at all. Of this organization I don't know anything. I don't remember ever having contact with them. I know I have never been in their office or had anything to do with their internal machinery. I may have appeared someplace, because I was running around singing any place I could in those days, but in my mind, I have no recollection of any definite thing about the organization in regard to myself."

"This organization being the League of American Writers, which has been cited as Communist by the Attorney General?"

"Yes; and I have nothing in my mind that I can remember that has any connection with it."

"I put it to you as a fact, and ask you to affirm or deny, or comment on this fact, that according to the Daily Worker for October 19, 1948, an article entitled 'Five Hundred Leaders in the Arts and Sciences Back Wallace,' reflects that Burl Ives joined as an Independent in the support of the candidacy of Henry A. Wallace through a statement issued by the National Council of the Arts, Sciences and Professions."

"I don't recall having endorsed Mr. Wallace for President. However, I did appear at one party where a collection was taken up for the campaign, and that was in Hollywood. As far as signing anything for Wallace, I don't remember, but I don't want to say definitively that I did not, because personally, I had met Mr. Wallace, and I regarded him as a very honest man, though I don't believe he would have been a good President, and I think it was proper that he should not be elected. I think that he was a very honest man and I had a personal regard for him. I had been asked to sing for the Wallace convention and refused. I was also asked to sing for the Republican convention and refused. The Democrats didn't ask me. So, since I refused to go down to the convention, I am dubious if I did sign any statement for Wallace. However, as I said before, as a man I had a regard for him, and so I cannot really say, if I don't recall it. I could say who I voted for now, but I don't think that is proper, because I do think the ballot is a secret, one which we worked hard to get."

"Mr. Chairman, I respectfully suggest that this would be a good place to stop for lunch and then return at 1:30."

The chair gaveled a recess. Ives, surrounded by his counsel, hustled out a door on the side of the hearing room.

"Ella, we better get to a phone booth so you can call your office."

I gazed up into the worried face of the kind old gentleman. I quickly slipped into my gloves, stowed my notebook in my briefcase, taking as he guided me up the center aisle toward the exit. "My office is going to hear about those 'Joint Anti-Fascist Refugee Committee' questions."

"I should say so," Owen responded not only worried about my firm. Nelson, from the Abe Lincoln Brigade, was tied into JAFRC, too.

"Owen," a voice called out from behind us. We stopped and I found a handsome young man only a little bit older than me.

"Marion, how much of the testimony did you hear?" Owen asked the fellow whose eyes, I noticed, were focused on me and not on the senior partner of his firm.

"None. I managed to get here from Harrisburg the moment they took the recess."

"Ella, this is Marion Forman, the guy I was telling you about on the Nelson case. Marion, this is Ella Moses from Cedric, Brown, and Jacobs."

"A pleasure, Miss Moses," Mr. Forman told me as I headed toward the hearing room doors, obliging the crush of people rushing to get lunch and   call in their stories, too.

"I want to hear all about Nelson's sedition case," I almost shouted over my shoulder to be heard above the tumult. Most of the people in the aisle had no courtesy for three Negroes in suits. I used my brief case as a persuader gently but firmly edging us to the doors and the wide corridors of the office building. Owen was correct. Forman was a good-looking man. Maybe Owen knew what he was doing, after all.

"You two can talk about Nelson another time," Owen suggested. "Ella has to call in where the committee was going in the questioning of Ives and we've got to throw down a sandwich and coke, find a rest room, and get back here by 1:30."

We shut up and concentrated on exiting the Senate Office Building out-numbered by the white men and women who would not appreciate our earnestness, if they noticed us. Finally, having gotten outside into the sunshine with space to walk side by side toward Owen's and my favorite lunch counter, we filled in Marion.

"They acted like Ives had played benefit concerts for every known Communist in the country," I told him sounding frustrated.

"More importantly, Marion, he did concerts and parties for the Joint Anti-Fascist Refugee Committee," Owen commented to make it more specific.

"Shit," the young man reacted.

"Yes. Pretty bad," I reacted sweating into my best blouse in the warm spring D.C. afternoon. The three of us were silent until I crashed into the phone booth on the sidewalk outside the diner. I plugged a dime into the pay phone while the men stood at the window which served Negroes. Owen and I never were allowed inside the place. They made ham and cheese sandwiches for us and sold us cold bottles of coke which we had the honor of opening on a bottle opener screwed into the framing of the counter. I gave my office girl the gist of the morning's hearing and she promised to put the typed notes on Edgar Brown's desk. He was out playing golf with a client on a public course. When I finished my call, I walked for the park bench nearby where Owen and I always sat. Mercifully, there was shade, a breeze, and no competition for the seating.

"I was worried about Ives cracking there for a while but his last answer seemed to show resolve on his part," Owen offered hoping to cheer me up.

I couldn't manage to assess how much damage Burl had done to himself and the refugee group. Instead, I decided to change the subject. "What's the latest on the Pennsylvania case against Steve Nelson?" I took a bite of the sandwich Owen had bought me, taking my second good assessment of Mr. Forman. *This guy must have a girlfriend,* I couldn't help but think.

"We're securing an attorney who can plead before the Supreme Court."

"You're going to appeal?"

"The Commonwealth's sedition law is unconstitutional," Marion suggested with a warm smile. I noticed but pretended not too, as I caught an approving smile on Owen's face.

"Owen, no one in your firm can plead?"

"Not yet. We're working on it. But the people who pay the bills want to get Pennsylvania's boot off Steve's neck sooner than later."

"It's an issue to find a lawyer who will take the case for a Negro firm?"

"Not necessarily, but you've noticed only we will take these HUAC cases in the first place," Marion responded seemingly happy about it with a smile remaining on his face. *Was his smile about Black firms stepping up or was his smile for me?* I asked myself finally calming down enough to take a lingering impression of him. *I noticed it was a perfect face.*

After taking a breath I asserted, "I want to know the name of this lion tamer."

"Time to walk back, you two," Owen suggested, preferring to return to the hearing room in a leisurely way ahead of the herd. As we walked, I nursed the end of my coke noticing Marion was on my right and Owen was on my left. When we sat down in the hearing room, we sat as we walked. I didn't get all the detail about the Pennsylvania case I wanted. I wondered if Marion would be guarded about the defense they presented.

The hearing resumed and I decided to sketch Mr. Connors, one of the three investigators supporting the committee. As I started, Marion gave me a smirk. I had yet to learn Marion was an artist. I paged back through my sketch book to show him I had been working on illustrations all morning. He also noticed Owen and my notes to each other. His initial confusion gave way to a smile of acknowledgement. *I noticed I was smiling at him and swiveled my head transitioning to a serious, studious expression while managing those telltale, initial sensations of attraction to him.*

"Mr. Ives, were you at one time on the board of sponsors of the Peoples' Songs, Inc.?"

"Yes, I was."

"Did you know that the Peoples' Songs was cited as a Communist front by the California Committee on Un-American Activities?"

"No, sir, not at the time. As a matter of fact, I supported this organization that much by the fact that it was an organization interested in folk music, and during the war they did several songs which were for the winning of the war. As a matter of fact, I remember there is only one of them that I learned, but I did it on the air once. I think to put the words in might be good, so I will sing it for you."

Our heads popped up and there was a minor murmur in the hearing room as Ives sang for us. Mr. Connors kept his composure and dove right back into his line of questioning.

"Mr. Ives, do you recall who solicited your sponsorship of the Peoples' Songs, Inc.?"

"As a matter of fact, I don't remember the occasion, or even what I did, or if I signed anything to sponsor it, but whether I did or not, because of the folk music and the things they were doing at the time, I agreed and would have, and at least my heart was for it. The only person that I knew up there, or was acquainted with, was Pete Seeger, so it must have been he because I didn't know anybody else."

He gave up Pete Seeger right there, I wrote showing my note to Owen. His nod indicated agreement. He wrote,

Seeger hasn't been shy about his political views.

Marion tried take a turn on the sketch pad, gently grasping my hand which was holding it. I gave him the flattest expression on my face to signal him the touch was too much. His warm expression never changed but the touch ended and he wrote, *Ives didn't call Seeger a Communist.* Taking the pad back, I answered.

He shared Pete Seeger introduced him to an organization McCarthy thinks is Communist.

Ives never used the word Communist, Marion asserted.

The exchange sounded scripted.

It was a casual comment.

Ives is casual with Investigator Connors. That's my point, I challenged him.

Ives has deniability.

Watch how the newspapers write that moment and what his folk singing colleagues say when he goes back to touring the nation again, I reacted with a smile for him.

Marion and I continued jousting rhetorically for a while until the testimony interested us again.

"The Daily Peoples World, which is a west coast Communist newspaper, in its edition of April 12, 1947, indicated that Burl Ives and other national figures were listed on the program of the Save the United Nations rally to be held in the Shrine Auditorium on April 18,1947. Would you please comment on that?"

"I have never, to my knowledge, appeared at the Shrine Auditorium for anything, so that I can say that I was not there, and I do not know anything about this rally or its purpose. This is the first I have heard of it, when Mr. Connors has mentioned it."

"Then, can you categorically state, Mr. Ives," Connors asked, "that you did not lend your name to the Save the United Nations rally?"

"No, sir; I did not lend my name to that."

"Were you present, or do you recall being present in New York City on December 12, 1946, at a dinner at the Waldorf-Astoria Hotel, which dinner was sponsored by the Southern Conference for Human Welfare?"

"No, sir; I don't recall anything."

"To the best of your knowledge and recollection, were you in 1949 or 1950, or any time prior to that, a member of the Advisory Council of the Stage for Action?"

"No, I have never seen the Stage for Action. As a matter of fact, I don't know what they have done. I never have been at any of their meetings."

"Are you aware of the fact that Red Channels indicates that you were a member of the advisory council, and a sponsor of Stage for Action?"

"I did read it there, but I didn't recall any connection with it."

"Then your answer is that you had no connection with the Stage for Action?"

"No, I have not had any contact with them. I wouldn't have any idea who headed it or what it does, or anything because I have never seen their production or had any kind of talk about them in any way with anybody."

"The Communist organ, New Masses, in its edition of May 20, 1941, listed the name of Burl Ives as one of the sponsors and participants in a testimonial given by the United American Artists, which testimonial on May 17, 1941, at 135 West Seventieth Street, New York City. Do you have any recollection of that affair, Mr. Ives?"

"I remember going to some dinner. I was not at the dinner, but I remember I ran in and sang a song at some kind of a dinner, but I don't know if that was it or not. It is possible that I did appear there. At this particular dinner I went to, I remember the Almanac Singers were there, and I ran in and sang a song, and as I performed, I remember they joined in on the chorus and that made me angry."

"Have you any recollection of sponsoring or attending a bon voyage party program by the United American Spanish Aid Committee on February 20, 1941?"

"In 1941, I don't recall, but it is possible that I did, because at that time I would have done such. So I don't know, but it is quite possible."

"The New York Times for March 3, 1945, carried an advertisement entitled "For America's sake: Break With Franco Spain," which advertisement was published by Veterans of the Abraham Lincoln

Brigade, and the name Burl Ives was listed as a sponsor of that particular advertisement. Do you recall that incident?"

"No, sir."

Owen silently asked for the sketch pad.

The heat is on.

I'll say.

Marion faced me but didn't write a reaction.

"Do you recall having any affiliation whatever with the Veterans of the Abraham Lincoln Brigade?"

"Yes, before that, back in, I don't know, about in 1938 or 1939, I did appear for an organization called Friends of the Abraham Lincoln Brigade, and as a matter of fact, they paid me, as those were professional jobs and I went out and would get paid $5 or $10. I made part of my living that way. But I did appear for the Friends of the Abraham Lincoln Brigade, it was called."

"Let me ask you at that point, if you appeared on January 19, 1947, at the Belasco Theater in New York City on behalf of the Veterans of the Abraham Lincoln Brigade?"

"On January 19? No, sir; that would have been impossible. At that time I was working in the Chicago Theater in Chicago, Ill. As a matter of fact, I opened there on the 25th of December, 1946, and I did six shows a day there until February, well, I was there 32 days."

"So that on January 19, 1947, you were in Chicago, playing at a theatre in Chicago?"

"Yes, sir. I couldn't have been there."

"Mr. Ives, the subcommittee has no further questions as such at this time, but we would like to give you an opportunity to put into the record any statement or any documentary material that you might like to give us."

"Mr. Connors, now if you have a little time to spare, I would like to bring up two further points in this discussion."

"Take as much time as you wish."

"There are a couple of things I would like to clear up. At the Passport Division in the United States Passport Department, they told my wife in April 1952, that there were two accusations against me signed by some people. The first one was that during 1943 and 1944 that I gave $250 each week to the Communist Party. I want to go on the record as saying that this is absolutely untrue. The second point is that somebody has also signed a statement that I am a member of the Communist Party; three people have. I want to say that this is also not true. I am not a member of the Communist Party. The only affiliation that I have had with communism was back in the spring of 1944; I went to some open meetings, discussion meetings of an organization called the Communist Political Association. I did not go as a Communist, I went to find out what I could about communism, to see if it made any sense to me. I cannot give you exact dates on those, I can only tell you this; that I went for a few of those meetings over a period of time, and rejected this idea, and it has never come back into my mind, the possibility of being a Communist, because I am against that philosophy."

"I first talked to an old friend of mine. I am very sorry that I have to bring up names in this matter, because I would like to be able to not mention other names, but I can't. I will have to do it, because these people will have to do as I have done, and many others. They will have to make up their minds on this matter. So, in my heart, I have to mention these names, although a couple of them are very good friends of mine. It was through a talk I had with Mr. Richard Dyer-Bennett. He had just started into those lectures himself, and it was through him that I went there. I can also say that I had a conversation with him a few years back, and we had both come to the same conclusion, and he also rejected it and didn't go back any more after, I think he told me it was 1945 or 1944, something like that. He went at the same time that I did, and we were really going to find out what this was about. From what I could gather on it, I didn't like it. After a time I went no more and rejected the idea, and that is that."

All three of us wanted the pen. Marion was first.

In his apology preface and supposed conversation about rejecting communism, Ives gave up Dyer-Bennett.

I quickly wrote, *Clearly.* Passing the pad to Owen, he reacted:

That's the end of a friendship.

"Do you recall where some of the meetings were held?"

"Yes, sir; some of them were at Steinway Hall."

"Steinway Hall in New York City?"

"Yes."

"And the other meetings?"

"Well, I didn't like this one, so I said 'Well, this is not for me.' So they said, 'Well, wait a minute, there is a music group of musicians, and that will be more your stuff,' so I went over there a couple of times, and that was no good. Then they sent me to another study group, it was some kind of art club. Before that they gave me the name of this school which I went down to one time – to which, as a matter of fact, my wife with me. She wanted to see what it was about, so we went down there to one class."

"Was that the Jefferson School?"

"That is the Jefferson School, and I went there for one class and said – I was very bored, to tell the truth."

Mr. Earl asked, "Where was the class held that the Musicians' Group attended."

"That, I can't remember. I think it was some hall some place."

"Did you ever attend any of these meetings in the home of any person?" Mr. Connors followed up.

"No, sir."

"Do you recall approximately or exactly how many such meetings you did attend?"

"No, sir, but it couldn't have been more than seven altogether."

"Did you pay any dues at any of these meetings?"

"No, sir. I remember once they took up a collection for something."

"Were you ever issued a card by any official at any of these meetings?"

"I don't remember. Let's see, now, I believe I was given some kind of an entrance card."

"Do you recall whether or not you were issued a membership card in the Communist Political Association?"

"I don't know, but I may have been. I may have been issued a card, because I remember I had something that got me in."

"Mr. Ives, do you recall who else, with the exception of Richard Dyer-Bennet, was present at those meetings?"

"Let me see. The last one that I went to, I went there with my publicity man at the time, who was Mr. Allen Meltzer. He was present then. I am very sorry to use his name, but he will have an opportunity to say his say."

Marion asked for the pad. He wrote,

That's three names today. Heaven knows how many names he gave up in the pre-interview.

Wouldn't they want Ives to name everyone on the record? I asked.

Not always. Now and then they like to call in suspects without tipping their hand. It's clear they surprised Ives a couple of times.

"Is Mr. Meltzer a Communist, to the best of your knowledge?"

"Well, he was there, and I assume that he was affiliated."

"Do you have any evidence of his present political persuasions?"

"As a matter of fact, I haven't seen him in 3 or 4 years, I have not seen him."

"He is no longer associated with you professionally?"

"No, sir; we made a change, and I have not seen him for a very long time."

"Can you recall anyone else who was present at those meetings?"

"No. This was the last thing that they sent me to. There were some familiar faces there, but I cannot think of another name. But at one of the other I can. At the music thing there was a pianist, Ray Lev, she was there. At the music thing there was a boy by the name of Herb Kay, he is a conductor. And those are the only ones I can remember. The rest of them were strangers."

"After you ceased going to the meetings of the Communist Political Association, immediately after you ceased going to them, were you solicited to return and continue your attendance by any person?"

"I got telephone calls saying there would be meetings, or they would send pieces of paper or letters, but I just didn't go any more."

"To the best of your knowledge and recollection, would it appear to you a fair statement of the facts to say that this particular chapter or group or club of the Communist Political Association might have considered for record purposes that you were a member of that particular club?"

"I don't think so, because my position was one of – I wanted to learn. I wanted to check and see if this fitted my bill. So, as a matter of fact, on my last occasion there something happened which probably ended the deal. They wanted me to go out and pass out handbills about something, and I said, 'No,' and I was talking to some girl there, and I said, 'Well, I haven't made up my mind myself on this matter,' and from the look I got I was quite certain I was in the wrong pew. So that was really the end of my association."

"So that if any Communist Political Association records show you as a member, you would say that this was based upon an assumption on the part of the officials of the club making up the record?"

"Yes. My idea was that I wanted to find out, I wanted to hear a clear, concise speech or understanding of what this was about, because there was so much talk bandied about in the night clubs and in drawing rooms, and all that sort of thing, that it was a confusing thing, and I wanted to hear a clear picture of it, to see if this was something I could go with or not. And as a matter of fact, I never did hear it, all I heard was a bunch of nothing. So I finally decided that I was going to find out some other way."

"Do you recall the name of any of the persons who addressed those meetings who were more or less instructors there?"

"Let me see, I remember one of those meetings where they had a book review of a book about Thaddeus Stevens, and some lady gave the speech, but I cannot remember her name. I think she wrote the book but I am not sure. She may have."

"Were any of the speakers or instructors introduced as functionaries or officials of the Communist Political Association?"

"No, I don't recall that they were. At the meetings there was really no talk of Russia or communism. It was sort of a win-the-war tack that they took, and it was strictly American. As a matter of fact, they never did get around to any kind of talk on communism. I guess that is why they had me down to the school. So my wife finally said, 'Listen, if you want to learn about communism, go and get a book and we will read it together because, the goings on in the world have pretty well cleared up any kind of question as to what it is, in, I think, everybody's mind.'"

"Then, since 1944, or approximately that time, you have attended no meetings of the CPA or the CP?"

"No, I had nothing to do with them. I don't know exactly what the date was when I was last there, I cannot say, but whatever it was, it was the last one and have had nothing to do with it and certainly would not."

Mr. Connors and Mr. Ives talked about his concert schedule which was put into evidence and letters of thanks sent to Ives for benefit concerts he had performed for various non-Communist causes. Before the committee was gaveled into recess, Ives made this final statement.

"Before the committee adjourns, I would like to say one thing: that it is human to err. I made some mistakes, and I want to thank this committee for the very fair and democratic way in which you have heard my story. I believe that in no Communist country would such a hearing be possible at all."

Mr. Connors responded by saying thank you. As Chairman McCarran gaveled the hearing to an end, a distinct mix of reactions from the gallery could be heard. Polite applause, hoots of celebration, growls of consternation, and angry shouts were directed at Mr. Ives. Congressional staffers guided Ives and his entourage out of the hearing room through a side door.

We stood up taking in the observers' mixed reactions. Our clients would appear before the committee soon and they faced grim life choices.

Chapter 2

"Let's catch the bus to Reggie's, and have a Sloe gin fizz, and talk about how to advise our client," Marion suggested.

"As much as I would love to get you talking about your sedition defense, I have to catch up at the office for a few more hours," I lamented, giving Marion my first intentional smile of the day.

"Give me your number. Friday night?" he hurried to ask as I took my first strides toward my bus stop.

"Cedric, Brown, and Jacobs. We're in the book," I teased him. I could have given him the number for the lobby of my apartment building, but I didn't want my landlord knowing my business or have Marion hear the background noise of the hallway. Owen was standing in the aisle of the hearing room smiling conspiratorially. I slowed my exit enough to throw him my 'you're hopeless' glare. I heard his booming laugh behind me as I threaded my way through the score of conversations which had broken out.

I had to admit to myself as I exited the House Office Building, I would be disappointed if Marion didn't call me at the office. But Friday night was girls' night. Marion would have to risk doing-the-dozens with my friends. I preferred to get to know Owen's fix-up with three or four friends checking him out, too. My Friday night group was a mix of teachers, businesswomen, and nurses, all professionals. None of them would be cowed by smooth-talking Marion Forman.

As the city bus took me closer to my office, I scribbled some notes about the new exposure Dr. Barsky and his associates had suffered in Burl Ives' deposition. He would come off the Blacklist and his career would have new life but the good doctor would face losing his medical career. The pressure from the House Un-American Activities Committee and the subsequent risk of losing patients, benefactors of the hospital he served, and sanctions that might keep him from easing the misery of patients loomed large.

Walking into our office building, I took the elevator to the third floor where the staff attorneys officed. I shared a large room with another newly minted attorney and two typists. It was a noisier setting than I would have wanted, but the four of us got along. When I needed to think, I hid in our   law library which I often had to myself. The offices had been built at the   turn of the century. The appointments were rich but dated. The firm did   well but intentionally avoided modernizing choosing a classical decor over any updated touches.

"Ella," the familiar voice of Mr. Cedric called from my office doorway.

I interrupted writing the notes I was finishing.

"Yes, sir?"

"I know you haven't finished the HUAC notes but Mr. Brown and I are leaving early for a client dinner. Could you come upstairs?"

"Of course, sir."

I carried the notes in my steno book and he walked toward the law library where a wrought – iron circular stairway rose into the offices of the partners. Since the previous summer when I was hired, I had been on the partner floor frequently but sitting in a meeting with two-thirds of the named partners was rare.

"Sit down, Ella."

Mr. Cedric pointed to a leather side chair opposite his desk. Mr. Brown was seated in a chair to the side of the desk.

"Hello, Ella."

"Good afternoon, Mr. Brown."

"Ella, the phones have been ringing off the hook since Mr. Ives finished his testimony. He didn't do us and our client any favors."

"We hear he put on an impromptu folk music concert," Mr. Brown announced with feigned disappointment.

"It wasn't one of my grandmother's songs," I quipped sarcastically.

The two septuagenarians roared.

I regained my composure hoping I hadn't overstepped.

"I take it, Mr. Ives' benefit concerts over the years for the Veterans of the Abe Lincoln Brigade were a feature of the investigators' attacks."

"The Abe Lincoln Brigade was one issue. A variety of other music organizations and several other groups involved his name."

"And Dr. Barsky's charitable organization?"

"Mr. Ives has ties to it, too."

"We thought Dr. Barsky might get called. His fund-raising success is a big beacon," Mr. Cedric shared.

"You'd think they would use Ives to set up other musicians and actors. But they used him to set up Dr. Barsky," Mr. Brown worried.

"He gave up four musicians and his agent. Seems meager but you think they were setting the stage to call in Dr. Barsky?"

"Ives was small potatoes really. Dr. Barsky created a mobile battlefield hospital for the Loyalist army and international volunteers in the Spanish Civil War," Mr. Cedric explained.

"He returned from Spain and established the refugee support organization, the Joint Anti-Fascist Refugee Committee. Consider how many donors it takes to raise $400,000," Mr. Brown suggested.

"Not to mention the many people the fund raising supported. Senator McCarthy and company would love to tar every one of those people as Communists."

I was stunned at the damage the House Un-American Activities Committee could inflict on all those people. "Will Dr. Barsky be a better witness than Burl Ives?"

"We don't know, Ella," Mr. Cedric shared.

"Anything else today, Ella?"

"Yes. Watkins and Townsend is trying to hire a white lawyer with Supreme Court experience for the Nelson sedition case."

"Owen mentioned the plan to find a SCOTUS veteran to you?"

"No. A young attorney named Marion Forman from Owen's firm was on the case up in Pennsylvania and attended today's HUAC hearing, too."

"They're hoping to send up the Commonwealth's Sedition Law for review?"

"Yes. The firm doesn't have someone to present."

"Let's see who they find. We might have some work for them, too, someday," Mr. Brown suggested with a smile.

"Thanks, Ella. Good work today," Mr. Cedric shared in a tone letting me know the meeting was over. I got up to go. "Oh, and say hello from us to Owen."

"I will, sir."

I left the well-appointed office, walls covered in photos of prominent clients, politicians, and awards. I walked downstairs through the law library heading back to finish more work before I could go home, but I was buoyed having contributed to the partners. It was a few minutes before six when I walked out onto the sidewalk waiting for my bus uptown. It was still warm but the shade from my building kept me cool supported by a little breeze. Thanks to streets choked with cars and trucks, the bus ride home was warm despite all the open windows. I usually held my jacket on my lap, the bus never moving for long to bathe passengers with any relief. I was carefree at this point in the day. No one of note would catch me bedraggled with curls pasted to my temples by sweat. That didn't mean equally damp young day laborers didn't try to chat me up during the two-mile ride and the four block walk home to auntie's place.

The opening verbal gambit started a variety of ways. 'Baby, you need cheering up…,' or 'Hun, let me carry your bag for you…,' or 'Your man ain't boostn' you, Sweetie…,' or 'Take me home with you, girl…,' to which my list of replies were, 'I change enough diapers as it is…,' or 'Does your momma know where you are?' or 'My boyfriend is a cop,' or 'I've got polio (cough-cough),' while I never lost stride. As I got closer to home, real friends were checking to make sure I was okay.

Ned, at the barbershop, saw me through his window and waved. Maxie, checking his fruit piled outside his store, handed me an apple, and Lena at the salon spritzed my face from a water bottle lamenting my wilted fatigue.

I walked up the stoop of my building inside to the lobby climbing two flights letting myself into Auntie's apartment with my key. I dropped my briefcase and jacket on a table inside the door, loosening my string tie and walked into the kitchen to help finish dinner. Uncle Ray was seated, polishing off a piece of buttered bread.

"Hi, El,'" he mumbled, mouth full.

"Hi, Unc," I replied continuing on.

"Ella. Right on time. Can you mash those spuds for me?"

"Certainly," I replied, opening a drawer where the ricer was stored. My aunt was a nurse's assistant at Sibley Memorial, working third shift. She made dinner, slept for a couple of hours, and caught a bus to start work at 11p.m. Unc was a bricklayer working that trade all his life. D.C. in the fifties was always tearing down something and putting up new buildings in their place. Between the three of us, we were comfortable enough financially. Unc and Aunt Flora didn't ask for my whole salary. They knew I had to dress professionally every day and I was out at least one night a week with my friends.

I added a little butter and milk to the pulverized potatoes and stirred them vigorously until the mass in the bowl was whipped. One more pad of butter got added on top and it slowly melted.

"Can you glaze those carrots?"

"Yesum," I responded starting to relax into the comfortable confines of my home away from home.

My mother was a farmworker back in Holly Springs, preferring the North Carolina countryside, fresh air, and sun in her face over city life. She could take a bus from Raleigh if she wanted to see me. My father had gone west when I was twelve settling in Las Vegas working as a maintenance man in a casino. Letters from him tended to arrive around my March 20 birthday always including a five-dollar bill. I prayed he could really afford to be so generous.

We ate talking all the while about Unc and Floras' family and the latest news. Unc was one of five siblings and Aunt Flora was one of seven. There was always something new. It was comforting to me, separated from my mother down in North Carolina. I was grateful for the stories. They filled up my life with laughter and the love that always sprung up, knowing more about cousins by the hundreds. The high point of the year was the Winters Family Reunion each August in Staunton, Virginia where the accumulated family stories would come to life in the face to face get together.

Aunt Flora always interrogated me about the existence of 'my young man.' She didn't ask me every night, mercifully, but usually Saturday morning when I emerged from my one sleep-in day, it was the topic of conversation after my previous night out with the girls. Nine months after joining my firm, there was no man of record.

After supper, I washed out some things, hanging them out to dry on a line we shared with a neighbor outside the window of my room over a walkway between buildings.

The rest of my evening was spent sitting in the parlor reading something other than the law with my uncle's radio programs playing in the background. My aunt, having napped was going out the door to catch her bus as I slipped into bed.

Going to work the next day featured no propositions on the way to the bus because the neighborhood suiters were due at work much earlier than I or because they were sleeping off an over-indulgence of some kind. A springtime thunderstorm had provided a cool start to the day. Everyone on the bus seemed delighted if, as always, silent. Four older gents had found a way to rig a small table and were playing pinochle providing the only noise on the ride.

I got off at my stop, crossed to my building and took a quick elevator ride to my floor exchanging greetings with the operator. A little after ten a.m. the phone rang in our shared office and one of the typists chirped, "El,' it's for you."

"Hello," I answered wondering if there might be a development in Dr. Barksky's case.

"Ella, it's Marion Forman. How are you doing?"

"Mr. Forman, yes, the two typists, my colleague Attorney Fellows, and I are quite busy," I replied letting him know my situation while managing an excited sensation in my chest such a good-looking guy was calling me back.

"Oh, you're not alone. I see. I wanted to buy you dinner so we could talk about the Supreme Court."

"We don't get much time to discuss Supreme Court cases. Mostly wills and trust work gets done in our little group."

"Wills and trusts are always fascinating. How about Friday night?"

"A group of colleagues have something on the calendar."

"I'd like to join you. Your friends will love me. They'll think I'm perfect for you."

"If you're sure you won't be bored at such a meeting," needing to test his interest before I let the possibilities of this new man become more real.

"Not if you're there. Where will you be?"

"There's a law firm at Good Hope and 13th."

"I've never typed a letter to that address," one of the typists commented.

"Me either," the second one confirmed.

I glanced at Janice Fellows, her eyebrows raised in happy acknowledgement. Janice knew what kind of 'law firm' was at Good Hope and 13th. Janice often met me there and would again this Friday.

"Do you mean 'Jellie's Crab House?'" Marion asked with a laugh.

"That's the place."

"I'd take you somewhere nicer."

"Maybe someday."

"I have to run the girlfriend gauntlet?"

"Seems so."

"I'll see you Friday night at Jellie's."

"Thanks for letting me know."

"Bye."

"Bye."

I hung up the phone and returned to my desk.

A minute later, Janice was standing next to me. She was smiling, 'What?" She asked expectantly. I pointed to the hallway and got up to lead her out of the office. "Who was that?" she asked.

"Have you ever heard of a lawyer at Watkins & Townsend by the name of Marion Forman?"

"No. He's new to me."

"I met him today at HUAC. He's been working on the Nelson sedition case."

"He asked you out to dinner?"

"Yes, but I'm having him come to Jellie's so you can assess him."

"He'll have to be with us, too?"

"Yes. You get a vote on whether he's good for me."

"What fun. No holds barred?"

"Let's see what he's made of."

We dug back into work. When my day was over, I did my same routine home. The guys trying to pick me up were out there again. One of them, taking a new tack, didn't lay a line on me but played bodyguard driving the mashers off. We got to my stoop.

"My name's William. My friends call me Bulldog."

I took in his boyish face, earnestly trying not to intimidate me with his 6' 2," 350-pound frame. A sense of calm enveloped me.

"William, you're a nice boy. Thanks for walking me home. I'm Ella."

"Goodnight, Ella."

As I entered our tenement he stayed, dutifully, and he was gone.

Later, when I was reading in the parlor with Unc. I wondered how different William and Marion really were. I was only one generation away from being a sharecropper. Could William be an attorney? What disaster had Marion dodged to get his JD? Being Negro was the beginning and the end of my thought process.

~*~

The work week proceeded. The cases were relentless, my routine didn't change. William was there as soon as I stepped off the bus. He walked a step behind me and swept the catcallers out of my way. Friday afternoon, he followed me up the stoop to the front door of the building.

"What do you do at work?"

Standing there right in front of me, I sensed an earthy, not unpleasant fragrance from a body in the sun all day.

"I'm a lawyer."

"Nah. That can't be right"

"Why not?"

He took a deep breath. He thought about it. "The kind keeping me out of jail?"

"Yes. The kind keeping you out of jail."

"You'd work for me?"

"Of course." I opened my briefcase and grabbed one of my cards. Here's my phone number at work."

"Ella Moses, Cedric, Brown & Jacobs."

"That's right."

"Thank you, Ella."

"You're welcome, William."

I walked into the apartment, hung up my suit jacket, put my tie on the dresser, and helped Aunt Flora with dinner and left for a bus getting me near Jellie's. When I got there, half my friends were already on their first drink at the bar. When everyone else arrived, we would go to a table and have boiled crabs. We were masters at cracking the shell and picking all the luscious meat from within it. Jellie's seasoned their boil perfectly.

I walked up to the rollicking conversation.

"Ella, is this guy worth ruining our Friday night?"

"We'll see. I met him Tuesday," I replied trying not to betray any inkling of interest.

"He's an attorney at your firm?"

"No…at another firm defending clients in front of McCarthy."

"Is he smooth?"

"More of a buck, I think."

"God's gift to woman-kind?"

"It's the impression I've gotten from him. I was curious what he would do with you all."

"Will he show up?"

I didn't get to answer. The last three girls walked in and our normal Friday night conversation ensued. Marion faded from my mind. I had received my second Rum Runner when suddenly, he was next to me. I studied his face and gave him a smile and he became animated shifting from faking inward cool in a bizarre situation to his usual at-home calm.

"Is this Attorney Forman?" Janice asked noticing him. The heads of all the rest of the girls assessed him thanks to her question.

"Janice, this is Marion Forman," I replied. "Janice is an attorney at my shop."

"Ah, happy to meet you, Janice."

"Millie, this is Marion. Millie teaches high school English."

"A pleasure, Millie,"

"Marion," Millie acknowledged lifting her daiquiri slightly.

"This is Joyce. She's an RN in an M.D.'s office."

"Joyce…"

"Mr. Forman, nice to meet you."

"Gloria, meet Attorney Forman."

"Hello, Gloria."

"Marion, what makes you think you can crash our Friday night?" Gloria teased him sarcastically.

"One moment, Gloria," I interrupted laughing. "Gloria," I explained to Marion, "is a partner with another one of her friends who run three beauty parlors in Anacostia."

"Enterprising," he replied smiling. A verbal scuffle had begun.

"This is Martha. She is an emergency room nurse."

"Welcome to our weekly crab boil, Marion," Martha offered with anticipation.

"Thanks."

"You didn't know you were going to be in the pot tonight, did you?" Gloria chided with a smile. The girls laughed. Marion's smile in return was sly like he knew something none of the rest of us did.

"When Ella invited me out with you all, it seemed a great way to know her better." He stood there with his drink trying to appear like he owned the place.

"We'll let you know if you are going to get to know her," Joyce teased with a warm smile.

"Where did you go to school?" Janice asked.

"North Carolina University and their law school," Marion shared.

"North Carolina, Ella," Martha noted.

"North Carolina is special?" Marion asked.

"I'm from Holly Springs," Ella answered softly.

"Oh, I'm from Graham."

"Really?"

"Is this old home week?" Gloria protested. "What makes you think you are good enough for our girl?"

"I have a good job and I'm gorgeous," Marion ventured gamely trying to weather the interrogation.

The girls oohed and laughed.

"All well and good but maybe you're also used to beating on your girls," Gloria countered.

"After all, you're kind of a big shot in this community. Are you likely to throw your prestige around?" Janice challenged him doubling down.

"I'm an officer of the court. In my line of work, it's attorney rule number one not to get arrested." The girls laughed. "Ella's a colleague. I have a lot of respect for her abilities," Marion replied calmly.

"No priors, then?" I teased.

"No arrests, no indictments, no convictions," he responded with a little smile and a lilt of amusement in his voice.

"Gonna buy us dinner tonight, Big Shot?" Millie harassed him further.

"Not all of you," he protested in jest. "But I will pay for Ella's dinner and drinks."

"It's not the answer I was hoping for, but it will do," Joyce begrudgingly replied breaking into a smile as the girls laughed.

Two waitresses carried the crab dinners to a large table nearby and we each claimed a plate, Marion sticking close to me. It was good he did, since he had never cracked a crab open before. He poked at it to make sure it was thoroughly cooked causing all the rest of us to roar with laughter.

"You need to help me with this," he quietly advised me. Expertly, I cracked open the shell pointing out all the sweet meat he could pick at with a small fork. After he ate a bit, I cracked open a leg to show him how to suck the savory treasure from within those appendages.

The girls ignored us continuing their normal Friday night news sharing.

"Mmmm, this is so delicious," Marion reacted enjoying the crab, the slaw, steak potatoes, and a fresh drink the waitress brought him. I noticed him relaxing, sensing we were being left alone. "Outside of work, I'm pretty boring," he offered.

"I like how on top of your job you are. I want to hear your conclusions on what the Committee's up to. I already know you're not shy about your perspectives."

"Yes. I have strong opinions. I don't have lot of people with whom I can share opinions being with the firm only a year and a half."

"I have the same problem," I replied.

"Family doesn't need to hear me rant. With them, it's like preaching to the choir."

"My aunt and uncle have their own daily challenges. Could we walk and talk after dinner?"

"By all means," he responded, his smile brightening. I let my smile curl up more broadly allowing a little nervous exhale to escape noiselessly from me.

We exchanged reviews of the food and the potent drinks celebrating an excellent meal in my community hangout. The tastes, the feeling of satisfaction, and the comfort of being with my own cherished friends each Friday revived me. 'Jellie's' was only ten blocks from home and owned by other Negro business leaders making their mark. It was an important release from performing for the D.C. crowd in the House Office Building.

Having demolished the meal, we sipped the last of our dinner drink and enjoyed my boisterous friends. They had relaxed in front of Marion and they got after each other like it was a regular Friday night.

We paid the waitress, adding a generous tip. As my friends and Marion walked toward the door, they harassed us again.

"I better hear good reports," Janice warned him.

"We know where your law firm is," Joyce threatened gently.

"Ella will tell us everything," Millie cautioned scowling, leaning in closer to him.

"No, I won't," I responded causing everyone to laugh and Millie to shrink back quickly. We all left the place into the early spring night. We stood there as the girls dispersed to catch their buses. I told myself I was okay being alone with him. I would suggest walking toward home, however, a minor concession to first date etiquette.

"Which way should we walk?" Marion asked deferring to my thorough knowledge of the neighborhood.

"Let's go this way," I suggested pointing toward familiar streets.

"They are a great bunch. I had a great time."

"They weren't too rough?"

"They were backing you up. I understand."

"Did you like the food?" I asked.

"Once you taught me the combination for opening that critter," he teased.

I laughed. Marion was very new to me and I was consumed with defending Dr. Barsky, especially having seen the Ives disaster. The singer didn't see his testimony as a disaster because he would be taken off the Hollywood Blacklist since he had implicated others. I didn't think I had time to take on a boyfriend. But Marion was a definite temptation.

Dr. Barsky would get called by the committee and he would face the same decision. Confess his political support for Loyalist Spain during their civil war, reveal the donors to his refugee organization, and the recipients of grants from his foundation. The doctor could spill the beans, or the committee could refer him to the Justice Department under contempt charges. I wanted my client to resist HUAC. I couldn't believe a monarchical Spain in 1936 would keep the United States from protecting Spain's allies, after fascism had been defeated in WWII. Yet, here was McCarthy in 1952 attacking anti-fascist Americans.

I realized I had been silent with Marion for much too long.

"Do you know this part of town?" I asked hoping he wasn't regretting this walk.

"A little bit. Friends recommend restaurants and bars over here. Never 'Jellie's' so I can return the favor after tonight."

"There are other places you'd like?"

"Is there a place where I can sit in a corner and drink after a bad day?" Marion asked.

"Oh, yes," I promised.

"Keep it in mind with the rough play going on in post-world war D.C."

"FDR's gone, the enemies are vanquished, and our old friends are now enemies in Korea," I sketched out.

"Bingo. Patriotic unity gone, the always downtrodden are under the jackboot again…"

"You didn't have enough to drink," I quickly but softly teased.

"I'm sorry. I hate losing and having to put on a happy face."

"You don't have to seem happy for my sake and the game isn't over.   There are innings yet to play."

"Yeah."

"Besides you met this fabulous young attorney."

"I did. Why am I…"

"It's all right," I interjected interrupting him. "If anyone knows what you're going through, it's me."

"How is it to work for Cedric, Brown, & Jacobs?"

"Like anyplace, they load up the new attorneys, but I figure the harder I work, the faster I learn."

"A healthy attitude that will take you far."

"Besides, I have no hobbies except helping my aunt make dinner," I smiled grimly.

"Your first year there is almost behind you. Maybe it's time to pick up a hobby." At this he gave me a playful bump with his shoulder.

"I'm not sure I would be very good company and when would we have the time?" I wondered warily although a larger and larger part of me hoped I could find a way.

"The girls didn't veto me. Did you?" he asked

"No. I simply don't know what kind of friend I'd be. Friday nights, the girls perk me up but any other weekday, my mind would be worn out."

"I understand. But think of the value a conversation would have."

"A friendship is more than conversation."

"If we get past conversation there are other things," he ventured laughing nervously. "You have dated someone before," he added with some sarcasm.

"Third year."

"What happened to him?"

"He relocated back to L.A. What makes you think two lawyers could get close to each other? We're attack dogs."

"You did it in third year, besides someday we could go out on our own. Moses and Forman."

"Such pandering…"

We walked on considering our options. I remained skeptical about dating an attorney again. Marion didn't make any demands. He was sweet and it was maddening. I was fighting it partially because I had gone without a boyfriend for a year and I was comfortable not having one. The farther we walked and the longer we talked, I kept getting this picture of Owen Townsend with a silly grin on his face. Despite how much I enjoyed Owen, I could hear his quiet satisfaction as matchmaker in every conversation, if Marion and I started dating. I continued to resist the idea.

Chapter Three

We were within two blocks of my street and William showed up to check if Marion was a masher.

"Hello, Ella. Is this guy bothering you?" the big man asked stepping between us grimacing down at a startled Marion.

"Hi, William. No, he's a friend. This is Marion Forman. Marion, this is one of my neighborhood friends, William."

"Hello, William," Marion replied with a hint of relief in his voice.

"Your name is Marion? Do people pick on you?"

We laughed.

"Not anymore, William."

"By the way, do you have a nickname?" I asked Marion peeking around the large soul between us.

"My nickname is Bulldog."

"That fits you, William," Marion replied warmly, trying to dodge my question.

"What's your nickname, Marion?" I smiled at them both with William so ably keeping us on topic. We were standing under a streetlight with illumination also coming through the windows of the business where William had stopped us. I could see Marion's reluctance adding wrinkles to his forehead. Childhood nicknames were not always happily remembered in adulthood.

"My nickname is Bullet."

"What a great nickname," William reacted. "Can I call you Bullet, when I see you?"

"Sure, William."

"How did you get that name?" I asked wondering if he had traveled with the wrong crowd.

"I played a lot of baseball and one of my coaches said I reminded him of Bullet Rogan who played for the Kansas City Monarchs."

"Oh, wonderful," I responded. We started to walk on. William followed us, now providing security for us both. "Do you miss playing these days?"

"Yes, but now and then a group of guys I know get together and play a pickup game."

"Do you let people watch?" I asked teasing him.

"Girlfriends come sometimes," he replied teasing me back.

"Let's see if I get to such a lofty status. This is my building," I announced pointing at my stoop. William watched the street for us.

"I can borrow a car. Let's go for a drive tomorrow." I shook my head no. "Sunday, then."

"I have church and chores. There isn't any time."

He didn't insert himself knowing the amount of time a church commitment could take and not ready to invite himself. "I don't want to call you at work. Isn't there a number you can give me?"

"We have a phone in my lobby. AS3-7938."

He opened a pocket calendar and wrote the number down. "Thanks for inviting me to 'Jellie's'"

"Thanks for buying."

"I'll call you soon."

"William, make sure Bullet gets to his bus okay."

Marion smiled.

"I will, Ella."

"Good night, you two."

"Good night, Ella," they responded in unison.

I couldn't help but laugh.

I entered the apartment and sat with my uncle listening to the radio. I replayed my evening trying to sort my feelings about Marion. I decided I was more interested in the idea of a boyfriend than Marion in particular. I also decided he was a decent sort. I reflected on work, deciding my focus had to be there. I was climbing the ladder at work and I couldn't let anything else get in the way. But Marion Forman was an interesting temptation.

~*~

The work week started again and with no McCarthy hearings on the horizon, I sat second chair on more mundane legal proceedings. I had to know my cases inside and out and have the case file well organized for the lead lawyer. This week I was working with Bertram Charles, a middle-aged guy who had a pretty good reputation in the firm. He was polite to me but quick to complain if I couldn't lay my hands on the right document at the right moment.

We were defending a local business owner who hadn't filed the correct paperwork for her permits. We were working with the court to reduce her fines and allow her to keep her beauty parlor running. Bertram sent me into the corridor to prep her for testifying.

A great deal of humanity passed by me as I watched for her. It was like going to a Washington Senators game. Every tier of D.C. humanity was in the courthouse. No one was immune from needing the courts. Outcomes weren't necessarily balanced. I could spot the attorneys from big, prestigious firms. Their clients were equally well-dressed.

When Lavinia emerged from the crowd, she was coiffed and dressed as finely as a Vanderbilt walking out of the Biltmore Estate. My smile widened as she turned heads. She was thirty. Lavinia had worked her tail off to add her shop to the Howard University neighborhood.

"You are a vision, Ms. Lavinia," I gushed quite impressed.

"I'm not seeing straight with worry."

"We have this all worked out, as you remember."

"I know, but between the clamor, the cat calls, and the…" she lowered her voice… "the crackers, I am plumb off-balance."

"Come over here out of the crowd. Attorney Charles has a terrific plan to make this appearance brief."

"I hope so. I have a full shop and a great group of girls but I'd like to get back."

"You'll be pleased how quick this goes."

"You're such a comfort, Ella."

"Come into the court room near us and you'll get called soon." I took her hand feeling the strength of a woman who worked with her hands but softness from a technician who knew how. She sat a couple of rows behind us until Bertram's case finished. After the previous client left, I guided Lavinia to her place at the table next to Mr. Charles.

The clerk started the proceedings. "Your honor, Mrs. Lavinia Miller is charged with failing to license a business and paying the appropriate fees."

"What do you plead, Mrs. Miller?"

Standing up Bertram took the lead. "We plead no contest your honor. We petition the court to levy one-half the fine. We have all the District applications with us to file to properly set up her beauty parlor, if it please the court."

"I'll rule on that, Mr. Charles. Mrs. Miller, I have a few questions for you." Bertram gently motioned for her to stand as he sat down. "Are you willing to pay half the fine, Mrs. Miller?"

"Oh, yes, your honor."

"Why did you fail to file your permits, Ma'am?"

"I was so very excited to open and so many friends wanted to come to the shop, some important 'to do' items were not attended to."

"I can understand. If your own sense of style is any indication you will be a great success. If only all the defendants before me presented themselves as handsomely. I agree to your motion, Mr. Charles. Pass your file to the clerk. Next case."

In the hubbub of the break in the proceedings, Lavinia was almost in tears.

"Mr. Charles, Ella, thank you so much."

"You're welcome, Mrs. Miller."

"Lavinia, you spoke well before the judge."

"I was so nervous, Ella."

"You did fine. I'll see you in the shop Saturday."

"Wonderful. Bye bye."

As she walked out, I could see our next defendant get up and walk to our table. Sitting next to his chair was William, which startled me. He was in dress slacks, a white shirt, and a vest. I waved at him and mouthed the word 'why,' wondering what put him in the courtroom. William pointed at Mickie, our client.

This case was more complicated.

"Next case, your honor," the clerk announced. "Mickie Robinson, possession of an unregistered, loaded pistol."

"How do you plead, Mr. Robinson?"

"We plead guilty, your honor. We ask for time served."

"Nice try, Mr. Charles. Such a plea won't fly. Mr. Robinson…" I signaled Mickie to stand. "What were you doing with a loaded pistol on the bus on a weeknight?" Judge Willis asked.

"Your honor, I work at my cousin's warehouse and we keep my piece around just in case."

"Mr. Robinson, it was less than two years ago a couple of yahoos tried to assassinate President Truman outside Blair House. As you found out, if you walk through the streets of the District of Columbia, the seat of our national government with a loaded pistol, you will be noticed."

A ripple of light laughter rippled through the room. Judge Willis didn't gavel quiet because he was enjoying his own moment of humor.

"I understand, your honor."

"Your honor, this is Mr. Robinson's first court appearance of his life."

"No, I'm sorry, Mr. Charles. If this case makes the papers, the Capital Police will pay me a visit. Two weeks in the District Jail, Mr. Robinson. Please present yourself to the bailiff."

"Thanks, Mr. Charles," was all Mickey got to say as the bailiffs escorted him out of the room.

"I'll be over to see you, Mickey. There's more I can do."

I gathered up our files into a small box and followed Bertram to his car. William walked with us.

"William, you're well-dressed today."

"Hi, Ella. It was fun to watch you work."

"You were here for Mickie?'

"Yes. He lives near you."

"I know. I suppose I shouldn't be surprised you know him."

"He wasn't careful enough."

"No. He shouldn't have had the pistol on the street at all."

"He knows."

"Do you know now?" I teased him with a smile.

"I won't carry anything ever again."

I gave him a big sister scowl to shut up. He was grave in response. "Were you carrying a weapon when you walked me home?" He got a sheepish grin on his face saying nothing. "Bull Dog, you are big enough not to need hardware?"

"Yes, Ella."

I exhaled, my serious face brightening as we walked on. "Was this your first time in the courthouse?" He nodded a sheepish 'no.' "Let's try to keep you out of here."

"Can't I come to watch you work?"

We got to the car, I put the files in the back seat and I gave William a big, warm smile. "I'll see you tonight at home."

"Bye, Ella."

Bertram drove back toward the office.

"He's the biggest man I've seen in a long time. He's a friend?"

"He lives near me."

"He's a mountain."

I set the box of files on my desk so I could add notes from the six cases we defended earlier.

"Ella, check your inbox for a memo," Janice warned.

I picked it up. It was from Mr. Cedric's secretary.

'Ella, Mr. Cedric wants you and Attorney Jacobs to take the NYC train Thursday for a breakfast meeting with Dr. Barsky Friday. Pack an overnight bag. You're staying at the Aloft Harlem Thursday night, returning on the afternoon train Friday.'

I picked up the phone and dialed 'Lavinia's.'

"'Lavinia's,' This is Clarice."

"Clarice, this is Ella Moses. I have an appointment on Saturday. Can you reschedule me to this Wednesday night?"

"Let me see, Ella... Yes, we can fit you in."

"Thanks."

I hung up and glanced at Janice. She gave me a knowing smile.

Attorney Jacobs' father helped create the firm with Mr. Cedric and Mr. Brown. The Jewish – Negro business partnership had been lucrative and strategic. Benjamin Jacobs had made partner a year before his father's retirement. He was forty-plus, sharp as a tack, lean, and well-spoken in the courtroom. I had seen him work in court on a big case. It was a master class for me. Ben Jacobs had acquired the Barsky case for us. It was a gift to go along on the meeting to prep the client for the House Un-American Activities Committee appearance.

Somehow, I managed to get back to work after the New York trip surprise.

When I walked into the apartment later, I jumped into making dinner.

"I have a change to my work schedule this week."

"Really?" Aunt Flora responded catching the contented tone in my voice.

"I've been invited to go up to New York with Mr. Cedric and Mr. Jacobs to have a meeting with Dr. Barsky."

"Your big client?"

"Yes. It's an overnight trip. We'll take the train up on Thursday and come back Friday afternoon."

"You'll be in New York overnight? Oh, Ella."

"We're staying in a Harlem hotel."

"Wonderful, Darling. You are doing a good job there."

"Thanks, Auntie. I changed my hair appointment to Wednesday so I can't help with dinner."

"Oh, good idea."

"I'm sorry."

"It's not a problem. We want you ready for your meeting."

I helped her finish the meal and had put the first forkful into my mouth when I heard a distant 'Ella' come from the building lobby. I cocked my head quizzically at Aunt Flora.

"The phone," she counseled.

I got up from the table. "Excuse me."

"Of course, Dear."

"Who would call now?" Unc asked.

I got to the landing…

"Ella." The call out sounded more urgent.

"Coming."

I scuttled down the stairs like a teenager, taking the handset off the top of the pay phone. "Hello?"

"Hi, Ella. It's Marion."

"Hello, Marion," I responded recovering from my descent.

"I wondered if I could take you out for a drink Wednesday night?"

"I have a hair appointment because the next day I'm going with two partners to prep Dr. Barsky for his HUAC date."

"Really? Congratulations. It's a honey of an assignment."

"Sitting in the hearing room for weeks has paid off."

"Let me borrow the car and pick you up and drive you home Wednesday night."

"It would be nice not to mess my do. Thanks."

"Where?"

"Lavinia's near Howard U."

"I know Lavinia's. I'll explain why when I see you."

"Dating stylists these days," I teased.

"Nothing as fun as I wish it was," he laughed.

"I should be done around seven."

"Excellent. See you then."

"Bye."

I hung up and walked upstairs slowly thinking through Marion's midweek request for an after-work drink. As I walked into the apartment my musings showed on my face.

"Bad news?"

"No, Auntie. Marion Forman wanted to take me out for a drink after work Wednesday. Instead, he's bringing me home from Lavinia's."

"He owns a car?"

"No, but someone in his family must. He's going to borrow it."

"It'll protect your hair if the weather is bad. Invite him up when you get home."

"He's not a close friend to bother you with."

"Unc and I have noticed it's been a while since there's been one. We'll be on our best behavior when there is a special boy."

"Thanks," I replied smiling at her hospitality.

~*~

The week seemed to accelerate as I tried to get ahead on my work to make up for my absence. I couldn't really justify leaving work at 5:30 on a Wednesday but I wanted to strike all I met as New York worthy the next day. I caught the buses required to get to Lavinia's. Her place was filled with customers when I sat down to wait for my turn.

"What have you heard from your boy, Matilda? Is he getting back from Korea any time soon?"

"I don't know, Ruth. I haven't had a letter for a week."

"Do you listen to the news?"

"I stopped. I know his unit number and I'd rather not think about where he is in the fight."

"So many boys joined up after the last war ended because the jobs were all taken by the returning veterans. Who knew they'd have to fight again so soon?"

"I've been hearing too much bad news about our boys coming back banged up."

"There isn't enough good news."

"Ella? We're ready for you," Suzanne called out. She always did my hair. I didn't think I'd get her on a Wednesday. "Heard you saved our bacon on Monday," she began.

"You're welcome, but we had to handle a lot stickier situations with lugs not as attractive as Vinnie."

Suzanne laughed. "What do you want me to do tonight?"

"I have a meeting in New York the next two days. I need big city sophistication."

"Sounds great. How's this cut?" She unlocked a drawer and handed me an old, worn, high school three-ring binder with the names of her friends written on the cover. She quickly paged through to the styling she suggested to me.

"Swept back on one side, curls almost to my shoulder on the other. I like it," I reacted nodding with approval.

The talk among us included struggles in the Howard University neighborhood, the dead, captured, and missing in action Negro men in Korea, and never enough money to convert from renting to owning. McCarthy wasn't on the radar of my stylist or the women around us. Racial disparities were also on their minds. That subject was in their face every day and with every other Negro. The only way I survived many of the slights was being a lawyer in my firm.

I was standing at Lavinia's cash register when Marion walked in. He stood there waiting for me not risking a further incursion into such a female haven. The conversation among the women in the front of the shop slowed to a stop.

"Your guy?" Lavinia asked softly.

"If he's lucky."

She laughed hard and all the women nearby wondered what I said.

Marion wondered, too.

I walked toward him with a little grin.

He took in my new upswept cut and forgot about my joke.

"You are ready for New York."

"I'm happy you like it."

"Let me take you out for one drink and show you off."

"I'm a status symbol for your rep?" I teased him.

"Yes," he confessed. This time I laughed.

We left the shop in the car he had borrowed from his father. He suggested an upscale Howard U bar called 'The Top Hat' faculty frequented.

A jazz quartet was working. We took a table far enough away from the musicians so we could hear each other sitting almost next to each other. I sipped my drink as he told me how important it was Attorney Cedric was including me in the Barsky briefing. He was excited and I just sipped my drink slowly trying to keep my composure. I needed him to change the subject or I wouldn't get any sleep. I would be a nervous wreck in New York.

I leaned toward him and kissed his chattering mouth. He was startled into silence measuring me trying to understand what had happened.

I took another sip.

He was stunned. My anxiety level eased as all I now heard was the quartet.

"I'm sorry. Too much, right?" Marion asked.

"I promise a lingering date over dinner on Saturday to talk about reality after the prep session. Time to take me home."

He took my hand and I let him. He opened the car door for me. When he sat in the driver seat, he couldn't hold my hand because he had to run the car through the gears.

"I'm happy for you."

"I'm not completely happy because I think Barsky is going to lose."

He was quiet again through the drive home, exiting the car, and approaching my stoop. I was willing to walk slowly because being with Marion was going to be the last fun I would have in the next seventy-two hours.

"Thanks, friend." I told him.

"Good luck, Moses," he replied softly.

"See you Saturday, Marion."

He stepped closer and kissed me this time. It was a soft, tender one. I put a hand on his shoulder easing myself away from him. Mixed feelings of attraction swirled, worrying I had started something at the bar I shouldn't have when I should be focusing on the big moment ahead of me in the next two days. I smiled at him squeezing his hand and stepped on my stoop. When I got to my door, I checked on him and found him smiling. I paused for a second and slid through my building's front door.

~*~

Aunt Flora lent me a small suitcase for the short trip to New York. I didn't pack too much. My one wild extravagance was to include the closest thing I owned to a cocktail dress. The suitcase on the bus wasn't a struggle. On the other hand, it was an unusual feeling walking into our office with it.

I worked at my desk until 10a.m. when we caught a cab to the train station. The three of us were going to take 'The Marylander' to New York. The cars on this train catered to business travelers. Mr. Cedric had gotten tickets for a salon compartment which included a round table with relatively comfortable chairs so we could meet and plan for our breakfast appointment with Dr. Barsky while enroute.

The porter served us sandwiches, coffee, and cookies for lunch.

Mr. Jacobs oversaw our preparations. I had read the biography Ben had prepared regarding the doctor's active support of 'The Abraham Lincoln Brigade' made up of Americans and other international soldiers in Spain during their civil war.

Dr. Barsky had fund-raised for and outfitted a full field hospital with all the critical staff needed in Spain. After the war, he had set up a benevolent organization supporting refugees from the conflict who had come to the United States to escape the vicious troops of General Francisco Franco. Because the only country supporting the Spanish Loyalists was Russia under Stalin, McCarthy's team was quite suspicious of Barsky's efforts.

"Dr. Barsky has been quite defiant about the House Un-American Activities Committee calling him to testify. He hired us. But I need to know what advice we should give him and his associates," Ben asked.

I pivoted to Mr. Cedric.

"The atmosphere in Congress is not very open to anyone who has worked with Russia or provided support," Mr. Cedric replied. "Congress has funded and supported President Truman's pursuit of the Chinese Communist invasion on the Korean peninsula."

"Although Burl Ives and HUAC's investigators worked together to script his testimony, they still laid bare in the hearing his supportive activity of progressive causes to ensure his compliance," I added.

"You're both suggesting Dr. Barsky is going to face tough questioning."

"You said he was defiant. He'll be a hostile witness. They'll hold him in contempt," Mr. Cedric responded.

"Ives is going to suffer because he cooperated with the committee. Which kind of damage can the doctor best withstand?" I asked Ben.

"We'll get an update tomorrow morning but in the last call I had with him he will not give up names."

"They could keep him in jail a long time; suspend his medical license. Does he have resources to keep his family afloat while he's not working?" I followed up.

"The Jewish community is not monolithic in New York, but the doctor's philanthropy is well known at Beth Israel Hospital and beyond. People would come to his aid."

"Good to know. Could he teach without his license to practice medicine? Is he in good health himself?"

"He could teach once he's out of jail. He's fifty-seven and apparently in good health."

"I don't want to tell him the future is grim," I replied sadly.

"He's Jewish. He's philosophical about such things but your intention not to overwhelm him would be well-received."

"The other side of the choice he's facing is whether he has the personality to be the face of the anti-HUAC movement. Progressives might try to anoint him," Mr. Cedric suggested.

"The Negro community has tried to elevate such a leader," I noted.

"I think he has the constitution for it. His family has done big things. I think he would take up the mantle. He'll impress you."

"Watkins & Townsend are searching for a Supreme Court experienced attorney for their Nelson sedition case. Who can we call on to reverse a congressional referral for prosecution?" I asked.

"I saw your notes," Ben acknowledged and I've started talking to candidates and, so far, I've found two who would love to reverse a McCarthy driven conviction."

"Excellent. Is it too soon to let Dr. Barsky know we are preparing to defend him before the Supreme Court?" I asked.

"Never too soon," Ben replied. "He's a sharp man. Don't be surprised if he lays out his defense already aware of our concerns."

We continued to talk through strategy for the defense. The train raced on. Pennsylvania was outside our window. When we took a break, we were already in New Jersey. Mr. Cedric left to find the bar. Ben and I were more interested in the rest room. I returned and poured a large glass of ice water and sat down. Ben came into the berth and sat opposite me.

"How are you feeling about the firm after you've been with us for a year?" he asked as he sipped another coffee.

"I've learned a lot. A wide range of work has come across my desk."

"Is being a defense attorney satisfying enough?" The follow up question hit her wrong. It struck her like an interview question rather than idle patter.

"We have so many needy clients."

"Working with people from your community is satisfying?" Ben instantly assumed Ella was talking about Negroes when she used the word 'needy' she thought.

"Very."

"How about our well-to-do Negro clients who have businesses and legacies to protect?"

"This week we helped a businesswoman get out of a jam."

"Good. We're starting to see Negro businesspeople amassing legacies. More of my work these days is helping them protect their success, create a succession plan, choose lucrative investments, or a well-intentioned will."

"It's great to know we help successful Negroes with their businesses."

"I wanted to see you in action on this trip. Everything I've heard made me think you could help me with these clients."

"I appreciate the compliment. However, it would take me months to be any help. I'd have a lot to learn."

"I wouldn't put you under any undue pressure. In three months, you'd know enough to do initial estate planning. Another six months, you could be writing legal covenants, and at eighteen months, you would start to have your own clients."

"I have to say I'm attracted to this plan," Ella reacted, a bit startled, never thinking this career opportunity existed.

He smiled. Ella took his smile as encouragement for a talented young lawyer. "We need a Negro attorney doing this work. Our successful clients need to see one of their own staffing legacy planning and succession. A brochure with both of us pictured would show the firm's interests in them are real."

"Estate matters received only a glancing reference at Howard Law."

"From what I've heard, you have the intellect to tackle something new."

"You are kind to say so."

"Talk about it more over dinner tonight?"

"Absolutely." I wouldn't know how to turn Ben down. He was our contact to Dr. Barsky who's case was one of the biggest, high-profile defenses the firm had taken on in years. The Spanish Civil War veteran needed a D.C. law firm dogged as he was by Senator McCarthy's committee.

Mr. Cedric popped into the salon berth. "We're minutes from arriving at the station in North Jersey. Ella, we transfer to a bus which will take us to a stop a few blocks from the hotel."

"I'm happy you have this all figured out." The two partners laughed. I didn't realize each man laughed for a different reason.

As we took the short cab ride to the hotel, Mr. Cedric gave us a detailed description of the neighborhood. He pointed out historic Harlem landmarks, multi-generational family businesses and how vital the economy was. The small businesses in my own neighborhood were doing well but this part of Harlem was one or two levels brighter. It was my first time in New York and despite being from D.C., I was a little star struck.

The hotel was an older structure but when we walked into the lobby, it was richly appointed and quite welcoming. It had its own restaurant and several retail shops on the first floor. A wide, central staircase rose to a ballroom where a convention was in session for The National Negro Funeral Directors Association. A lot of well-dressed men and a few women were gathered in conversational knots on the staircase and outside the hall. Open doors gave me a glimpse of an ornate ceiling with a chandelier.

We stepped up to the elevator bank and were invited in by a cordial operator who swiftly took us to our floor.

"I'm going to take Ella to dinner, Walker, and find out if you've been over-working her while you catch up with family."

"I try to keep her busy," he teased in return.

I laughed.

As we exited the elevator, he asked me, "Dinner in thirty?"

"Yes, I'll meet you downstairs."

"Great," Ben responded.

I hadn't felt I had been interviewing for a new job when Ben raised it earlier, but dinner was an audition. I was in work mode on the train, a little more ready for his offer. Tonight, I was feeling more nerves. The agenda would be wide open. I had my recently completed law school experience to draw on, but I worried dinner conversation would feel like a final exam. I was hoping the food would be good.

My hotel room was small but had the basics, a full-size bed, small dresser, mirror, a single desk chair with modest writing table, and a bathroom with a makeshift shower curtain rigged around a stand-alone bathtub with feet. I changed into the dress I had packed for my Harlem night out, checked my hair, and caught the elevator.

I walked into the restaurant and the maître d' met me.

"Welcome, miss. A table for one?"

"I'm having dinner with Mr. Jacobs."

"Oh, yes. His table is over here."

He walked me toward an empty table for two. It was the most elegant restaurant I had been to and it was Negro owned and operated. My eyes swept across the many tables in a large room, filled with Negroes dressed well and enjoying the richly appointed dining room. I was filled with a feeling of pride and many more places in the United States needed to be populated like this room. I sat so I could see the entrance out of the corner of my eye. The maître d' left me with a menu. I saw many dishes I liked. One night in New York would not be enough. I was getting spoiled with this little trip and I was not complaining.

"Sorry to make you wait, Ella," Ben apologized cheerily.

A waiter joined us before I could respond.

"Cocktail?" Ben asked.

"A Sloe gin fizz?"

"Certainly, miss," the waiter responded.

"A Manhattan for me."

"Yes, sir," the waiter answered and stepped away.

"So nice to get to the unscheduled part of this trip. Edward asked for an early breakfast meeting. He has surgeries all day. Afterward, we'll get right back on the train."

"It's my first trip to New York. I'm grateful for the opportunity."

"We had to have you come along. Your first-person experience in the hearing room is crucial."

"I'll have to appear solemn when I'm back at work tomorrow afternoon. Don't want them to know I had fun."

Ben laughed and was less anxious than when he found he had left me sitting.

"Are you from D.C.? I know you attended Howard University Law School."

"I'm from a little town outside of Raleigh."

"Nice country there."

"Yes, although my town's most famous historical moment was when almost all the white men were killed at Pickett's Charge."

"Really?"

"True story. The town shut down for a while. The women had to flee to relatives to survive."

"Amazing. Did your parents relocate you here?"

"No. My mother is a farmer there. My father lives in Las Vegas. He does maintenance in a casino. I live with my aunt and uncle."

"They must be proud of what you've accomplished."

"They are."

The drinks arrived and we celebrated our glasses together and took a first sip.

"Have you had a moment with our menu?" the waiter asked.

"Ella, you go first."

"I'd like the petite fillet with asparagus."

"Dressing on your salad?"

"Your house dressing, please."

"Excellent. I'll have warm dinner rolls for you in a moment."

"Lovely."

"For you, sir?"

"A T-bone, baked potato, salad with house dressing."

"Very good, sir." The waiter was dressed impeccably. He was tall, slim, maybe fifty years old carrying himself like royalty.

"With school and now work, do you get time to get out?"

"I meet my girlfriends at a crab house every Friday night."

"Boys?"

"I've met a few young attorneys through work but newly minted Negro attorneys all work long hours," I teased with a smile.

"New careers are a challenge to a social life," he teased back. "You've noticed you aren't alone in struggling to find someone."

"Our divorce attorneys are always proving being careful is wise," she cautioned. "I'm not in any hurry."

"I think we're too hard on ourselves in this culture. The pressure to get a friendship perfectly right once in a lifetime is out of hand."

"If I weren't an attorney, I'd think you were shilling for the law firm."

"I'm being totally philosophical. Didn't you take a social studies class or anthropology in college?"

"Yes. I remember the studies."

"Legislatures need to make it less heinous for couples to divorce, to take the moral turpitude out of the process."

"You're probably right, but you're selling an issue to someone who's too young yet to consider it." I took another sip of the Sloe gin fizz as he realized it was not a topic for someone who had never married. "Tell me the academic mountain I would have to climb to do Estate Law."

He seemed to take my change of subject seriously after a moment. He began to launch into the law I would need to learn. He suggested an accounting class wouldn't hurt. He had a tax accountant who had been guiding him for years and he promised time with him to help me learn the ropes.

I sat back until the bread arrived. I broke open a warm roll, put a bit of butter on it, and sat back to listen to the sales job I was getting.

I could see the career advantages. It could lift me out of criminal defense work leading me to more lucrative billings but my heart was in the courtroom defending Negroes from the legal trouble a dominant culture used to keep us poor, held back, and downtrodden. I finished my drink and was about to walk out on him when the steak arrived. It smelled wonderful and was prepared appealingly. I picked up the steak knife.

"I should use this on you, but I'm hungry."

He laughed and started in on his food, too. I savored the petite fillet. It was the best I'd ever had. The asparagus was perfect, the salad cold, fresh, and expertly imbued with the dressing. I ate enough of each to feel rewarded for putting up with the Neanderthal across from me.

I ate a little more and said nothing else.

He ate, too, waiting for me to follow up. I sat back, sipped from my water glass, not speaking another word.

He finished eating. I still said nothing.

"Ella, think about what I am offering you. No more worries. You get to concentrate on your career with me watching your back."

It's 1952. But you're trying to offer me more than a career enhancement. All I see is turbulence, Ella thought. She paused to gather herself. She decided to try the truth. "Frankly, I want to stay with being a defense attorney for our firm and our working-class clientele. My heart's in their challenges."

"You could do both, especially while you're learning our approach to estate law. You would be working with the Negro community all day long every day." Ben sat there managing a hurricane of emotions himself.

I sat there without comment, not willing to give him any hope I might go for what he was really selling. Personally, though, his pitch touched me. I wanted to believe I could do defense work and estate work with successful Negro businesspeople. I wondered if he would leave my personal life alone. I wasn't going to allow his sordid fantasy.

The bill for dinner was left on the table. He signed it and added his room number. "Let's go find a jazz club."

I nodded and we walked out onto the sidewalk.

The Doorman hailed a cab for us as we noticed how the street life had shifted to celebration from commercial hustle. The cabby described our options. We chose 'The Midnight Club.' It was a warm, early summer night with light almost until nine, but when we walked into the club, it might as well have been two a.m. There were little stubs of candles burning in small glass chimneys on the tables and lights hung above the performers but no other lighting. The bar was lit up a bit, but it was almost sixty feet behind us. The group working when we sat down included piano, drums, trumpet, trombone, and string bass. A tall, thin, mournful Negro girl sang now and then. She didn't seem more than 19. Her voice was like satin.

I ordered a glass of wine. Ben ordered another Manhattan.

Talking would have been hard. The music wasn't loud, but all the other patrons were focused on the music. Fortunately, Ben picked up on the vibe of the room. I sat next to him, but he was over my left shoulder as the performance continued. It was the best jazz I had ever experienced. I was at home. The longer I listened, some strange thoughts swirled in my brain. Why not take Ben for all he would give me professionally. I'd make sure I would only work with Negro clients in their criminal defense or helping them secure a legacy for their next generation lifting them out of forced segregation. I wanted to be able to give a significant portion of my salary to Aunt Flora and Unc and make sure I made partner.

The combo took a break to an ovation from all in the club.

"Do you need a fresh drink?" Ben asked me.

I shook my head, no.

He signaled to the waitress for another drink. When it arrived a few minutes later, he took a sip. Exhaling, he assessed me, choosing his next step. His pitch continued. I had no music to hide behind. "I live in Georgetown. It's a stand-alone colonial four-bedroom, two bath home, with a garage. The back yard is all garden with a nook in the back to take your morning coffee and the paper before work or a Sloe gin fizz on a weekend evening. My car is in the parking lot at our office building. I'll drive you home to my place."

"In a neighborhood where Negroes serve only as domestics? Do I have to work in the kitchen?" I asked him suspiciously.

"When a meal gets cooked there, I hire someone who knows what they're doing."

"A bowl of Wheaties in the morning and martinis at night?" I asked teasing.

"I live there alone most of the time except when the kids are over. I have a part-time cook and a cleaning lady who comes in once a week. You're welcome to create a favorite meal there," hoping a partner's power could move me.

I laughed over escaping what he tried to do.

"You can't have a black shiksa as a girlfriend." I teased back.

"You're welcome to move in."

"Your place may not be nice enough for me."

"Okay, Ella. You let me know," he replied with a confidence I hadn't seen since the meeting on the train. I asked for another drink. He saw to it. The combo returned. We stayed until their next break catching a cab back to the hotel, the jazz bouncing around in my head mingled with the discordant choices Ben had offered me. Together they added up to a new, wildly dangerous offer Ben threw at me. It raised a craving in me but the image in my mind was of Marion Forman. Even Marion wasn't a logical thought, not a lawyerly decision. It was, however, part of a longing for everything I never had. The feeling to add a serious relationship, even with a Negro man frightened me and hummed almost violently within me at the same time.

Ben walked me to the door of my room. As many feelings raced inside me, I managed to put a hand on his shoulder to keep him from kissing me.

"Good night, Ella," he replied to my repulse of the kiss. There was no tone of defeat in his comment. Clearly, he was still on the make.

~*~

Mr. Cedric knocked on my door at 5:30a.m. to make sure I was awake. We would have our bags with us when we met at Carnegie Deli to prep Dr. Barsky. As I got ready, I realized I was a little hung over having mixed drinks the night before. More surprising was getting any sleep at all. My head was alive with turning down Ben and suddenly yearning for Marion. I felt no regret. I wanted to go be Dr. Barsky's lawyer. It was a higher caliber feeling. Growing up I often thought about being an attorney with a higher calling. Today it was a palpable conviction.

I gave the desk my key and stood with Mr. Cedric. A moment later Ben checked out.

"Good morning you two," Ben robustly barked.

"You are full of it this morning and without any coffee," Mr. Cedric noted. I didn't speak to what was behind Ben's mood.

"It's a lovely morning to screw over Joe McCarthy," he replied.

We laughed. I noticed the confident stride we all took up as we walked out to the cab stand.

Ten minutes later we entered Carnegie Deli's bustle. Ben walked us over to Dr. Barsky who set down his coffee cup, dropped a newspaper to the table to stand, giving Ben a bear hug.

"Edward, this is Walker Cedric…"

"A pleasure, sir…"

"And Ella Moses."

"I'm happy to make your acquaintance," Barsky told me.

"It's great to finally meet you."

"I've already ordered for you," he announced waving to his man behind the counter.

We sat.

Dr. Barsky was short, wiry, fifty-seven years old but as intense as any man I'd ever met.

"So, this is what we need to do," Barsky began, a wide smile erupting on Ben's face.

Chapter 4

We sat there, amazed. The good doctor had outlined our defense before we had a chance to speak a word.

"Ella, are they going to try to interview me before the hearing," Dr. Barsky asked.

"I think they will, and you should respond taking one or more of us with you. They'll reveal more of their plans. Their approach isn't subtle. Their FBI unit shakes down people who know you with fear of prosecution. In the interview, they'll tip you off to whom they've spoken."

"I know it will take you away from work and family, but I think you should do the pre-interview," Mr. Cedric agreed.

"I'm refusing to name names hoping fewer vulnerable people will get abused by McCarthy," Dr. Barsky explained.

"Which brings us to the issue of organizing support around your family should you face incarceration. We'd like to work with a network of your colleagues and friends to quietly develop an account Vita could draw upon," Ben suggested.

"I appreciate your help. I think the way to do it is to contact my rabbi, Joel Berman and have him give you a list of my friends. You can also have the administrator of Beth Israel Hospital, Alex Reitman, build a similar list from my medical colleagues."

"Ella, would you offer any support needed to those two contacts?" Mr. Cedric asked.

"Of course. Whatever I need to provide."

"We don't know HUAC's timeline. It could be months before they call you, Edward. I want all our plans in place in the next two weeks. The more time they give us to plan the better," Ben suggested.

"I appreciate your point of view, Ben," Dr. Barsky shared.

"For instance, I want you to stay with me when you're forced to come to D.C.," Ben added. My head popped up from my notes having agreed to provide logistical support. He noticed. "Ella, send me an office memo to get the grocer to provide Edward's favorite foods. Oh, he drinks Chivas Regal."

"Will do," I responded, head down writing stiffly avoiding any reaction which Ben would read inappropriately.

"He likes dry wines."

"I really don't drink like I used to," Barsky protested drawing laughter out of the rest of the table.

Ben and Edward fought over the check. Edward won.

We shared warm goodbyes with Dr. Barsky after which he ran off to catch a cab to get to work, a day of surgeries awaiting him. We waved goodbye from the sidewalk. When he was out of sight, we grieved the fact most of our work would be about providing support to Vita and their child and mounting an appeal to whatever sentence he got. Finding the attorney who could present in front of appeals judges and the Supreme Court was another challenge. A defense fund should be raised as well as replacing his salary to support his family. We packed into a cab, luggage, and brief cases in its trunk. I sat up front with the driver. He took us to our bus station to catch the ride to the north Jersey train station. The train left at noon. We had to wait for a while. Walker and Ben stood away from the trackside to discuss some firm business separate from where I was. I checked my notes from the breakfast meeting.

We were called to our train and enjoyed the comfort of our salon suite once again. Mr. Cedric left us for the bar. The porter offered us lunch. I took a bowl of soup and a soft drink. Ben had a sandwich and a glass of milk.

Could I catch Marion on his home phone? I decided to try but also to leave a message on his office's after-hours service before I returned to my aunt and uncle's apartment for the night. I'd call the service from work to start the conversation.

"How do you think your aunt will react if you decide to move in with me?"

"It's one of the big reasons I'm not planning to move in with you."

He smiled but he didn't laugh.

We sat in silence for quite a while. The Negro porter entered the berth to pick up our dishes. "I have some snickerdoodles, if you'd like a cookie," he offered.

"Oh, yes. I haven't had any in years," I replied.

He smiled and left.

"A what?" Ben asked.

"A snickerdoodle. You'll love them if they're baked right."

The porter came back with a plate of three for each of us. It gave us something upbeat to talk about for a while.

"I want to take a long weekend at the end of the month. I have a townhouse in Ocean City, Maryland. It's rented out now and then to short term visitors, but I have big blocks of time reserved for me. Summer, mid-fall, Christmas week, early spring when winter eases. The kids like to go. You'd love it."

"Tell me about your kids."

"Lauren is twelve. Charles is sixteen. They're both bright, excellent students with lots of friends. Lauren likes music. Charlie plays three sports."

"How are they handling being away from you?"

"They're doing well. They like my wife's new husband. He's an executive for the Washington Senators."

"Ah. A little flashier than being an attorney."

"Yes. He's an assistant general manager. He's involved in acquiring players."

"Perhaps he's an attorney, too?"

"He is," Ben replied revealing the first moment of unease I had seen in him.

"Have your children ever met a Negro professional," I asked with the wild visage of a gambler. I was walking on iffy ground risking my possible rise in the firm.

He exhaled. "Actually no, but I'm sure they are ready," sounding even more tentative as the words came out of his mouth.

"Perhaps you wouldn't introduce me to them, if I dated you." I was slightly more confident this conversation wouldn't go beyond the train ride home.

"Do you want me to describe the house?" He asked changing the subject which got a wry smile out of me.

"I'm sure it's worthy of Georgetown."

"Oh, yes."

"How many Negros live in your neighborhood?"

"Some college faculty, hospital executives, and several NAACP staffers I know of."

"More than I imagined."

"One is an estate client. More may become clients with you representing the firm, too."

"I noticed I'm going to help host Dr. Barsky's visit to our fine city," I teased him. "How often do you host parties for your friends?"

"I'm cut off from my former friend group since I'm single. I get out to the theater and the symphony. I have some favorite restaurants and I go to Senators' games although I haven't been invited into the general manager's box." I laughed. He smiled. "I know this is going to have some awkward moments. I'll work hard to make daily life livable. I want this to work out."

"You do realize you've only known me for a few minutes."

"I'll confess I noticed you months ago."

"Oh, really?" I teased him.

"You hardly saw me around. I didn't stalk you," he added.

"Evidently, you've been really sneaky."

He laughed.

Mr. Cedric returned. The conversation lost its predatory quality and the three of us described how our lives developed to put us together. By the time the train slowed to a stop in D.C., we had professionally debriefed each other.

I put my suitcase next to my desk about 4:45pm. My office mates gathered around for a report. I kept it to headlines promising more scoop after the weekend. I kept Janice by me for a minute.

"Honey, I may invite Marion to the crab shack, again, on girls' night. Can you put up with him one more time?"

"What happened to you?"

"I'll call you Sunday night when I see how the conversation goes with Attorney Forman."

"Promise?"

"Promise."

I called Marion's office. "Could I speak with Attorney Forman?"

"I'm sorry. He's in a meeting with a partner."

"Could I leave a message?"

"Yes."

"This is Attorney Ella Moses from Cedric, Brown, and Jacobs. I'm hoping he can make our meeting at the Crab Shack tonight."

"The Crab Shack?" the secretary asked finding the non-professional nature of my call rather gauche.

"Correct. The Crab Shack," I replied gently with crazy feelings of going too far rumbling in my chest. Ben's inappropriateness seemed to have spawned some of my own.

The secretary agreed she would give him the message.

I continued to type Barsky meeting notes until 5:30. Unfortunately, I was burdened with a suitcase as I rode the bus toward my neighborhood and The Crab Shack. Since it wasn't a girls' night out, I planned to sit at a table and slide my bag under it.

Whether or not Marion would show up, I needed a drink after my business trip.

The neighborhood changed as the bus trundled away from work. Every store front was open and commerce thrived. The law firms, banks, and engineering firms were in the rearview but business was open along my main drag. There were apartments on the floors above the retail establishments, the side streets were full of tenements. Some apartment buildings rose four stories.

Many businesses along the bus route sported colorful awnings hawking the goods inside. Shoes, hardware, fabrics and sewing goods, groceries, paint, kitchen goods, and cobblers were all in attendance.

The farther along my route the bus motored, I began to see stores I walked to from my aunt and uncle's apartment. The Crab Shack was a block away. I got up to exit at the stop.

Once on the sidewalk, I walked to the corner. I felt a little silly entering a neighborhood haunt with the overnight bag. Luckily there were a couple of open tables right inside the door. I hadn't been sitting a minute and one of the waitresses I knew walked up.

"What can I get you, Ella?" Sara asked smiling.

"Hi, Sara. How about a Sloe Gin Fizz and a crab salad?"

"Coming right up."

Right after work the place wasn't as busy as it would be into Friday evening. Only two people sat at the bar. A smattering of people at the tables relished crab meals after a long work week.

Diners left replaced by a larger crowd. My meal arrived and I dug in, sipping my drink close to the bottom of the glass.

"Another drink?" Sara asked as she cleared my plate.

"One more."

When I got it, I sipped it as slowly as I could. My hopes of seeing Marion on short notice were fading. I began to worry my messages left in several places might have upset him or at the very least confused him considering how tentative I had been with him. I had to admit to myself my own hasty turn away from a total commitment to the law was a reaction to the relationship Ben had suggested. Crashing back in on Marion was a knee-jerk reaction. So much for my principles. By the time I gave up, the Shack was packed. I tried to go through the door to the street to walk home when a person blocked my way.

"Where do you think you're going?"

I smiled seeing Marion gazing down at me. "Sara…" I called out to the waitress. She noticed Marion and me.

"I've got a little table by the kitchen," she announced smiling broadly.

We followed her through the hubbub a little out of place in suits and my awkward overnight case. I was quite happy to be at the far edge of the dining room. Marion sat with his back to the kitchen door.

"A Ballantine and a crab sandwich," he requested.

"An iced tea for me."

She left us.

"Don't you want a drink after your big trip?" Marion insisted.

"I've already had two."

"Oh, I'm sorry. I made you wait so long."

"You're here now…"

He exhaled. "How was the conversation with Dr. Barsky?"

"Pretty upbeat considering we're going up against McCarthy."

"Had to be nice being in the meeting with the partners and the client."

"Someone has to do the real work of this case."

He laughed. "You get to do what?"

"I'm in charge of marshalling the resources to support his family while he's in prison."

"I suppose it makes sense to prepare for the worst."

"He's a Jew who was on the same side of a war underwritten by Communist Russia."

We let the searing inevitability of failure sink in, knowing the wave of support McCarthy was raising thanks to his rhetorical cudgels. Eventually, I risked a summation. "I thought Negroes had cornered the market on high-handed white shenanigans."

"A little cabal of brown shirts inflict pain in the States whom our forces stopped in Europe a few years back," Marion noted.

"Working against HUAC is important to me but my heart remains defending people in municipal court. It's where Negroes suffer most."

"It's good you are committed to municipal court cases on one level but don't you want to do well?" Marion asked with a snide smirk.

"Funny you should ask."

"Oh, really?" Marion's levity melted. Someone was beating his time.

"Do they teach you guys to wave your wallets at poor colored girls thinking we'll jump in the sack with you?"

"I never attempted such a gambit since my wallet is too thin to stir hearts."

"You're always generous," I protested.

"For the correct person," He replied, his face turning serious. "Someone tried to purchase your affections?"

"I think it was a function of the setting. New York City evokes an empire mentality in some men, it seems."

He laughed. "Some guys have to have a fat wallet when their empire fails them."

Ella smacked his arm. "You're nasty."

Marion laughed some more. "Is this goodbye? Are you some high roller's doll?"

"I have no plans to say goodbye," Ella replied with a coy smile.

"If you don't watch it, I'm going to think you really do want to see me." Sara put his food in front of him, getting an earful of his last comment. Her smile got wider. I sat back, sipping my tea, not saying a word. Marion picked up his sandwich and took the first bite. As he lifted the sandwich a second time, he noticed I was smiling beatifically at him. "Wait a minute."

I started giggling.

"You want us to be a thing?" he asked with expectant exasperation.

"Let's define 'thing.'" I replied breaking out into noisy laughter.

"Why haven't you been answering the messages I leave you at work?"

"I had to think about you a little bit."

"You could think about me while we were at the movies or something. I heard nothing from you."

"I called you today," I reacted with the word 'today' showing a bit more high-pitched tension.

"Owen thought one of your partners might have made you an offer you couldn't refuse."

"Male partners either hate women are going into the law or they are targeting us as wife number two."

"Someone did make a play."

"One of the named partners put me on Dr. Barsky's case and it got me a little more visibility. I simply prefer your street corner come on to having homes in Georgetown thrown in my face."

"You do? What's wrong with you," he teased.

I relaxed and gave him a sour expression from which Marion did not shrink.

"Sass? Sass is what I get?" I faux complained smiling.

"You said…"

I wanted his arm, my smile continuing. He slid his hand into my gentle grasp holding my palm with affection. Marion noticed me begin to blush but it didn't mean I was retreating. Instead, I laced my fingers into his.

My additional grasp of affection created in him panic he tried to mask. His eyes darted back and forth as he searched for the most suave verbal response.

"What did you think of Dr. Barsky?" immediately realizing he had already asked this but putting engagement on his face to cover his mistake. He did not let go of my hand. I did not try to slip away.

"He was remarkable. He wasn't afraid to set up a field hospital in Spain during their civil war. He's not frightened to go to battle with McCarthy or to lose to him."

"Interesting. Owen was telling me he's hearing Negro leaders starting to talk about challenging anti-Negro laws in targeted places. Our lawyers have been challenging the 'separate but equal' doctrine of Plessy v Fergeson in South Carolina, Virginia, and Delaware."

"Really? What we do with McCarthy is instructive to a legal strategy for us."

"It's another front to make challenges. The NAACP already has an active legal arm."

"But the NAACP headquarters are in Baltimore. Close, but are activists at Howard talking about action?" I asked.

"My old girlfriend, Wanda, works with American Teachers Association affiliates…"

"Tell me about your old girlfriend," I interrupted sitting forward with interest.

"I was starting to…"

"How long ago was she your girlfriend?" I teased.

"When I was a first year," he replied with a smirk on his face enjoying my apparent jealousy.

"What's she doing now?" I probed.

"She travels the mid-Atlantic states organizing local teachers' unions for the ATA and she is an adjunct professor at Howard in the education school."

"Do you still talk?"

"She asks for free legal advice regularly since part of her job is being a contact with the NEA to build interest in joining forces."

"I'd like to meet her."

"Interesting, because she wants to meet you. Even more now," Marion shared.

"You talked to her about me?"

"She thought it was funny you didn't immediately go crazy for my handsome self and law degree."

"She likes it when you fall on your face?"

"Yes. Why exactly are we together again?" Marion asked, seriously wondering.

"You aren't afraid of McCarthy," I reacted.

"I think McCarthy is scary."

"But you are defending clients at HUAC."

"It's true I asked for a McCarthy case," he confessed.

"See. We're a match."

"HUAC makes us a match? What happens when our cases against McCarthy's fascism are over?"

"There's no shortage of unconstitutional garbage going on in this country."

"True enough. You do think I'm cute, though, right? My handsome face is part of what makes us a couple, correct?" Marion teased.

I sipped the last inch of my iced tea making sure to gurgle through the straw. Finished, I smiled at him.

Chapter 5

"You've had an intense couple of days away from home. Let me drop you at your aunt and uncle's place."

"Great. I want you to come up and meet them."

"You want me to meet your people?"

"Yes. Once they meet you, it will be easier for me to explain why I'm not coming straight home some nights."

"You think so?"

"You appear to be the consummate professional."

"I suppose seeming businesslike is more important than being handsome."

I laughed. "My aunt won't have any trouble picking up you're well put together."

Marion paid and tipped Sara and walked to his car carrying my suitcase. After I was in the front seat, he put my bag in the back.

"Should we stop at a phone booth and give them notice? They're not expecting me,"

"My aunt always has the place ready for guests, although it's been quite a while since someone's been over."

Marion parked and took my bag as we entered the building and up the stairs. I noticed I wasn't nervous bringing Marion home. It was a feeling of excitement and balance as Marion was just a year older than me. It wasn't as precarious a friendship as had been offered me during the Barsky trip. The one nagging worry was would this relationship slow my career trajectory?

As we took the stairs, Mrs. Washington checked to see who had entered the building. "Ella, who is this man with you?"

"He's an attorney from Watkins and Townsend."

"Well, La Di Da."

Her door shut loudly in protest.

The hallway on the second floor was quiet except for someone's radio as I put my key in the lock. As we entered, my uncle was already in the parlor with the paper. My aunt was in the kitchen fussing over the dinner dishes. As she heard my entrance, she remarked without focusing, "Ella, how was …" She stopped, seeing Marion. Curiosity blossomed on her face.

"Aunt Flora, this is Marion Forman. He's an attorney for Watkins and Townsend."

"Welcome, Mr. Forman."

"It's nice to meet you, Mrs. Winters."

I walked Marion further into the apartment. "Marion, this is my Uncle Ray."

"This young man is a lawyer, too?"

"Yes, Unc."

"It's good to meet you, Attorney Forman."

"Happy to meet you, Mr. Winters."

"I made a strawberry – rhubarb pie, if you'd like a slice," Aunt Flora offered.

"A little slice would be nice. We just ate," Marion replied.

"Ella, the coffee is fresh. Pour everyone a cup."

"Yes, Auntie."

"Sit down here, Marion." He set my suitcase next to a chair in the parlor. "Thanks for getting her home after her long week."

"Ella did well in New York," Marion shared.

"Did you meet Ella at the capitol?" Unc asked.

"Yes. I'm happy to hear I was mentioned in conversation," Marion replied smiling. I gave him a smirk sitting down after finishing my serving duties. "Mmmmm, Miss Winters this pie is amazing."

"Thank you, Marion," she replied trying not to seem flattered but failing.

"I haven't had a good piece of strawberry – rhubarb pie since my last reunion."

"He's from Graham, Auntie," I shared.

"No."

"Yes, ma'am. I lived there until I attended college."

"It's a joy to have a fellow from Graham at our table," Aunt Flora observed with a smile.

"Thank you."

"Do you get back there often?" Unc asked.

"Usually only for reunion. My parents own a car repair shop here."

"It's the same for us. Work keeps us quite busy," Unc explained.

"Ella tells me you're in construction. What are you working on right now?"

"I'm helping to finish the Engineering and Architecture Building at Howard University."

"Marvelous."

"You've been defending people at the House Un-American Activities Committee?" Auntie asked.

"I recently got back from Pennsylvania where we successfully defended a member of the Abraham Lincoln Brigade from a charge of sedition."

"The Brigade was the international military unit which fought on the side of the monarchy. It was the first mixed race American regiment since the revolution, correct?" Unc replied.

"Correct. They fought against the same enemies we faced in WWII. I'm afraid I need to get the car back. Everyone in the family wants to use it."

"Understandable," Unc responded.

"Take a piece of pie with you," I suggested.

"I couldn't. You've been so kind already."

"I insist," Aunt Flora replied. "Ella, could you fix a plate for Marion?"

"Of course, Auntie." They continued to chat up Marion as I put a slice of pie on an everyday dessert plate covering it with wax paper. Having said his goodbyes to Auntie and Unc, I stepped into the hall with Marion, closing the door behind us for privacy.

"A walk under the cherry blossoms after church Sunday, 2pm. I'll pick you up."

"I'll be waiting," I replied, his lovely face beaming I had said yes to a date. He slipped his arm not holding the plated pie around my waist gently holding me close. He kissed me with a slight touch of our lips. Stepping back a bit allowed me to see a fuzzy, happy appearance of new love about him. I hauled him back into the clutch and kissed him more firmly.

"Sunday," he uttered softly.

"Sunday," I responded with a big smile.

He snapped out of the moment. "Gotta go."

"Thanks for the ride."

He descended the stairs and got to the building's front door. He checked realizing I might still be there and waved. I returned a wave and he was gone. I confessed to myself a feeling of wanting to be alone with him. From somewhere images of us entwined flooded into my brain. I shook myself to break the spell. *Imagine. Daydreaming about Marion in so lurid a way.* As I walked back into the apartment, I realized I was grinning like a teenager. I decided there was no reason to suppress my happiness.

~*~

I got up early the next morning to beat the crowd at the laundromat down the street. We had a couple of machines in our basement but there was a McCrory's next door the neighborhood laundromat and I needed a strange combination of items at the store. Besides, the laundromat had large windows front and back which were more welcoming than a basement. I started two washers and began my wandering through McCrory's aisles. I had a list but it was a Saturday morning treat to inventory everything. I grabbed a packet of three different sizes of sewing needles and a card of replacement buttons which were perfect to repair a work blouse. I bought a new, large comb barrette to pull my hair back quickly and easily some mornings when I didn't want to fuss. The most expensive thing I bought was an envelope of linen stationery which had a lovely floral pattern at the top plus a new pencil and a fresh little sharpener. My old one had worn out.

My last stop was their penny-candy counter where I found William deciding on his selection.

"Good morning, Bulldog."

His head swiveled sharply but his face relaxed as he saw it was me.

"Hi, Ella."

"What are you going to get?" I asked, curious about his favorites.

"I can't decide. What do you like?"

"Mary Janes."

"They are too chewy."

"You don't chew them. You let them melt in your mouth."

"Who wants to wait. Maybe Mike & Ike's."

"They're good."

To the woman behind the counter, he requested, "Twenty-five cents of 'Mike & Ike's.'"

She used a little scoop to get a bunch to ladle into a scale pan to measure out his order. She put his pieces into a tiny brown bag. She did the same for my 'Mary Janes.' "I'm doing laundry next door," I explained.

"Can I help you?"

"You can sit with me. I don't think you want to help with a girl's laundry."

"I have sisters. I know everything."

I smiled at him. My machines were still in spin cycles. We sat on the broad windowsill of the street-side windows.

"Let's play tic-tac-toe," William suggested.

"Go get the newspaper over there. Let's finish the crossword."

"Crosswords are a pain," he replied getting the paper, nonetheless.

"Sharpen my new pencil." He jumped to it. "Over the trash can, Silly," I objected softly, laughing. William sighed as if hanging with me was hard work. "What's an eleven-letter word for 'drawing ads?'"

"Artist," Bull Dog replied wearily.

"Eleven letters," I reminded him.

He sat there a while. "Another word for drawing?"

I waited. I showed him some letters had been revealed: an 'i,' an 'r,' and an 'a.' "Starts with an 'i.'" He brightened slightly.

"My great-grandmother used to ask me to write stories. She would draw the pictures. She said she was an…illustrator." A smile broadened across his face.

"Your suggestion works." I wrote it into the little blocks.

"I'm getting the hang of this."

"Okay, next."

"Not another one."

"Crosswords need a lot of words to make a puzzle." He exhaled. "A motorcycle's third seat," I read out loud.

"What? Only two people can ride a motorcycle."

"Not the one in which Officer McNamara rides around the precinct when he has his dog with him."

"Oh, yeah. The dog sits in the little bullet thing."

"What's the bullet thing called?" I asked smiling.

"I don't know," he said in frustration. He noticed the beat cop walk past and he bolted outside to ask him

"Cheating," I teased him when he sat down again next to me.

"It cost me some 'Mike & Ike's,' too," he reacted laughing.

"The answer is?"

"Sidecar."

"Correct." I wrote in his answer.

"What's the next one?"

I smiled. He was hooked for the moment. "Nine letters: graceful and flexible dancer. Here are the letters we already have," I announced. He checked the puzzle.

"It starts with an 'L' and ends in 'm' and 'e.' What's the clue again?"

"Graceful and flexible dancer."

"Ballet is too short."

"We need the word equaling 'graceful and flexible.'"

"Striptease?"

I laughed hard at this try. "The word starts with an 'L.' You probably haven't seen a ballet."

"Nah."

"I'm going to provide this word." I wrote it into the puzzle.

"How do you even say…lightsome?"

"Close. It's pronounced lithesome."

"What kind of dancers get called…what you said?"

"Tall, thin ballet dancers."

"You couldn't be called…what you said?"

"I'm kinda curvy."

"I don't think so."

"I'm not sure you've given me a compliment," I replied laughing.

"I think you're above average."

I smiled noting he was not smiling. "Okay, here's a new clue, you'll get it in a snap."

"Hit me."

"Nine letters. The clue is 'a bludgeon.'"

He was counting the letters in his head on his fingers. "Could it be 'blackjack?'"

"You are correct. I've got to put my clothes in the dryer." I kept him working on the puzzle until my clothes were folded. He carried the basket to my place for me.

"Can I have the newspaper? I want to finish the crossword."

"Certainly. Let me know how it goes," I replied with a smile.

"Bye, Ella."

"Take care, Bull Dog."

~*~

"We got a nice day for this," I observed as Marion and I walked hand-in-hand taking in the pink glory.

"True. You hardly need a jacket."

"Thanks for bringing me."

"I've never been on this path before. Seen the trees from a distance, but close-up is spectacular."

"Young lawyers need inexpensive ways to date."

"Thanks for understanding."

"You provide the vehicle. It's a big deal."

"It's part of the family business. Next time, let's start working our way through the monuments."

"I've been to the zoo," I announced cheerily.

"Me, too. We should go there together."

"I haven't been to the National Museum of Natural History," I added.

"I hear it's loaded with famous artifacts."

"The First Lady gowns."

"It's on my list. Is work on your mind today?"

"One thing I didn't share from my New York trip was Mr. Cedric, a named partner, wants me to add Business Succession and Estate Planning to my portfolio. Another partner has a solid reputation leading Negro business owners in this area and Mr. Cedric wants a Negro attorney as part of this legal team."

"How do you feel about his idea? It's usually a higher billable hour rate than municipal defense."

"I like having another way to serve families and business owners. I think it will be a tough learning curve. I only took one class on estates in law school."

"If your mentor is willing, pick their brain all you can."

I paused hearing this suggestion knowing Ben would love it if I were heavily dependent on him. "Mr. Cedric wants me to be running estates in three years."

"If you make his deadline, you'll be in the middle class."

"Do you think we have many business owners in D.C.?"

"Do you go to any businesses which aren't Negro owned?"

"But they're all mom-and-pop stores."

"Every one of them wants their economic power to flow to a relative."

"I start Monday. So, it's good?"

"You can teach me as you learn."

"Estates, you?"

"Eventually, we're going to open Forman & Forman, attorneys at law."

"You sweet talker," I teased smiling at him.

"Hot dog?"

"Just mustard, thanks."

There was a Negro guy with a cart about a block away. We each got a 'dog' and a beverage finding a shady bench where we ate while the weekend crowds enjoyed the southern spring breaking out. I got him talking about a couple other women he dated. None of them worked out. I asked why in my best tone of neutral curiosity.

"They thought I would be a highflyer with deep pockets. When I told them I was more interested in Negro rights, they knew there would be no big billings and they dumped me."

"No girlfriend pining for you back in Graham?"

"There was a girl, but the friendship fell apart a couple of years into college. She married an insurance agent and had three children."

"Just dating since then?"

"As soon as they found out I was a poor student, it would end."

"You won't be poor anymore."

"I'll be one of your estate planning clients."

"Yes, you will," I replied smiling. "Where is your parents' business?"

"They have a great location. Their repair bays are always filled. We live upstairs. We connected two houses, so my sis and I live next door to my parents. My brother is married and lives with his family nearby. My little sister is studying to be an LPN."

"Your mother works with your father?"

"She's his receptionist and scheduler."

"Who's going to keep the business going with your brother and sister heading off in different directions?"

"My dad's terrific at taking on apprentices and turning them into masters who go on to start their own garages."

"He has a reputation as a teacher?"

"He does."

We walked away from the crowds, alternating in the spring sun and leafy shade, our conversation flitting from one news story to another. Korea, the early stirrings of the presidential election, the return of warm weather, the joys of making money, paying off education bills, and having a savings account with a significant balance.

We risked a kiss here and there as we headed toward his car. When we sat in his car, I took advantage of the bench seat. I was expectant and he tilted his face down kissing me lovingly and long.

"I'm liking this boyfriend thing," I teased.

"The sound of the word boyfriend does all kinds of good things for me."

I giggled.

He took me home.

~*~

I had been sitting at my desk at work about an hour when the phone rang in our workroom. "Ella, you have a visitor. An FBI agent."

I froze for a second.

"I'll let the partners know," Janice reacted. "One of them will want to sit in."

"Thanks, Janice."

I stood up, checking my mirror in my purse, and started to make my way to reception. As I descended the stairs, I saw him. Black suit and tie, crew cut, muscled, stocky build, old enough to have served in WWII and get his J.D. afterward.

The receptionist's phone rang.

"Yes, sir. I'll tell her. Ella, Mr. Brown asked you to wait for him before you start your meeting."

"All right, Julia," I replied as calmly as I could. "I'm Ella Moses."

"Yes, I know."

That's a creepy answer. "And you are?" He removed a leather folder from an inside jacket pocket. His folder revealed an FBI badge and a card identifying him as Peter Curran. "Welcome, Mr. Curran."

Mr. Brown walked up. "Good morning, I'm Edgar Brown, Attorney Moses' counsel. Won't you come into our conference room?"

"Of course," Curran replied. Before he sat down, he repeated the process of presenting his credentials. Mr. Brown nodded in response. Curran sat at the end of the long table. Mr. Brown motioned for me to sit in the first chair to Curran's right and he sat next to me. The two of us waited for him.

"Miss Moses, you realize you are providing legal support to a known Communist working to subvert our government."

"I don't recognize any of my clients by your description," I replied matter-of-factly.

"You are in serious trouble, young lady. Your reputation is being trashed by defending Barsky."

"Two things, sir. That's Dr. Edward Barsky to you and my work is memorialized in the Constitution."

"You're going to throw the Constitution at me?" Curran's face hardened even more.

"Investigating people for their thoughts and beliefs?"

"Barsky provided aid and comfort to Communist backed troops."

"His doctors and nurses treated troops of the Spanish Republic and the Nazi insurgents."

"Did you come to our offices to arrest Attorney Moses?" Mr. Brown asked.

"No. This is a courtesy call to warn her how much trouble she could be in for representing a Communist."

"If you're not going to arrest her, allow both of us to go back to work. We have a lot to do."

"You both are fellow travelers…" he announced with a quiet determination.

"Mr. Curran, please put evidence on the table to back up your wild accusations."

"You can't accuse me of anything considering who you represent."

"Sir, you come with nothing but hearsay."

"The possible charges will be well supported," the agent offered with the tiniest of a smug smile.

Mr. Brown picked up the phone asking Julia, "Would you send Georgie for the beat cop?"

He put the receiver in the cradle.

Curran let a derisive hiccup escape him. "You sent for the police? You're out of your mind." FBI agent Peter Curran broke into a manic smile which put a chill into me. It was a smile of someone who felt he owned the offices where he sat which the original Cedric, Brown & Jacobs partners had created over a hundred years earlier.

"We consider this meeting over," my named partner asserted. All I could think of was to get ready to run. "Attorney Moses, please return to your duties." I was afraid to move. "Mr. Curran, you can wait here, if you desire." I willed myself to get up and walk out. Mr. Brown followed me. He gestured for me to get back to work. I used the staircase instead of the elevator to watch how this moment would end. Mr. Brown stood there for a minute. Georgie returned with Officer Murphy. Attorney Brown quietly explained to the veteran officer what was going on and the cop shook his head as if one of the neighborhood kids had been truant. The partner returned to his office. Murphy entered the conference room. I couldn't hear anything from where I was. I began to worry about the receptionist who was left to watch and possibly handle what happened next. I read her face and recognized the grimace she gave me when she wasn't going to endure my nonsense. It was a visage my aunt used when I needed it. It was her "no you don't" nonverbal.

After a moment the beat cop, listening wearily to the FBI agent, walked him out the door of our offices. He acknowledged what Curran was saying but the cop managed to persuade the McCarthy staffer onto the sidewalk.

Mr. Brown chuckled. He had returned to Julia's side. They exchanged a nonverbal acknowledgement of this wearying experience having absorbed another indignity of Jim Crow D.C.

Chapter 7

I returned to my desk but found I could not get to work. I was shocked by the intrusion, by Curran's accusations, and being harassed for keeping my oath. I could not see anything I should be doing sitting in front of me. All I could think of was the superiority in the face of the government employee. I couldn't understand the grievance aimed at me for representing my client. The agent was an attorney as well. He knew what my job was but didn't want to acknowledge the appropriateness of my role under the Constitution. I was sensitive about the Constitution's protections as it was. It created a paralyzing combination of emotions when an officer of the law denigrated those protections.

"Ella…"

I glanced at Janice. She pointed to the doorway of our workroom. Attorney Brown was standing there. He motioned me to come into the hallway.

"Let's borrow Bertram's office and talk for a minute." He led me into the office and closed the door. At first, I felt embarrassed as a stream of people walked past the windowed office watching me get feedback from a partner. "Ella, you were terrific with Agent Curran."

"I'm upset about it," I confessed.

"You handled him perfectly. I wanted you to know I thought so."

"I made you work so hard."

"I stepped in because he was out of control. He's been bitten by the red scare pandemic bug. His ability to be guided by founding documents has been lost."

"His nonsense has me angry and distracted."

"Which is understandable. I want you to go to the law library with your resource materials for estates and business successions for a couple of hours."

I paused as I considered his suggestion. "I have a lot of notes to do on closed cases."

"Notes will wait. Change the subject."

"Okay," I replied reluctantly.

"You're too excellent an attorney to get derailed by this interview."

"Thank you for saying so."

"It's true. You have some important work to do for Dr. Barsky and many others."

"Okay. Estates and successions, it is."

"Excellent, counselor." He walked away leaving me to screw up my courage to prepare my head to work with Ben.

I walked back to my desk, picked up my study materials and walked off to the law library for quiet and the emotional space to recover.

"Ella," Janice whispered from the library door.

I sighed seeing a friendly face. "Hi, Honey," I replied seeing the concerned frown she was giving me.

"Are you all right?"

"I'm a Communist now, evidently."

"For representing Dr. Barsky?"

"Yes."

"The agent showed up to harass you?"

"I suppose it would get him a feather in his cap if he forced me to leave the doctor's team."

"You're going to resign?" Janice asked in alarm.

"Of course not," I reacted noisily with a defiant smile.

Janice recognized the real me was functioning despite my rude visitor. She smiled as she sat back at her desk.

I dug into estates and successions eventually losing myself in the law forgetting for a couple of hours what I had gone through. At noon I was back at my desk, poured a cup of hot coffee from my thermos, and started to eat a chicken salad sandwich Aunt Flora made from the leftovers of Sunday's chicken dinner. A peanut butter cookie was waiting.

The phone rang in the office and one of the legal secretaries picked it up.

"She's here." Holding out the receiver to me she whispered, "It's Marion."

"Hello, Marion."

"How's your day going?"

"I'm so happy you called," I answered instantly getting emotional again.

"What's happened?" he responded hearing my composure crumbling.

"An FBI agent showed up here and tried to frighten me off the Barsky case."

"What?"

"He called me a Communist for defending him."

"Outrageous."

"Mr. Brown sat in and made sure it wasn't a long meeting."

"Thankfully. Are you feeling all right?"

"I could use a hug."

"I'm on the way."

"You're kidding."

"Hang up…" he replied laughing.

I set the phone receiver in the cradle and ate some more. Marion showing up blew away my discomfort about Curran's red baiting. I was back in the library studying successions when Julia, our receptionist, poked her head into the library.

"Marion Forman is here."

I got up and followed her to the front door of our building. Seeing him, he opened his arms and I melted into his embrace. A sob escaped me.

"I'm part of your family now. I'm ready with the hugs."

"You are an answer to prayer." I let the hug do its work. I could feel the nervous tension leave my shoulders. He didn't let me go right away. I felt too cared for to step back.

"When Attorney Brown asked the agent if he was going to arrest you, he didn't answer?" Marion asked.

"No. Should I worry?" He didn't answer right away and I wanted to know what he was thinking. Was he thinking hard about something? "Should I worry?"

The hug was over and the newly trained legal minds discussed what the charges could be for an attorney representing a traitor. We stood there discussing the law as we knew it. Eventually he noticed the time.

"I've gotta go."

"One more hug," I replied.

I smiled. A hug and a kiss later he was out the door.

I got off the bus and started walking toward home. I felt more tired than usual. It was a much bigger day than I was used to. One positive was all my usual friends on my walking route were out to welcome me back home. As I approached the corner to turn for my stoop, there were more neighbors than usual gathering in clumps talking.

I started to wonder what Auntie Flora was making for dinner. I was hungry for whatever it was. I was running my favorites through my mind as I rounded the corner onto my block. I almost walked right into FBI agent Peter Curran. As I kept from stepping on him, I could see he had a colleague with him this time. There were groups of neighbors on the sidewalk and standing in doorways on both sides of the street. I slipped by the agents and headed for my building. Curran and his colleague jogged past me and blocked my way again.

"Uncle Ray is working a Howard University building site," Curran began.

He surprised me. I observed him, picking up the slightest smirk. My mind raced as I processed the intended implication. "Something about bricklaying unconstitutional?"

"Aunt Flora's supervisor know she's harboring a Communist lover?"

"Inuendo is quite professional on you," I quipped hiding fear for my loved ones, a fear I could not avoid feeling which angered me even more.

"Consorting with another commie lover, Forman," Curran hissed quietly, his darting eyes giving away his sense of the nearness of my neighbors.

"Pete..." his friend urged with a cautionary quality in his voice.

I didn't miss the direction of Curran's thought process. "Don't hush him, unknown agent. Today isn't the first day in my life someone has shantytowned me."

"Nigger," Peter quietly growled on the corner of a Washington, D.C. Negro neighborhood. Heads popped out of their windows, more neighbors stepped out onto their stoops, and workers interrupted their tasks. The FBI agents noticed.

The next thing I knew, William swept up, smiling broadly, and stepping between the two agents making them flinch as the large, young man took my arm.

"I owe you an Italian Ice," he announced smiling idiotically and leading me away. A minute or two later we walked into 'Luigi's Confections' and he ordered for me.

I didn't have to check back to know the FBI boys had left my block.

The next morning, Ben had me reading through a case file for a recent succession plan he wrote for a family which owned three restaurants in D.C. I was impressed with the woman who had inherited the company from her husband after his sudden death.

She worked with Ben to restructure the management of the restaurants designating job titles, salaries, and profit sharing while bequeathing the value of the company to her three children. Larger shares of her legacy would go to a son and a daughter who worked in the company's management. A generous portion of the company's value was bequeathed to a daughter who was a professor at Virginia Union University in Richmond.

The wisdom of the business owner was incredible to view. What she had done to empower her employees and family was immense.

Ben walked into our office area and sat in the plain wooden chair next to my desk.

"Mrs. Simpson," I remarked holding up her file.

"She worked out a sharp plan."

"You didn't create this succession?"

"I didn't have to do much. She knew what she wanted."

"I'm impressed."

"She's a smart cookie." He paused and I waited for his reason for dropping by. "Edward is coming into town on Thursday night for his Friday HUAC interview."

"Really? Will we have time to prep him? Who's going to sit with him facing the committee staff?"

"Walker's assigned you and me. Edward is taking a late afternoon train and a cab here, which will mean working late Thursday. Nine a.m. interview at the House Office Building."

"I'll be ready. You heard about the FBI agent's visit, yesterday?"

"Yes."

"Two agents were on my street after work."

"I heard that report, too. Impressing you with their knowledge of your family?"

"Scary stuff."

"They've been at my kids' school."

"No."

"Fortunately, our nanny is a tough broad with a sharp tongue."

I sighed with a little smile thinking I needed a nanny or needed to see more of Marion.

Ben left. I worked on more succession files. Mr. Walker had sent me a memo alerting me about a new succession client. I would be working with Ben on it and doing all the initial work with the client.

Friday I'd be at Dr. Barsky's interview and Monday, the new succession client would be in the office to start planning the future of his business after he was gone. I had been removed from Municipal Court cases for a while.

Ben had mentioned in passing, the firm was starting to talk to a couple of Howard Law School third years about working for us. Such news made me determined to hang onto some Municipal Court work.

Close to quitting time I called Marion at work.

"A better day today?" Marion asked.

"Yes, much."

"Good to hear. Are we getting out this week?"

"Change of plans. Dr. Barsky is coming in Thursday. I must work late. Can we get out on Wednesday?"

"Yes. How about I pick you up after work and we'll go to a restaurant near DuPont Circle?"

"Lovely. Can't wait."

"Same here, Ella."

I put down the phone and immediately got buzzed by Julia in reception.

"Mr. Harpole, Attorney Jacobs' new succession client has dropped in. All the partners are out. Could you give him a tour?"

"Of course. I'll be right down." I hurried down the stairs into reception. A nattily dressed older Negro gentleman stood in front of Julia. "Mr. Harpole, so nice of you to stop by."

"I don't want to interrupt your workday. I'm expecting good things at our meeting on Monday and I wanted to see your offices. I've heard enough to make an appointment for next week but I wanted to see the level of professionalism in your facility," he offered smiling.

"Of course," I replied cheerily. He was tall, slender, in his 60's, and dressed professionally. I especially noticed his perfectly polished dress shoes. He didn't surprise me. We got this scrutiny often. "Let me show you the conference room on this floor."

"Oh, this is an elegant room," he reacted smiling, indicating the upscale décor matched his elegance.

"People come here with important goals. Meeting rooms should be appointed seriously."

"This is very business-like."

"We'll take the elevator to the partners' offices. What business are you in?" as I guided him to the elevator.

"We're a shoe and family clothing store in Anacostia."

"If you are serving families, your store must be spacious."

"We are one of the bigger buildings on our avenue," he reported with quiet pride.

"Here is the partners' floor. The corresponding and legal secretaries sit out here and these three offices are for Mr. Cedric, Mr. Brown, and Mr. Jacobs. Ladies, this is Mr. Harpole. He'll be in to see Mr. Jacobs on Monday."

"Good afternoon, hello, welcome," responded the staff.

"Good afternoon, Ladies."

"Let's sit in Attorney Jacobs' office for a few minutes."

"Thanks."

I invited him to sit in one of the chairs in front of Ben's desk and I pivoted the second chair toward him and sat down.

"How did you decide to sell shoes and clothes?"

"My grandfather was a drummer who sold shoes and notions out of a box truck in all the little hamlets in Maryland and southern Virginia. He had a set of stairs he put out so the customers could sit in the back of the truck as he fit them for new shoes."

"Enterprising."

"When I was in third grade, he would take me along on days off from school and Saturdays and I would help."

"Did you think non-school day work was fun?" I gently teased.

"Not at first," he replied, smiling at the memory of it.

I laughed.

"What changed your mind?"

"The work and travels grew on me. As I got older, I could do the math of his transactions, learned to wait on customer's fittings, and learned how to find stock on his truck shelves."

"Excellent. When did his business turn into a brick-and-mortar store?"

"As he got extremely old, my father and mother talked him into getting rid of his little warehouse and renting a store front here. He was never happy about it but my parents helped him at work every day, adding product lines. After he died, my parents relocated the business to a larger place. By the time I graduated from college, we were in our current building."

"You've always worked for your family's business?"

"Yes. My parents put up with my suggestions for more business-like methods. I used to drive them crazy. I always told them they were getting their money's worth out of my business degree."

I laughed again. He was simply delightful.

"Is your business going to stay in the family?"

"Yes, but I want to plan for the day when I can no longer lead."

"I think your business education continues to pay dividends."

He smiled warmly.

"I think I've chosen the correct law firm."

"Thank you, Mr. Harpole. We are honored. Can I get you a cup of coffee?"

"Oh, no thanks. I've taken enough of your time."

"It's been our pleasure."

"Monday, should be very helpful."

"We'll welcome you back."

He stood up and I led him to reception and bid him goodbye.

Chapter 8

After work Wednesday, I made sure to be on the sidewalk when Marion drove up. I was yearning uninterrupted hours with him. Our weeks were long, two dates a week were all we could manage. Aunt Flora and Unc liked him. They liked the boy I dated in Law School, too, and they grieved with me when he abandoned me for L.A. They liked, as did I, Marion's firm plantedness as a D.C. native. It dawned on me to ask him if he ever wanted to live somewhere else.

He rolled up to the curb and I got in.

"Hello, Ella. I'm so happy we could get together tonight."

I smiled as I slid over sitting close to him. He was signaling for a kiss and got one.

"I agree. Maybe Wednesdays are a better date night. I don't have to wait so long."

"Tuesdays are too long a wait."

I laughed.

"Next week, three date nights."

"I love it," he reacted, which thrilled me.

"We don't need to spend money every time. I'd love a chance to talk."

"Me, too. And if you don't mind, a bus is the best way to take in the monuments."

"I'm happy with the bus."

"Tonight, I'm taking you to 'Ma Raney's Carolina Restaurant.'"

"Oh, I've heard it's marvelous."

"Since you grew up in Holly Springs, I wondered if it would pass muster?"

"My tastebuds are ready for this test."

"Good."

"I wondered if you ever wanted to live somewhere besides D.C.?"

"I enjoyed being away for school and my parents have taken us to the Maryland shore for beach weekends."

"They found welcoming hotels or vacation cottages?"

"We would go to Highland Beach. It's only thirty-five miles from town. Negroes have been going there for almost a hundred years."

"Where would you stay?"

"My parents rented a house, but something smaller would be all we need, *like a hotel room,*" Marion thought. "I know the best place a block from the beach."

"When it's warm, let's go."

"The waves would be fun. Here's 'Ma's.'

Marion led us in and a hostess put us at a table handing us menus. I couldn't believe the offerings. It was a blueprint of my grandmother's recipe cards.

A waitress hustled up asking, "Is sweet tea going to work for the two of you?"

"Yes," Marion answered.

"Sweet tea for me as well."

"I love to come back to this place because I have so many favorites."

"I can see why. What are you going to have tonight?"

"I think the gumbo."

"I think I'll have smothered okra with shrimp."

"You'll like your choice," Marion confirmed.

The waitress returned with our beverages and a basket of small, warm muffins and butter. I took a cornbread muffin and Marion selected a darker orange muffin he said was a yam muffin.

"We should simply come here on all of our date nights with an occasional stop at the crab shack."

"We must include a barbeque place not far from here."

"Good barbeque?"

"You'll swoon."

"It's great to see the extra benefits of knowing you. A friendly beach, great restaurants, and a place to get my car fixed if I owned one."

"I can help you buy your own car, too," he boasted.

"You sell cars on the side?"

"No," he laughed. "My father does repairs on cars from a couple of the local used car lots and he recommends particular cars in better than average condition to customers wanting to upgrade."

"Your father's under the hood analysis before buying is a huge factor in how cute you are," I teased.

"I'm a blue-ribbon guy, right?"

We laughed as I admitted to myself, he was, beaming warmly at him. As we lay on the beach mid-summer 1952, he told me this moment at 'Ma Ramey's' was the moment we had finally clicked. I told him it had been weeks earlier but I agreed my guard had completely dropped as we talked over southern cooking.

After dinner, we got back in his car.

"It's not too late to stop to see my parents, is it?"

"No," I responded.

"I'm not clear who all we be home, but let's see."

"Sounds marvelous."

Marion parked in a spot in front of the repair shop. It was still open and bustling. He led me into the midst of the repair activity quietly waiting for an older, bear of a man discussing with a young man barely twenty how a brake job needed to proceed.

"Hi, Daddy," Marion interjected.

"Marion," the older man replied taking me in instead of his son, his professional intensity melting.

"Dad, this is Ella Moses."

"It's a pleasure to meet you, Mr. Forman."

"I wondered if you really existed. It's nice to meet you. This is Wheels Baker, one of my mechanics."

"A pleasure."

"Hello," Wheels reacted sounding like he had always wondered if Marion actually liked girls.

"Is Mommy upstairs?"

"Yes, she's gone up. Nice to meet you."

"You, as well."

Marion led me to a door in the back of one of the repair bays revealing a staircase to the flat above. At the top of the flight, we walked into the kitchen where food slowly simmered. Walking into the living room, we found Marion's mother sitting at a desk while a radio played. She was working on the books of her business.

"Marion is this Ella?"

"Yes, Momma."

"It's so good to meet you, my dear."

"It's a treat to meet you, Mrs. Forman."

"Oh, none of this Mrs. stuff. Call me Gladdy like everyone else. Have you had dinner?"

"Marion took me to 'Ma Rainey's.'"

"Oh, such a good place. They do the old recipes right. We eat later here after Marion's dad finally decides the workday is done."

"It was fun to see your shop after hearing about it so much."

"We're so fortunate to have a faithful following here. We've been blessed."

"I can tell you are a neighborhood institution."

"She's as nice as you said she was, Marion."

We all laughed.

"I'm going to show her the rest of the house."

"Of course, Honey. Great to meet you, Ella."

"And you, Gladdy."

He led me to the connecting door which opened into the second floor of the apartment where Marion and his sister roomed.

"This is a terrific idea connecting these two buildings."

"It's given us room to spread out as we grew older. The living room is down here."

We took the stairs down where a couch, some side chairs, and a record player filled a warm, engaging room. Out the front window, the side street revealed a solid residential atmosphere.

"All these records. You even have a handful of 45's."

"It's my parents' collection."

"What a treasure."

"Would you like lemonade?"

"A little glass would be nice." I peeked at the record covers. It was a catalogue of singers I loved to hear on the radio. He handed me a glass of lemonade. "Ella Fitzgerald," I noted with admiration.

"Here. I'll put it on."

Ella started singing and we settled back on the couch. His hand found mine.

"She can sing," I reacted. Marion seemed quietly happy. I couldn't ignore him. I set my glass on the side table turning back to him laying my hand on the side of his face. He bent toward me and kissed me softly holding this affectionate moment for several beats. He took me in with a quiet intensity which I soaked up and tried to return.

A key slipped into the front door's lock and our heads tracked the sound. It was Veronica, Marion's sister. "You must be Ella. I'm going upstairs for supper."

"Okay, Ronnie," Marion replied. He got up and put the needle on another record. When he sat down, he adjusted me so I was facing him. I kicked off my heels and put my knees on the couch so I wasn't in a weird twist and he offered his arms to cradle my torso and shoulders.

"Mmmmmm," I murmured as I settled into the cuddle.

"Comfy?" he asked with a tender smile.

"Couldn't be happier," I responded with a whisper and intense eye contact.

He kissed me again. The first was followed by a dozen more. I remembered being in an embrace like this with my law school boyfriend. When Marion kissed me again, I put my left hand on the back of his neck to keep my face inches from his. His right hand was freed up and he slipped it inside my suitcoat jacket on my left breast. It felt warm and sensual there. My increased excitement was revealed in soft, husky breathing. His kisses became more invasive and I met him measure for measure. We were loath to get up so we tolerated the needle riding on the inside edge of the last song we listened to. The rhythm of the needle almost matched my increased pulse.

"I have strong feelings for you, Sugar," Marion confessed.

"I'm thrilled, Counselor," I teased him with a smile. "Nobody but you," I added with a little heat in my voice.

I knew his bedroom was only steps away but his family was close by, also. We hugged and kissed and talked. The increased physical intimacy released a host of as yet unshared thoughts about each other. We were in a new place together.

I reluctantly agreed when he suggested he drive me home. When we got off the couch, I hugged him, our bodies fully together the wish was clear.

"Thank God, I found you," he confessed vulnerably.

"I thank God I was found."

Chapter 9

Thursday had gone quickly which was a blessing. I was excited to see Dr. Barsky again but Friday morning's interview with the House Un-American Activities Committee's staff attorney would be difficult. I sat in with Ben late morning as he began to discuss a succession plan with a Negro business owner. Wilber Jaffrey owned a foundry near the Anacostia River, an industrial area immediately south of D.C. His firm manufactured soil pipe angles, curves, and custom fittings for specific applications. His company could make custom pipe, pouring metal around pre-baked cores. They had a central furnace from which they poured molten metal into lost sand molds on a vast molding floor. There were a dozen lines where workers prepared molds and poured the metal creating pipe.

"Tell Attorney Moses and me your musings about who would succeed you at Jaffrey Foundry?" Ben asked him.

"I don't have anything firm yet. Let me describe my situation and see what you think."

"Please do," Ben replied.

"I'm blessed with strong leadership in sales, production, and accounting. My instincts are to make my sales manager president because she is the oldest."

"Is there anyone in your family who can serve as owner or president?" Ben asked.

"My children are educators, important for our community but neither of them are attuned to manufacturing. They will be co-owners after I retire or pass but silent to day-to-day operations."

"Can your finances support promoting the production and accounting managers to vice-president as your sales leader becomes president or perhaps include these two in profit sharing?"

"I have done bonuses for some time. Perhaps a larger percentage could be offered."

"You could also design a future succession plan naming future presidential positions for the production and accounting leaders, when your president resigns."

"Such a future supporting concept is interesting. It might help me keep these strong leaders."

"When we meet next, let us know how you'd like to shape top management. We can start working on a draft revision of your will."

"Excellent."

"Shall we get back together in two weeks?"

"I would find another meeting helpful, Attorney Jacobs. It was nice to meet you, Attorney Moses."

"Thank you, Mr. Harpole."

Ben walked him down to the reception area. I returned to my desk. A few minutes later, Ben stepped into our work room. "Ella, while Edward's train gets in at four, I don't know how long it will take a cab to get him here."

"It's okay. I have plenty of work on my desk."

He smiled. "I'll buzz you as soon as he is settled."

"Thanks."

I was representing three clients in Municipal Court in the next week. Bertram Charles, usually sitting first chair, was on vacation on the barrier islands of North Carolina. Growing up I heard great stories of the beauty there but also the devastation when hurricanes blew ashore. Without hesitation, he passed the case files to me.

The succession cases I had read and the two clients I was managing involved wealthy Negroes. I certainly valued the effort to protect their legacies and to pass their wealth on. But this financial planning wisdom needed to be taught to every member of our community. I wanted to talk to Mr. Cedric about raising awareness. For instance, would he allow me to talk to my pastor about promoting the idea of wills for all? Would he think the firm could absorb new work?

I wanted to encourage fellow members of Richmond Missionary Baptist Church to seek out an attorney they may already know but to protect their legacy no matter its size. It would lift the next generation.

Representing defendants was crucial. But getting all working adults into thoughtful planning was pro-active.

I returned to the criminal cases on my desk. Before I noticed it, my three office mates had cleared out for home and the entire floor was quiet. It was after six and Julia would have left and our front door locked. Instantly, I became worried about Dr. Barsky. Had he arrived before Julia finished her day? My phone buzzed.

"This is Ella," I responded.

"Dr. Barsky and I are ready to meet," Ben explained.

"I'll be right up."

I grabbed a pad of paper and a couple of pencils and hustled up the spiral staircase to the partner suite. The center of the room was quiet. All the secretaries were gone. Mr. Cedric was standing in Ben's office doorway.

"Hi, Ella."

"Mr. Cedric, could we talk when you have time. I want to promote wills and trusts at my church. Succession law is an important tool."

"You don't need my permission to raise the value of wills to your congregation. But let's talk about how we expand the message beyond one church."

"Of course, thank you, sir."

"I'll have Julia put you on my schedule."

He walked toward his office.

"I appreciate it, Mr. Cedric."

He stopped and faced me again. He wearily smiled and headed for his door. I stepped into Ben's office. Dr. Barsky stood.

"It's great to see you again, Ella," he began.

"I'm happy to see you again, sir."

"Please call me Edward. We're going to become family through this ordeal."

"I will, Edward," I replied with a smile. I sat down, and simply focused on Dr. Barsky without another word.

"I want to start by explaining what it's been like in New York. FBI agents have been stopping and unsettling colleagues with inuendo, half-truths, and veiled threats. They've been concentrating on select members of my surgery department, but they've started to harass the soldiers and medical staff from the Abraham Lincoln Brigade they can dredge up in town."

"We've been experiencing a bit of the same here," Ben replied pointing at me.

"You, Ella?" Edward asked.

"On my way home, in front of my neighbors."

"I'm sorry, my dear."

"I have a better appreciation for your circumstances."

Ben and Edward laughed despite the bitter truths revealed and confirmed in this meeting.

"Communications with committee counsel have been tense. I've sent you what they've mailed me. Here's the latest, inviting me in for a pre-interview asserting a date with the full committee is a forgone conclusion."

Ben passed me the latest House Un-American Activities Committee correspondence.

"Secondary evidence of the Dies Committee's activity are carbon copies of affidavits from 'witnesses.' They include negative stories of our fundraising and organizing to put a hospital in Spain and our work to care for refugees and injured fighters who have returned to the states. There is a fervent minority in support of Dies and McCarthy's intentions."

"Are these 'witnesses' people from within your organization?" Ben asked.

"They always seem to be relatives of members of the Lincoln Brigade. As one former fighter described him, 'my crazy uncle.'"

We laughed again.

"The crazy uncles seem to surface when the demagogues find a microphone," Ben acknowledged with weariness.

"Like Ella, a half-dozen of us get followed daily. It gets tiresome when you can't walk down the street in peace to get to the deli."

"We'll go to one of my favorite delis tomorrow after the interview," Ben promised.

"Excellent."

"Have you changed your mind about how you are going to testify?" Ben asked him.

"No. I've told you time and again, I won't name one name or give them our list of donors or recipients of the immigration fund."

"You remember what I told you they would do?"

"Refer me for prosecution to the Justice Department and a trial will follow."

"Correct. The wrinkle since we last chatted is my partners and I have found a party who's willing to fund appeals as far as we can take them."

"Oh, really?"

"The donor wants to get this silliness to the Supreme Court."

"I'm for appealing it to them. Would you present at the high court?"

"Probably not if we want to win," Ben joked. We reacted with a laugh. "We're starting to have conversations with attorneys who have experience at the court."

"Interesting."

"Since you are sticking to principle, we turn to Ella. She has the latest regarding the receipts for your family fund."

"Ah…," Edward replied focusing his attention on me.

"We have almost $20,000 in your account here and pledges of $9,000 more." I handed him a carbon copy of my ledger page.

"The response is amazingly heartwarming. You can give me a list of these fine people? I will work on my thank you notes from the slammer."

Ben and I laughed but not robustly.

"As the public HUAC hearing is in the news, we expect to have close to 30 thousand in hand and more promised," Ben asserted.

"Vita will be able to manage nicely. Such a comfort."

"We'll let you know how the fund is doing but now let's get you to my place for a hot meal. Are you okay getting home, Ella?"

"Just fine, thanks. Good night."

"Thanks for everything, Ella."

"You're welcome, Edward."

I put my notes from the meeting in my pencil drawer when I got back to my desk, grabbed my jacket and purse, and exited to the street to catch my bus.

I put work behind me lifting my spirits by planning a call to Marion. Tomorrow night was a girls' night at Jellie's Crab House. I wanted him there with a chance for a long talk afterward. As I walked home the last couple of blocks from my bus stop, I decided to call him as soon as I walked into the building. I set my bag down by the phone, fished out a nickel out of my change purse, slipped it into its slot on the top of the phone, and called the number at his apartment.

"Hello?" Veronica answered.

"Ronnie, it's Ella. Is Marion around?"

"Hi, Ella. Yes. Let me get him." I heard her yell, 'Counselor, your favorite female lawyer is on the line.'

I chuckled at her sibling abrasiveness. I escaped this dynamic in my family but knew it well from my friends.

"Ella?"

"Hi, Marion."

"How was Edward?"

"Defiant."

"It is such with the principled."

"Can you come to girls' night tomorrow at Jellie's and take me out for a drive after? I have an idea to try out on you."

"I'm all ears. See you for girls' night," he replied with a laugh in his voice.

"Bye, thanks."

I walked upstairs, my head swimming with all the irons I had in the fire.

~*~

I was standing on the curb at eight a.m. in front of the office with my briefcase as Ben arrived with Edward in the front seat. I sat in the back listening to them share personal stories like they were going to a Washington Senators game. It dawned on me who these two were. They were world tested professionals going up against political hacks of the lowest caliber. I took a deep breath and began to enjoy I had a front row seat. Within ten minutes we were in the House office building walking into one its smaller conference rooms. A House page was standing by the table nervously.

"Mr. Tavenner will be here in a moment."

"Thank you, sir," Ben replied.

The boy stole a glimpse at me. I imagined I was a relative oddity in this building on a non-hearing day. "Why don't you sit while we wait?" I asked.

"Pages don't sit."

"Where are you from?" I asked the boy, official but nervous in his uniform.

"Chevy Chase."

"Umm… How do you like working in the House?"

His head was now up, a more open expression forming. "It's the most amazing thing I've ever done."

"Do you want to come back here when you're an adult?"

"Maybe when I'm much older. I'll be working in my father's road-building business."

"Ah, roads…" I reacted as the committee's counsel entered the room. The page disappeared.

"Good morning, Dr. Barsky. Is this Attorney Jacobs and Attorney Moses?"

"Yes," Edward responded matter-of-factly.

"Members of the committee may drop in from time to time during our visit. They all have standing committee responsibilities this morning."

"All right," Ben responded.

"Dr. Barsky, the committee and I need a couple of things from you before your hearing date. We would like the list of people who funded your Joint Anti-Fascist Refugee Committee and the list of people who received cash payments from the group."

"I won't be providing any names to you," Edward replied quietly but firmly.

"Many, if not all, of the refugees you helped, fought or are dependents of fighters backed by the Communists."

"Russia was our ally in WWII and the Abraham Lincoln Brigade fought in Spain against the same fascist forces we fought in WWII."

"Times change, Dr. Barsky."

"Time hasn't changed the refugee's position in life, sir."

"We also need the names of your field hospital staff, the funders of your equipment and supplies in Spain, the Spaniards with whom you worked while you were abroad, your patient lists, your military liaison to the republic's forces, and the mayor of the town in which you were located."

"I won't be providing any information," Edward replied matter-of-factly.

"We need the list of the board members of the JAFRC, any office staff, the owner of the building where your offices are located. Before you answer, understand your unwillingness to cooperate could result in many years in a federal penitentiary, the loss of your medical license, and financial penalties."

"I understand."

"Have you really thought through your answer? Your life could be changed irreparably. You could die penniless and be ostracized for all time by your nation as a Communist."

"In the end, my life will have been well-lived."

"Attorney Jacobs could you and Attorney Moses talk some sense into your client. I'll leave the room if you'd like to help him reconsider."

"We've tried our best already."

"Dr. Barsky, you're certain?"

Representative Willis walked in and the proceedings stopped. The committee's counsel walked up to him before he could sit down. They chatted conspiratorially out of earshot for a minute. One of Willis's staff members put his name card on the table for us to see. He was familiar to me from the Burl Ives hearing.

Willis sat down.

"Dr. Barsky, my advice is to think twice about not cooperating with the committee. Think about where your case will go if you don't share what you know. We'll refer you to the Justice Dept. for criminal prosecution. The current Attorney General is James P. McGranery who recently revoked Charlie Chaplin's re-entry permit due to his Communist activities. The attorney general won't hesitate to indict you for obstruction and conspiracy."

"With all due respect, Representative Willis, being included in the same sentence with Mr. Chaplin is delightful."

A little smile crossed Willis's face. "Do you have anything else for Dr. Barsky?" the legislator asked his counsel.

"No, sir."

"We'll see you before the full committee, Dr. Barsky," and Willis was up and gone.

"Thank you for coming in today. We'll be in contact with your counsel."

"Good day, sir," Edward replied standing up.

Ben dropped me at the office going on to take his friend to Grand Central Station.

Chapter 10

After work, Marion and I walked into Jellie's and joined my friends at the bar.

"Is this guy still hanging around?" Janice quipped.

"I'm the boyfriend now."

"Oooooh," the girls responded with derision.

When the reaction died down, I added, "Ladies, you have some catching up to do."

"Sass is the way it's going to be?" asked one.

Another asked Marion, "Know any other attractive Negro attorneys?"

"Actually, I do."

The questioner slipped an arm through his and asked him to pour forth.

My friends confided in him and dealt for some matchups. Phone numbers were exchanged.

We ate and began the private part of our evening taking the drive into the country we planned. In the D.C. of 1952, it didn't take long to get into the Virginia countryside.

"I had an idea."

"Yes, Honey."

"It's one thing to help Negro business owners to pass their wealth to their heirs to preserve legacies. How about all the working stiffs? Why not create an effort to write wills for more of our blue-collar community?"

"What a marvelous idea. Could people with a modest income get the work done 'pro bono?'"

"I would love it but Cedric, Brown & Jacobs can't absorb all the work."

"There must be a dozen Negro law firms in the city," Marion replied.

"Oh, what a good way to tackle this. Create a project backed by all Negro D.C. firms."

"It could be promoted in our local newspapers."

"How about on WOL?" I asked.

"Everybody listens to it."

"Mr. Cedric suggested I start with my church until a plan can be put into place."

"Have you talked to your reverend yet?"

"I did. He invited me to speak on Sunday morning."

"May I escort you to church Sunday?"

"I would love it if you would."

Marion headed back toward town. He stopped at a community owned ice cream parlor and we each chose a cone with two scoops.

"Seeing you more is making me happier," as I rescued a rivulet of melting chocolate ice cream from dropping onto my work suit.

"I'm noticing the happiness effect myself. My co-workers have commented on my sudden affability."

I laughed.

"I'm seeing a lot less of Aunt Flora and Unc, but they're happy I've met someone substantial."

"I like the word, substantial."

"It's not easy to find someone special once you are out in the working world. My firm's partners are old enough to be grandfathers except for Ben."

"What about Ben? He's available, isn't he?"

"He's divorced and has two children. I want to create a family of my own with a peer not an already wealthy Brahmin. I want to build a successful life with someone who shares the worldview of my generation."

"From everything I've heard, Ben is a rare bird, already committed to civil rights."

"Our generation will take it to a new place, reshaping it into a cause."

"I think you're right. Our firms being active on Capitol Hill is another foundation stone for our people."

"Building is what I'm talking about. It's one thing to pass a generation of Negro wealth to the up and coming. It's another thing to change the stature of Negroes to the level of those who wrote The Constitution."

"The groundswell is rising from everything I'm hearing," as Marion crunched into his cone.

I smiled.

"See. No one like Ben would be caught dead biting into an ice cream cone." Marion almost choked with laughter his mouth full of the treat. I handed him a napkin in self-defense. He swung away to keep from spritzing my face with cone debris. We giggled in youthful simplicity. "I rest my case. How could anything be better than this?"

Recovered, he leaned in and kissed me sweetly. As the cones were finished, we sat at one of the picnic tables arranged next to the stand among other ice cream lovers.

"Can we fit children into our cultural revolution?" Marion asked shocking me with this abrupt change of subject.

"How did you know I was thinking about the family we might have?"

"Have you?" Marion reacted not expecting my open response to his question. By all rights, it was frightening early in our friendship for this topic.

"Meeting your family put into stark relief my own situation."

"Wait a minute. Your aunt and uncle exemplify the best of family."

"They do, considering I foisted myself on them rebelling from an agrarian life back home."

"A lot of us gravitated to city life."

"True. I envy what your parents have done. They replanted the family ethic not forsaking the power of Negro interconnectedness."

"They chose D.C. before they started a family."

"You didn't have to do the migration?"

"They taught us about it so we know of their upbringing in rural North Carolina. The three of us see Graham, North Carolina as our hometown."

"How did your parents juggle working and children without a larger set of relations surrounding them?"

"Their church family provided surrogate grannies who took care of us."

"The community saves the day."

"Always."

"I was hoping Aunt Flora could be our mother's helper. It would finally get her on day shift."

"With both of us working, we should be able to rent a big enough place, they could move in with us. Then, when they need caring for, reaching great age, they will already be in a safe place."

"It's been the way to go forever here. I'm happy family is the answer for you."

"I'm happy about it," he said smiling, "but why did your law school boyfriend choose California over you?"

"Southern California is his home. He struggled through the winters here as mild as they are compared to New England. The occasional big snows drove him crazy."

"But he knew you."

I smiled. "Yes, I was wonderful me."

"What was his plan for the law?"

"Real estate."

"A mismatch with your instincts?"

"We fought. I was 'too serious.' I always had to lay off the 'struggles of our people' talk."

"But Howard has always been known for its change makers."

"He was often the odd man out when we were building the community."

"Maybe you weren't totally broken up about his return to the west coast?" Marion ventured.

"He talked about going home all of third year. The final decision was no surprise but he was my first adult relationship. I was numb emotionally after graduation. In fact, I was still recovering when I met you at the Burl Ives hearing."

"For a while there, I felt something was in the way."

"My history and the possibility of marrying up."

"Ben," Marion commented filling in the blanks so I didn't have to. "Are we getting ahead of ourselves, too?" he asked in a much softer tone fearing the answer.

"Maybe, but the conversations have a shared history undergirding them. I enjoy our ability to talk about all the tricky subjects," I observed.

"Why are all issues open to us? Are we fools speaking the truth to one another? We seem to be running toward the issues which would crush other friendships."

"I think we both happen to be pyromaniacs," I joked.

His head dropped in laughter. When he recovered, he remarked," a reckless urge to find the fault lines."

"Exactly," I replied.

"You don't come across as a madwoman."

"More and more you know what you are getting."

He smiled.

"Who knew in this Carolina girl's down home demeanor one would find a firecracker."

"You don't know the half of it yet," I teased.

"Okay, you're driving me crazy. My place before I take you home."

"Sounds perfect," I replied trying my best smolder on him. He took my hand leading me to the car. As he drove, I rested a hand on his knee. There wasn't much talk afterward until he walked with me up my stoop steps. "Any questions, Counselor?" I asked in my most sultry voice.

"All I can say is I'm serious about you."

"I can tell. It's a good feeling."

The good night kiss was long enough William showed up.

"Ease up, Bullet," he growled.

"You're right, Bull Dog."

I laughed and slipped through the door flashing a happy, sassy smile at Marion.

Chapter 11

"Thanks for giving us a ride to church this morning, Marion," Aunt Flora remarked as he drove the short trip a couple blocks from home.

"My pleasure," Marion replied.

"It's a short bus ride for us but the ride is nice."

"Your father has this car humming," Unc observed from the front passenger seat.

"Ella, you and I have to get over to Howard and see Unc's new building."

"I've been meaning to. The last time I was there, the walls had barely begun to go up," I replied.

"It's one of the bigger jobs I've been on in a long while."

Marion found a spot at the curb two doors from the church and he helped me out of the back seat. Unc helped Aunt Flora to the sidewalk. I was wearing a burnt umber colored dress with a hat to match. Auntie wore a floral pattern and a red hat which matched one of the colors in her dress.

It was as dressy as Marion had ever seen me, my work suits running in the black and brown pallets.

Walking into the building, Marion caught the interest of Aunt Flora's friends. It was a warm, admiring gauntlet he passed through accepting the approving language of my church family. There wasn't much not to like. He was tall, athletic, and handsome.

Prelude music indicated the service was soon to begin. We joined Unc in a pew leaving me on the aisle so when called, I could gracefully make my way to the front.

Reverend Abraham Michaels Crossley was our pastor and he welcomed those gathered, inviting us to rise and sing an opening hymn. Our robed choir filled four rows in the front. The congregation sang but the choir lifted us into reflection. We were happily separated from our daily challenges.

The hymn completed, Reverend Crossley prayed over us and read a lesson from the old testament.

After he finished, he walked up the center aisle toward me. "This morning, Sister Moses has an important community message to share with us. Please welcome her."

The musician played me forward, a warm smattering of applause surrounding me. I could only smile as I faced the gathering. "In my work in the law for Mr. Cedric, Mr. Brown, and Mr. Jacobs, I have a new task. I help Negro business owners plan how their firms will continue to be influential after they retire."

A murmur of approval responded to my opening statement.

"I know you value and patronize our business leaders."

"Yes…" voices responded.

"No matter our own station in life, we see their success as our success and it is heartening to know they are doing well."

"Yes, yes…" the voices in front of me responded again.

"But I think every one of you should plan to pass on your signs of success to your following generations. Whether you are a bricklayer like my Uncle Raymond, a nurse like my Aunt Flora, whatever you do should be protected to empower our family members coming up."

Some shouts welcomed my assertion.

"A document communicating your wishes is a will. Properly prepared, signed, and submitted to the appropriate authorities in the District, it cannot be changed. I prepare them as a part of my work and I will prepare yours at no cost."

Applause greeted me. I smiled. "As you can see, this is such a good idea, my social life could be seriously threatened."

The congregation laughed and checked Marion. He shrugged his shoulders and they laughed even harder. "As you pass your financial legacy in a planned way, you accelerate our influence in the years to come. We are already part of a powerful past. Let's multiply it. Thank you."

The musician played, applause rolled again, and I walked back to Marion and my family, their smiles beaming.

After the worship service concluded, I was surrounded by many interested couples and individuals. Even some young people wanted my work phone number.

The four of us left for Sunday Dinner.

"Ella, you are so right to encourage financial wisdom as we get older," Unc asserted earnestly. "We have the chance to put our community in a stronger place."

"I'm happy to hear you agree," I responded.

"You're exactly the kind of couple who can expand the Negro community's power. Two committed workers who have already been building up our neighborhoods," Marion asserted as the waitress set down the beverages and took our order.

"I think you give us too much credit," Aunt Flora shared quietly with a little smile.

"Your dependable commitment to your employers and supporting Ella during law school and her first year of work is major league."

Flora smiled and Unc shook his head affirmatively, pausing to speak, uncharacteristic of him. After a beat, "It's true. I never would have made it without you," I told them,

"Compared to other people we have a modest life but I like the idea of a will," Aunt Flora ventured more positively.

"You are young yet," Marion boldly teased.

"Now he's spinning, Flo," Unc retorted laughing.

"Yes, husband, he is using his summation styling on us."

We laughed.

"Does he sweet talk you, El?"

"All the time."

We all laughed.

"Flo, is it time to tell them?" She stared long and hard into his face. He smiled conspiratorially. She evaluated me and Marion.

"I think they're grown up enough."

A quick glance at Marion confirmed we both were quizzical, as we wondered what we didn't know about them.

"Your aunt and I have been dabbling in the real estate market for years."

"What?" I reacted.

"In what way?" Marion wondered.

"Over the years, we've been buying tracts of farmland in Alamance County. It's created two larger parcels. We have a broker working with us and we're trying to buy more land to connect them. At present, we own a little under five hundred acres."

"Wonderful."

"Amazing."

"The land includes three farmhouses which are occupied by tenants. We pay them to do upkeep," Aunt Flora explained.

"Now, see. You are perfect candidates for a will," Marion observed with a smile.

"Actually, we are," Aunt Flora confessed sheepishly.

"I already adored you but now I'm immensely proud of you." Ella emoted.

"Thank you, Baby," Auntie replied. "We might not be on the land anymore, but we want to stay connected."

"It's so important you are owners," Marion replied.

"We're fortunate. We've lived a fruitful life in the District, never wanted for work and kept our life simple."

"It's a terrific formula," Marion responded.

"Do you want to retire down in North Carolina?" I asked.

"I don't know if we'll ever retire completely but we're talking about spending parts of the year down there," Unc explained.

"Sounds perfect," I replied.

Our plates were put in front of us and our conversation relaxed into lighter banter.

We took them home and proceeded to saunter through the National Zoo to process what my aunt and uncle had shared. Marion was carrying a section of the New York Times. "This discovery simply proves our community needs the protection of wills and trusts," I stated.

"Clearly. Do their plans change your goal of having them move in with us someday?"

"No. They should make our home their intown base. They can travel when they want to."

"A plan for childcare would be more complicated."

"The church community will provide," I replied.

"It always seems to." Marion paused and handed me the section of The New York Times he had packed. "I wanted you to see a couple of the articles circulating around my office." We sat on a bench across from the lions. We could see several females lounging in the sun, a male laying on a rock nearby.

"Check this headline," I reacted. "Adlai Stevenson talked about race in Richmond on a campaign stop?"

"It's interesting how the speech starts," Marion suggested.

I read on.

"This is crafty of him. He's acknowledging southern whites' grievances, but also indicates Negroes feel the economic downturn, too."

"He's trying to hold southern Democrats in the party and weave us in alongside them."

I read some more. "Listen to this, 'But I do not attempt to justify the unjustifiable.' I read out loud. 'Whether it is anti-Negroism in one place, anti-Semitism in another, - or for that matter anti-southernism in many places… let none of us be smug on this score, for nowhere in the nation have we come to the state of harmonious unity between racial and religious groups to which we aspire…' "Amazing coming out of the mouth of a Democratic candidate for president, considering how things are."

"Read on," Marion suggested.

'No one could stand here in Richmond without reverence for those great Virginians – Washington, whose sturdy common sense was the mortar of our foundations, and Jefferson, that universal genius who proclaiming the Rights of Man when few men had any rights anywhere, shook the earth and made this feeble country the hope of the oppressed everywhere. And so it is today after nearly two centuries.'

"He sweet talks them but reminds them the 'hope of the oppressed' resulted from the idealism of a southerner. Brilliant," Marion observed recasting Stevenson's remarks.

"Adlai Stevenson said this?" I reacted. "I confess I haven't been paying a lot of attention to this election. His speech is not representative of a large portion of the country."

"But isn't idealism the way you want your candidate for president to talk?"

"Of course, but he's not going to get elected making speeches including us in the American portrait as much as I yearn for it."

"FDR and Truman have been in power for two decades. Stevenson should ride their coattails," Marion asserted.

"Truman didn't strike me as an active civil rights activist except for integrating the armed forces," I complained.

"But think how big Truman's action is," Marion asserted. "Negro servicemen serve side by side with whites and over time they'll rise into the officers' ranks," Marion forecasted.

"Isn't Adlai Stevenson's speech in Richmond too big a step forward?"

"Here's the other document I brought for you. It's a mimeograph of the Civil Rights plank of the Democratic Party's platform for the 1952 Presidential Campaign."

"A Civil Rights plank?"

I was reading a full page of goals for Negroes driven by Democrats. I read it through.

Civil Rights

The Democratic Party is committed to support and advance the individual rights and liberties of all Americans.

Our country is founded on the proposition that all men are created equal. This means that all citizens are equal before the law and should enjoy equal political rights. They should have equal opportunities for education, for economic advancement, and for decent living conditions.

We will continue our efforts to eradicate discrimination based on race, religion or national origin.

We know this task requires action, not just in one section of the Nation, but in all sections. It requires the cooperative efforts of individual citizens and action by State and local governments. It also requires Federal action. The Federal Government must live up to the ideals of the Declaration of Independence and must exercise the powers vested in it by the Constitution.

We are proud of the progress that has been made in securing equality of treatment and opportunity in the Nation's armed forces and the civil service and all areas under Federal jurisdiction. The Department of Justice has taken an important part in successfully arguing in the courts for the elimination of many illegal discriminations, including those involving rights to own and use real property, to engage in gainful occupations and to enroll in publicly supported higher educational institutions. We are determined that the Federal Government shall continue such policies.

At the same time, we favor Federal legislation effectively to secure these rights to everyone: (1) the right to equal opportunity for employment; (2) the right to security of persons; (3) the right to full and equal participation in the Nation's political life, free from arbitrary restraints. We also favor legislation to perfect existing Federal civil rights statutes and to strengthen the administrative machinery for the protection of civil rights.

"They expect to pass this agenda in the next Congress?" she asked Marion.

"If they win the president and the majority of congress. At least parts of it might happen," Marion suggested.

"We've had Democratic Presidents for quite a while but Stevenson is running against General Eisenhower, a popular figure to be sure."

"His Richmond speech shows he's a thoughtful person and has courage. He may be able to inspire the voters to choose Democratic leadership once again. But do you feel the country is ready to extend rights to us?"

"We must talk about this more. Sometimes I don't know what to think. I see many Negroes riding upwards in the post war economy, other people are frozen out of moving up with all the servicemen returning to the work force. I'm not seeing an expansion of rights, except in small ways and now we have Senator McCarthy's witch hunt added on to aspects of Jim Crow keeping the races from working together productively."

"I would like to talk about our community's strivings to have full rights in this country. It would be good to support each other on a higher level, maybe investigate ways together to take some positive steps. I think your wills effort needs to get much bigger, for example. We should urge Virginia congressmen to act on the platform."

"A group of lawyers could be persuasive," I suggested.

"Maybe take some clergy with us," Marion added. "But living in the District, we are at a disadvantage."

"True. We have no representative. Will Virginia congressmen even take a meeting with us?" I wondered.

"Between our two firms, one of the partners must know one of Virginia's congressional delegation or maybe we'd get a better reception from a northern congressman or Senator."

"I bet Dr. Barsky could get us a meeting."

"I know you're right."

"All I know is I'm ready for some progress getting full rights under the Constitution."

"Indeed. Ready to walk on?"

"Oh, yes." We walked hand-in-hand past Lemur Island stopping near the gorilla enclosure, seeing alligators and tortoises on the way. Spring had launched the glory of the foliage everywhere in the zoo. Sun splashed our walk lifting and deepening our spirits as we grew closer. Marion's arm would slip around my waist from time to time. I enjoyed his affectionate attention. We were a couple. We walked on past the small mammal area heading for the elephants. We lingered there, enjoying the massive animal's movements and use of their area in the zoo. We leisurely walked back through the zoo and out to find his car. He drove me home.

Parked in front of Auntie and Unc's, he opened my door, but I surprised Marion, leading him into the foyer of my building. I motioned to him to be quiet placing a hand on one of his forearms as I tipped my brimmed hat off my head. I was on my toes to kiss him. The first-floor hallway was quiet but we could hear children playing outside an apartment somewhere upstairs.

"Three dates this week," he whispered kissing me again.

"Three dates this week," I replied and started another kiss. He held me tightly against his body which made me want to be alone with him. I couldn't imagine how to arrange to be alone but I was highly motivated to figure out a way.

We must have stood there ten minutes.

"I better head home before I cause us some embarrassment," Marion teased.

"I'm ready for embarrassment," I whispered softly.

"Me, too, actually," he confirmed. "Think about where you'd like to go on Tuesday."

"I will," I replied brightly. He gave me another squeeze and a quick kiss and he headed for the building's front door. I followed.

"Thanks, Mister," I teased.

"You were great, Girly," he teased back.

"Thanks for lunch."

"Anytime," and he tucked himself into his car.

He drove to the corner, turned, and went out of sight. As I headed to Auntie and Unc's apartment, I prayed his interest in me would continue because I had it bad for him.

Chapter 12

Three weeks later and I found myself sitting in Mr. Cedric's office with Ben.

"We have a date with HUAC this Thursday. Edward will be here tomorrow. Put everything you're doing to the side or delegate it. Ella, confirm Rabbi Berman received and has deposited the check we sent him. Vita will probably need to draw on it if the Committee refers Edward to the Department of Justice."

"They can't jail him immediately," I asserted.

"No, but things will accelerate and if Edward wants to stay in town, we'll want to know the Rabbi has funds ready to get to Vita."

"I'll let you know after I talk to Rabbi Berman."

"Thanks, Ella. Ben, are you sure you want Edward staying with you?"

"Most definitely. I want him in a comfortable setting."

"We should arrange security for your house because his date with HUAC will be in the papers."

"Yes. Security would be important."

"There's a PI company in town owned by a couple of Lincoln Brigade veterans."

"Really?" I reacted.

"I'm going to give you their phone number, Ella. Please coordinate Ben and Dr. Barsky's security."

"Will do."

"Why don't you get going on those two tasks. We'll check in with you later."

"Of course." Back at my desk I put in a call to Rabbi Berman's New York office. His secretary promised to get him to call back. I called the security company.

"Columbia Private Investigations."

"Hello, this is Attorney Ella Moses from Cedric, Brown and Jacobs."

"Good morning, Attorney Moses."

"Mr. Cedric asked me to call to arrange security for Dr. Barsky when he stays at Attorney Jacobs' home later this week."

"Yes, Attorney Cedric asked us a month ago to expect a call. Could I stop in your offices before lunch?"

"Stopping in would be perfect. Tell me your name."

"My name is Noel Green. I'm on the way."

"Thanks."

I buzzed Julia. "Julia, I have a man named Noel Green coming this morning to discuss Dr. Barsky's security."

"Thanks for letting me know, Ella."

I started to gather the info Green would need. I called Representative Dies office.

"Representative Dies' office," a female voice responded.

"This is Attorney Ella Moses part of Dr. Edward Barsky's legal team. I wanted to get the details set for his testimony Thursday."

"Just a moment, please."

I sat there for five minutes hoping someone might come back on the line.

"Miss Moses, this is Bob Arthur of Representative Dies' staff. Could you have Dr. Barsky arrive at 8:30a.m.?"

"Yes, of course."

"On the Pennsylvania Ave. side of the building, drive your cars into the basement parking area and tell the Capitol Police officer the nature of your business and he'll admit you to the indoor parking area. There's an elevator there. Go to the third floor and I'll be waiting for you. What's your phone number?"

I gave it to him.

"Thanks, Mr. Arthur."

"I appreciate your call."

"See you Thursday."

I flipped open my law firm three-hole binder and wrote down Ben's address on my pad of paper along with the Committee staffer's instructions. Ben popped his head in our office doorway.

"Need any help with the security setup?"

"No. A company employee is arriving soon and I put in a call to Rep. Dies' office and got information where they want us to report."

"You've got this all arranged. Great," he replied. "Any conversation with Rabbi Berman?"

"His office promised a return call."

"Let me know how it all goes."

"Of course." He walked off.

I worked on some Municipal Court files until Julia let me know Mr. Green had arrived. I brought my notes and met him in reception.

"Mr. Green, I'm Attorney Moses."

"Please call me Noel." I smiled.

"Noel, we can talk in the conference room." I led the way and sat down. He sat across from me. He was a brawny Negro man in his late thirties, maybe six foot with a military bearing. "Mr. Cedric shared your staff were former members of the Spanish Civil War veteran corp."

"We are. The Abraham Lincoln Brigade was the first integrated fighting unit in American history not counting Bunker Hill."

"Makes Dr. Barsky's story even more interesting."

"For sure. We're happy to have this work protecting Dr. Barsky, Attorney Jacobs, and you."

I handed him a page of information I typed for him. I kept the carbon.

"I'll have Dr. Barsky's train arrival time later today."

"Call me when you get it."

"Mr. Jacobs' home address is there. We need someone to be in the house when they're there."

"We'll have someone outside, too."

"Terrific. You also see the Dies' staff directions on arrival Thursday morning?"

"Yes. Put your address on the sheet. We'll pick you up first."

"Here…" I slid the information sheet toward me adding my address.

"Call me with anything else which comes up or with details you need to add," Noel asked.

The conference room phone buzzed. I got up and answered it. "Rabbi Berman for you." She got off the line.

"Rabbi Berman, thanks for calling me back."

"Attorney Moses, thank you for the first check for Vita and her family."

"I wanted to make sure you received it."

"Yes. We've already given her some cash because Edward will be on the train the day after tomorrow."

"I'm happy she is already seeing the wonderful support all the donors have contributed."

"They have been generous. We have a nice nest egg for Vita."

"Have your staff give me a call when it's time for the next check."

"They will call. Bye bye, Miss Moses."

"Goodbye, Rabbi Berman."

"Support funds for Mrs. Barsky?" Noel asked.

"Yes."

"Great to hear his family has what they need. Thanks for all these logistics. We'll see you Thursday morning."

"Thanks."

I settled at my desk and ate the sandwich I packed.

~*~

"Hello, Marion," I bubbled seeing his face Tuesday. It lifted the weight of a day of work off my shoulders.

"Hello, Sugar. Let's go to McCrory's and get a burger and fries."

"Perfect."

"How was your day?" he asked as he eased into traffic.

"My days are going to be all about Edward for a while."

"When does he go before the Dies Committee?"

"Thursday."

"You'll be sitting at the table with him?"

"Ben and I."

"We'll have to go to the movies to catch you in the newsreel."

"Is it good to be photographed at a losing moment?" I reacted more quietly.

"It's important. It shows us chipping away at injustice and the misuse of Congress' oversite function."

"Some days, I'm perfectly happy to go to my neighborhood lunch counter surrounded by the community and not do any striving."

"You're awfully young to be retreating to the front porch rocking chair," he teased.

I laughed out a petulant selfish feeling. "I've been a damn adult all my life. I deserve to hide in the community and us."

"Hide in you and me anytime, Baby."

"Welcoming me is the beauty and new reality of feeling about you the way I do. I have a safe place to escape the law and seeking our rights."

"You do and you should," he reacted taking my hand while approaching our dinner spot.

"I will walk into white stores for something extra nice to wear and put up with the entitled attitude of clerks, but some days I want to escape the forced shabbiness they leave for us."

"Let's get into our little booth in McCrory's and feel down home," Marion agreed rolling up to the curb. He took my hand again and led me to the lunch counter. It was less busy than at lunch. A waitress stepped up.

"Soft drinks?" she asked as she slid two half-sheet menus in front of us.

"Yes, please," I responded trying to sound less crabby. Seeing the Seeberg Wall-O-Matic up against the inside edge of our booth, I grabbed my coin purse, put a dime in the thing and chose E-4, Larry Darnell's, 'For You, My Love.'

"Such a good song," Marion reacted.

Our eyes locked for a moment and he reached across the table for my hand. I eventually checked the menu but held onto him. A burger and fries sounded good in the car and nothing else on the menu could compete.

"Do you know what you want?" the waitress asked setting down two ice-cold drinks.

"Cheeseburger and fries," Marion replied.

"The works?"

"Yes."

"And for you, miss?"

"The same."

She took the menus and disappeared.

For a few minutes, we didn't say anything, but listened to the songs other diners had chosen. Then, the one I chose played.

"For you, my love, I'd swim the ocean blue," Marion reacted.

"I said goodbye to the mob and went and got a job," I replied and we both laughed. I took a sip of my drink. "Take me to the beach this summer," I requested with a smile.

"I'll get the number my mom has for rentals down there. Some week in June good?"

"I only get one week of vacation so I want to take it all with you."

"Sounds perfect to me. Do you own a swimsuit?"

"Not one I want you to see me in. I'm going shopping."

"I could go along."

"You can drive me but I won't be exiting the changing room. You must be patient."

"I have less and less patience the more I'm with you," he replied smiling.

"On the one hand, your feelings are a good thing but we have nowhere to go."

"I know. It's frustrating."

Marion put a dime in the jukebox and chose Nat King Cole's "Nalani."

The food arrived and we took first bites. Ketchup settled prominently in the corner of his mouth and with a napkin, I cleaned him up. "We were both hungry," I noted with a smile.

"Good, right?" he replied to my tender attention to his face, smiling.

"Great," I replied laughing.

"You know, I babysit my brother's kids on occasion. Want to help?" he asked with a gleam in his eye.

"Are they hard to get to sleep?" I asked already seeing where he was going with this idea.

"You read them one book and they are out."

"I'd be happy to help you with them," I responded with a knowing nod.

"How are you guys doing," the waitress swept up to ask.

"Two chocolate root beer floats," I requested.

Marion scowled at me like I had busted his budget. I simply patted my change purse. He smiled shaking his head at his quite willful girlfriend.

~*~

Thursday morning, I was standing on my stoop dressed for the House Committee Hearing Room, carrying my briefcase.

Dozens of people on my street were heading off to work. Some I knew waved a hello. After a moment an older model black sedan eased down the narrow street. Older, yes, but polished to a gleaming luster. Noel jumped out to open the door to the backseat.

"Good morning, Noel."

"Good morning, Ella." I got comfortable in the car. "We're going to swing over to Georgetown where a second car will carry Dr. Barsky and Attorney Jacobs."

"All right."

I was left with my thoughts, knowing I wouldn't have much to do today until we hit the deli with Edward later for a post-mortem. It was a helpless feeling as Noel deftly negotiated through D.C. We were not bucking traffic to get to Ben's place and by the time we headed for the House Office Building, seventy-five percent of the District's workforce would be clocked in.

We arrived at Ben's. The second car was parked deep into his driveway to have the men come out of his kitchen door. Without any delay, Ben and Edward climbed into the backseat of their car. The car backed down the driveway, accelerated up his street, and we followed.

It was a beautiful late spring day in D.C., belying the sadness of this moment for Edward, who would end up in contempt of Congress and referred to the Justice Department for indictment. It wasn't a situation for which we could offer a defense. Critiquing Congress' abuse of power would come later.

These big roadblocks toward "a more perfect union" often took the altruism out of me.

The first car slowed to a stop in front of the Capitol Police officer at the entrance of the House Office Building. Noel's co-worker explained who he had in his car. Cards were passed out to the officer so he could match the list the committee provided.

Noel and I repeated the procedure. I passed my National Bar Association card to the officer. We proceeded into the underground parking area. Out of our cars, Noel and his partner led us into the basement office area.

"Hello, Attorney Jacobs, Dr. Barsky. Thank you for your prompt arrival. I'm Bob Arthur from Representative Dies' office."

"Mr. Arthur, this is my co-counsel Attorney Moses and our security, Noel and Oscar."

"Welcome all. We'll follow this corridor to an elevator and we'll get you situated in a conference room next to the hearing room." We followed him and soon were in the small conference room. "You probably noticed the rest rooms across the hall. My staff has put a pitcher of ice water on the table. Noel and Oscar?"

Arthur pointed our security through the door on the other end of the room opening on the hearing room. They saw the layout and the proximity of visitors who would be sitting behind us. He directed them how to lead us to the witness table. "Thanks for coming in today." Mr. Arthur left us.

"Why so glum, Ella," Dr. Barsky chided me with a smile. "This is a wonderful day to defend the Constitution."

His buoyancy coaxed a smile out of me. "It is, actually," I responded.

Ben and Edward chatted about family, great places to eat, summer vacations, and the best places in Madrid to eat kosher. I asked Edward, "I hear Kurt Weill's new show 'Lost in the Stars' is about apartheid in South Africa."

"It's a sensation. If you and a friend can get away, Vita will get you tickets."

"Another visit to New York…" I reacted dreamily, smiling.

Eventually, Mr. Arthur returned. "The Committee's ready for you now."

Oscar led us out. As we were about to take our seats, I checked row three behind us and found Owen Townsend and Marion in the seats we occupied for the Burl Ives' interview. They smiled broadly, Owen acting particularly proud because Marion and I were a couple. I leveled Owen with mock disgust and I could hear his robust laugh despite the rumble of a hundred conversations expressing their curiosity at Dr. Barsky's presence at the witness table.

Congressman Connors was the chair and he wrapped his gavel to get quiet in the large hearing room. As a semblance of quiet settled on the filled hearing room, I could hear the faint whir of film cameras recording for posterity and the nascent, fifteen-minute nightly news programs.

"Mr. Adamson, you may begin."

Chief Counsel for the committee, Attorney Eric Adamson addressed the witness with this opening salvo. "Now, Dr. Barsky, I ask you, have you produced for the committee, in compliance with this subpoena, the papers, documents, and records called for in the subpoena?"

Dr. Barsky replied, "Mr. Chairman, I am here in response to a subpoena requiring me to appear. I have a statement here…"

Not being seated with Owen and Marion, I could not pass my notebook to them. I wrote contemporaneous notes for my own record. *Edward interrupted the committee counsel.*

"May I say that your subpena orders me to produce certain documents in my possession, custody, and control as described in that subpoena, and since I don't have either in my possession, custody or control the documents described in that subpoena, I am unable to comply with your order to produce them."

This could be a short hearing.

Representative Bonner responded, "He has answered it and given reasons in that first paragraph of his statement. Doctor, do you have any objection at this time to stating who does have the authority to produce the records?"

"I would say that the board of directors, the executive board, would have the ultimate authority to produce the records."

Does Edward really want to put his whole board into the hands of HUAC?

Rep. Rankin asked, "Are you the chairman of the board, you say?"

"Yes," Dr. Barsky responded.

Rep. Mundt reacted, "Just one question. Will you submit for the record here a list of the names and addresses of your executive board?"

"I could do that; yes. You mean now?"

"Yes," Mr. Mundt replied.

"No. I haven't got the list with me, but I can easily get the list."

Of course. Don't give them any more than they ask for.

Representative Murdock addressed the chairman, "Let it be put in the record here."

Representative Robinson asked, "Has the matter of producing their records or permitting the examiner of this committee to look at them been discussed or taken up in any of your board meetings?"

"Yes, sir."

Mr. Rankin resumed the questioning. "What did the board decide? I am supposed to have the witness, Mr. Robinson, but if you want to question him, go ahead. I yield."

"You say it was discussed?"

"Yes, sir."

"That it was discussed?"

"Yes, sir."

"And were minutes made of the meeting?"

"I am sure there were minutes made."

"Can you produce those minutes?"

"I haven't got them with me."

"What was the decision reached?"

"I put the proposition to the executive board and the executive board discussed it. The executive board felt from the discussion, as far as I could gather that the Joint Anti-Fascist Refugee Committee was purely a relief committee, that it is engaged in no political propaganda of any sort whatsoever; that it sends its financial support to the President's War Relief Control Board; also that it certainly is not engaged in any activities that could be considered subversive or un-American or designed to overthrow the government of the United States. They also discussed –"

"That may be all true, but what does that have to do with the subpena?" Rep. Robinson blurted out interrupting Edward.

"Those are the things they discussed," Dr. Barsky replied.

'Based on Edward's response here, the board knew they were in this situation together. They were all willing to end up in the docket.'

"In other words, you wanted to make up your own minds as to whether you should obey a subpena issued by the committee of congress?"

"No; I am just stating to you the discussion that took place at the meeting. They also discussed the fact that the press had a statement emanating from this committee derogatory to us, in regard to your counsel's request to the President's Control Board to withdraw our license before we had an opportunity to discuss it. This letter was sent down one day, and they refused –"

'Edward is accusing the committee of an unlawful act. Mr. Rankin is interrupting Edward's accusation.'

"Did they decide that they would not submit these records to the committee?"

"They refused to grant me permission to submit those records."

"And you are carrying out their orders in refusing to submit the records?"

"I suppose that is right."

My question for Ben is, "Did you know Edward was prevented by his board to release any records?" Soon after the hearing, Helen R. Bryan, executive secretary of JAFRC, would provide the names and addresses of the board.

Mr. Wood asked Dr. Barsky, "Would you be willing to permit one of our investigators to go with him and go through those and go through those books and records for the purpose of ascertaining the information we seek?"

"I will not allow an investigator look through our records."

"Mr. Chairman, I believe the witness has made it clear he will not respond to our subpena and therefore we have every right to refer him to the Department of Justice for obstruction."

"Dr. Barsky, we have no more questions for you. You are excused."

At these words, the room exploded as we got up to leave the room. Our security removed us from the table back toward the little conference room immediately off the floor. I gave Marion and Owen a look and they gamely smiled at me but there was no victory in their facial expressions. As I followed Noel Green off the hearing room floor, audience members were trying to grab me. Noel gripped my forearm propelling me forward, shielding me with his body and focusing on the conference room door. Throughout our exit, the chair did not gavel the room quiet or ask the Capitol Police to quiet the crowd. As I ducked into the little conference room, I quickly faced the doorway to be certain Dr. Barsky, Ben, and our other bodyguard made the room.

"So terribly rude," I asserted to Dr. Barsky.

He smiled beatifically. Ben stood next to him and he gripped his hand in thanks and shook hands with me as well.

"Let's get to the cars and go to lunch."

Without a word, Noel led us to the elevator.

The hallway outside the hearing room was calm. One enterprising Washington Post reporter walked with us to the elevator doors.

"Dr. Barsky, any comment for the Post?"

"It's lovely in Washington this time of year," he said to the journalist.

The elevator doors closed and Ben laughed uproariously slapping Edward on the shoulder. Everyone recovered and regained a businesslike demeanor as we proceeded into the parking garage. As our cars hit the street, we returned to anonymity.

The House voted to refer Dr. Barsky to the Dept. of Justice for prosecution for failing to respond to a Congressional subpoena. 399 members voted for the referral, 4 voted against, and 88 did not vote.

Chapter 13

While it was quiet in Noel's car, and the early spring scenery in D.C. never failed to be beautiful, my brain was replaying Edward's actions in the hearing room. The beauty of monuments, stately buildings, wide expanse of public spaces, and eventually the quiet elegance of Georgetown were in sight. Despite the beauty, I could not quell my anxiety about Edward's future. I tried to get back under control and prepare to be his attorney again, my grief internalized.

We stepped onto the sidewalk in front of Wagshal's, Ben's favorite deli. Noel and his partner watched the street as we entered. Noel stayed with us. Our second driver was outside. The three of us ordered at the counter and found a table. Edward and Ben relaxed into the welcoming aromas of the deli and the upbeat chatter of the patrons around us. The spicy tang in the air and the neighborly conversations were beginning to ease my nerve endings still rattled by the partisan cat-calling ushering us out of the hearing room.

A runner set our drinks on the table. I took a first sip of my soft drink to find Dr. Barsky focusing on me.

"Any questions, Ella?" Edward asked.

I paused to decide which question to ask. As I did, he smiled understanding tact was keeping me from complaining about not being briefed. "Your board is willing to go to jail with you?"

He hesitated to answer until he thought about my question. His tone was less defiant when he shared, "Some of the older members should resign in the next couple of days to save them from the prison experience."

"Going to jail saves your many donors and benefactors from HUAC scrutiny?"

"Yes. The refugees have been through a lot already. Sparing them from Franco's harshness includes keeping them out of the hands of the House of Representatives."

"It's frustrating Franco has such an impact here."

"You, Ben and I have to organize against autocracy in all its forms, domestic and foreign."

"Understood," I replied.

"You understand better than most."

I took a breath. "Your board intentionally delayed the document transfer?"

"They formally took it out of my hands. After lunch, I need you to call the board secretary, Helen Bryan, and fill her in on my testimony."

He slid one of his cards across the table with Miss Bryan's office phone number. "Ben's going to get me to the train station later this afternoon."

"Of course."

The food was delivered and we continued to recover from the fury of the hearing room.

"Are you going to take Vita and your daughter on the vacation you talked about?" Ben asked him.

"Thanks to your fund-raising efforts with Rabbi Berman, I can get off the surgery schedule. I want to take two weeks right away. My parents have a place."

"Isn't it up in the Catskills," Ben asked.

"Yes, a little outside of Windham."

"I'm going to need to reach you by phone," Ben urged.

"My parents have a phone there. I owe my mom a call this afternoon. I'll get it from her before I get on the train."

"Tell Vita, my place is always available to her."

"She knows, Ben."

"Did you know Ella is dating an attorney?"

"Ella, a lawyer?" Edward teased. "You can't find a doctor?"

"I do want to see him now and then," I retorted gently.

"Dating is a complication for doctors your age. How did you meet him?"

"He was checking out a HUAC hearing."

"I'm happy to hear something good has come out of this for you."

"Working for you is its own reward."

"You and the partners haven't knocked the idealism out of Ella, Ben."

"I don't think there's a way."

After lunch we dispersed in different directions, Noel drove, my brain filled with imagined depredations Edward would experience in prison. What would his sentence be? I would ask Ben.

I tried to remember what work was waiting for me but I was preoccupied with the decision Edward had made.

Noel parked in front of the office. "Ella, thanks for choosing us."

"You're my driver in the future, too, Noel."

"Having us back means a lot."

I got out, gave him a cheery wave, and walked in to see if Julia had anything for me.

"Hi, Ella. Stop up to see Mr. Cedric before you go to your desk. Here are your messages."

Marion wanted me to call.

I stepped into Mr. Cedric's doorway. He excused himself from the visitor in his office and joined me in the hallway. "Did Dr. Barsky decide to resist like he planned?"

"He did."

"All right. I hope he can handle what's facing him."

"He seemed resolved to do so."

"It's sad."

"Extremely."

"Thanks for today, Ella."

"You're welcome, sir."

I sat down at my desk and re-prioritized what was there and got up to call Marion. It was old news when I called him now. Everyone in the office got mushy about it but there was no teasing.

"Marion?"

"Ella, let me pick you up after work and I'll cook for you at my place."

"Sounds perfect, Marion. Call me when you're on the way."

"Will do."

After he hung up, I called my building and left a message with the downstairs neighbor so Aunt Flora would know I was eating dinner with Marion. We had a system. The downstairs neighbor would leave a note on the stairs for Auntie and Unc when he came home from his shift.

I started in on the business succession plan and will on the top of my stack. I typed the first draft at my desk which the client and I would edit later in the week when he had his appointment. When it was typed, I started on another one. I updated the notes I already wrote and started to type.

Janice lifted the receiver and took Marion's call when it rang in.

"Marion's on the way," she reported.

"Thanks, Janice."

I had the timing of Marion's drive from Watkins and Townsend down. I typed and the rest of the workers in my office left for home.

Ben tucked his head in my doorway. "Thanks for today."

"You're welcome, Ben. There's nothing you can do for some clients," I suggested smiling.

"Correct. You end up standing with them as they choose against your advice. Thanks again."

I waved goodbye to him. I typed another five minutes, left my page in the typewriter for the morning, packed up, and headed down the stairs and out onto the street.

A rain shower was playing around with sprinkles on my head as shafts of sunlight were hitting buildings way down the street. Soon congress would go home for the Easter break. Better weather would allow Marion and I to enjoy the beautiful parks and other public spaces in D.C. I was enjoying soft, warm 'excuse me' rain drops as Marion arrived.

"Hello, Ella."

"Dinner with my Baby," I emoted after my harrowing day.

"Dr. Barsky was defiant?" Marion asked as he drove toward home.

"He was and so was HUAC."

"Of course. How are you doing?"

"I need an evening with you."

"Happy to oblige."

I put a hand on his knee and exhaled. When we got to his place, we walked through the repair shop waving at his father and his mechanic.

We settled in the kitchen in his apartment starting to work on a spaghetti sauce recipe he took out of an accordion file his mother had filled with her and his grandmother's recipes. We leaned together over the recipe.

Veronica walked out of her bedroom and disappeared downstairs. "Your supper already smells good," she shouted out as descended.

"Thanks," I yelled enjoying the aroma of the garlic and onions sautéing in the pan.

"I'm eating with Mom and Dad," Veronica shared.

"See you later," Marion replied. Our faces locked on each other relishing dinner on our own. Marion gave me a tender kiss. "How bad was it, today?" he asked.

"Knowing he was going to lose, he and his board arranged it so Edward did not have permission to release anything to the committee today," I explained.

"Ha, ha, ha. A wonderful dodge."

"The McCarthy-ites were livid and besides themselves."

"He was able to walk out giving them nothing?"

"Since his board of directors prevented him from turning over anything, they asked for the list of his board. He promised the board secretary would send it to them."

"Amazing. He did walk out giving them nothing?"

"For now. We expect HUAC will refer him to the Department of Justice for ignoring their subpoena."

"How was he afterward?"

"He was appreciative of Ben and me, happy to be in a Jewish deli, enjoying lunch as a perfect antidote to the hearing room."

"So calm and collected."

"He's been under fire in a war. He has the intellectual courage and the physical dexterity to be a surgeon. Barsky has stood with his people through thick and thin and will willingly go to prison for them. Compare those credentials to his accusers."

"What's next for him?"

"He's going on vacation with his wife and daughter for two weeks."

"Why not. It'll take a while before he's in court again."

"Correct."

"You need a vacation."

"I need lots of nights and weekends with you. I want to get the wills and succession plan project going."

"I'll involve our firm in the project and between you and my partners, we'll get the other Negro firms lined up."

"I appreciate your help."

"Are you feeling good about us?" Marion asked with a smile as he added tomato paste and a jar of diced tomatoes to the big skillet. He rotated the knob producing heat under a big pot of water.

"I'm smitten," I responded intensely.

He made sure the food was cooking safely. "I'm so happy we are out in the open with our families and friends."

"We can relax and get to know each other completely," I asserted.

"We know we want to own a home, have some children, take care of Aunt Flora and Unc, start our own law firm, rise in our legal careers, and make the country a more perfect union."

"Music should play behind your summation, Counselor."

We laughed.

He dropped the noodles in the boiling water.

I set the table, poured us small glasses of wine, and tossed a salad with vinegar and oil. The kitchen was warming up so I took off my suit jacket and draped it over the back of the sofa. As I walked back into the kitchen, I unbuttoned the top two buttons of my blouse.

A moment later Marion poured off the water in which the noodles had been cooking. "Could you grate some parmesan, Honey?"

"Of course, Marion." He had the cheese sitting on a little cutting board.

"Please bring the cutting board over to the table when you're ready." He was plating the spaghetti.

I walked the cheese to the table and was sitting down when he set two pieces of carved wood in the center of the table facing me.

"What are these?"

"I'm revealing one of my remaining secrets to you tonight?"

"Not all of them?" I teased.

"Eventually. Remember we're going to the flea market Saturday?"

"Yes. I can't wait."

"We're going as sellers."

"What?"

"Inspect those two figures."

I picked them up. My mouth dropped open. "You've created us," I reacted with surprise. He took the first bite of his dinner. "There are three big boxes of carvings in the bedroom."

"Don't sit there. Haul them out here."

He smiled as he managed to get another forkful of spaghetti in his mouth. He walked away and disappeared into the bedroom. Returning, he put the three boxes on the kitchen counter and ate some more.

"Is this wood?" I asked.

"It's black walnut."

"Your daddy is not the only one good with tools."

He laughed.

"I could never get into fixing cars. But whittling became a passion."

"This isn't backyard noodling. This is art. Why didn't you tell me?"

"I wanted to wait until I had enough pieces for a flea market."

"This is spectacular. I'm extremely impressed. There's all different kinds of figures here."

"Come and eat. We can inspect them after dinner. By the way, those two…" he remarked pointing to the carvings depicting us, "are not for sale. They're for you."

"I'm going to treasure them always."

"Eat," he said laughing.

I took my first bite holding the wooden sculpture of Marion. He had captured himself quite ably. I slowly spun the piece as I ate, my mind completely overtaken, the HUAC hearing out of consideration temporarily. "I love you used this wood. Is it hard to work?"

"It's harder than some but I love the feel of it."

"I know. It's so rich."

"I'm happy you like what I've done. It should be interesting to see what the customers think."

"Yes. I'm curious, too." We ate and he savored his spaghetti and my praise. "Do you want to do some bigger pieces?"

"I do, once we are more settled and the basic household is set up."

"I love you have an artistic outlet."

"I love your singing voice."

"Oh, singing's nothing special compared to this."

"I love sitting with you in church. Your voice transports me."

"You're exceedingly kind."

"We have special things to share with our children. Somehow, talking about children reminds me, my brother is asking us to watch their dog next weekend."

I paused my meal giving him a coy smile.

"I told my brother we would both be happy to take care of Dodger."

"It certainly will take both of us to take care of their dog all weekend," I teased smiling.

"I thought the same thing."

"We both need some alone time together."

"Need isn't a powerful enough word," he responded.

"Good thing we have a night to practice," I suggested with a smile.

"Let's not rush into practicing. I have a surprise dessert."

"Dessert before practicing for sure," I reacted, "but I want to eat this wonderful meal slowly, too."

"I feel so terrific about us…, we are a couple now."

"We've been a couple for a while now," I responded. "Let's do the wills / succession project as a couple."

"We've got our list of Negro law firms. Let's divide and conquer, getting everyone on board."

"Watkins and Townsend is giving you hours to do the organizing?" I asked.

"Yes. I never use my quota of pro bono time so Owen was happy to see you were getting me on the ball."

I laughed.

"Owen's happy because he thinks he's responsible for making us a couple."

"I like him thinking so. It deflects from my real motives."

I slapped his arm. "Everyone knows you are a lothario, even Owen. He's trying to take you off the market so you don't sully the firm."

"Wait. I said a minute ago I was happy to be with you," he protested with a smile. "Whatever term could have been used to describe me is moot."

I laughed at him and grabbed his hand.

"I was amazed you were still available when we met. Handsome, an attorney, great family, successful parents, not afraid to take controversial cases," I chronicled.

"My history's not going to change," with a hint of warning in his voice.

"We won't make it if you stop taking civil rights case work."

"No worries. I have a lot of work to do protecting families from rights abridgement. We must hone the 14th and 15th amendments."

"I need you to stay on it because I think my work is going to stay in the succession law. We need Negro wealth flowing to the next generation. Our law firms need to protect our millionaires."

"We need to be on the millionaire continuum, as a family," Marion suggested. "We need a powerful next generation," he replied smiling.

"We got back to the subject of making babies pretty quickly," I teased.

"I don't see either of us slowing down on the baby issue," Marion observed.

"No, sir," I agreed, leaning toward him to get a kiss. He obliged making it soft, long, and intense.

"Mmmmmm. I need another one of those." We kissed again. "I'll never want dessert."

"You promised me dessert," I protested.

"Okay, Okay," he mock complained. Marion cleared the table. He opened the freezer compartment of the fridge returning with two bowls of pastel colored frozen treat.

"Sherbet?"

"Yes."

"I haven't had this in a long time."

"Today of all days you need a treat after the stress of the hearing."

"You and sherbet," I smiled letting the first spoonful melt in my mouth. Mmmmmm…" I ate my dessert slowly even though I wanted to be on the couch with him a half hour ago. He wisely led me to nourishment, conversation about us, and our future. The future and being with him constantly filled my head in the moments when I wasn't buried in work. We had talked so much, I only wanted to get started. However, the part of my brain my mother created in me as a girl, always seemed anchored in reality. The truth was, Marion and I had met six months ago. In such a short time almost half of the time had been a mutual sizing up. What had Alexander Pope written? 'Fools rush in where angels fear to tread.' Marion and I were fools about each other.

Although, I had a serious relationship with my law school classmate, we were never in a fever. Marion and I were different. Some nights, alone in my room at Auntie and Unc's, I wondered about us. Where and when would we struggle with each other? I had never known any couple without stress points.

My spoon scraped the bottom of the dessert cup. I investigated it to make sure I had it all. He laughed at me. "I am feeling no shame," I teased. "Sherbet was a treat and I loved it." I took a deep breath. "Shall we do the dishes?"

"I'll do them after I come back from taking you home."

"Are you sure?"

Marion took my hand and I followed him to the couch. WHFS had been playing since we arrived at his place. He extinguished the lamp, sat on the couch, and invited me to sit next to him with my feet up on the cushions to my right, my torso lying across his body. He cradled me and we locked eyes. I began to tear up, more stress escaping me from Edward's horrible day. Marion kissed the tears away, softly saying "Yes, yes, Baby, you are home." I cried more, shaking within his firm but gentle embrace.

Sources of my uncontrollable carousel of emotional tripwires spun to mind; Edward, McCarthy, Capitol Police Officers, FBI agents, Marion, Auntie and Unc, Mr. Cedric, Ben, rabid hearing attendees, and my distant parents. For a while this cloud of realities paralyzed me and it was only my love's strong arms keeping me from rolling off the couch onto the floor.

"You are home..." he whispered slowly over and over.

The visions of my, our, the community's active adversaries became a shorter and shorter list as Marion's chant took over me.

"Can your arms be my home?" I pleaded in a broken voice impaired by tears.

"They already are."

I rolled into his chest and desperately grabbed him with both hands thankfully clinging to the man who was now my true north. I remained in our restorative hug for some time. Slowly I released my panicky embrace but Marion held me close. I had no desire to get free. As I lifted my eyes slightly to take him in, he kissed me tenderly. New tears rolled out of my already tortured eyes. I felt an overwhelming feeling of gratitude, especially for his gentleness. Marion's intermittent kisses and my feeling of safety in his arms kept me on the couch for almost an hour.

"I'm going out with friends to the library...Oh, I'm sorry," Ronnie blurted. "Are you okay?" she squeaked in concern and embarrassment.

"She had a tough day," Marion replied softly.

"Oh. Was today the HUAC thing?"

"I'll be all right," I croaked out, trying to rally to greet her properly.

"I gotta go. Friends waiting. Feel better, Ella."

"Thanks, Ronnie," Marion replied. I sat up a little higher and she disappeared down the steps. Marion handed me his handkerchief again.

I dried my face and found his lips mere inches from mine. "I'm helplessly in love with you," I whispered huskily my throat swollen with emotion.

"I'm over the moon for you," he whispered back.

I leaned in to kiss him finding the kiss was a different kind of intensity. Once soothing, his kiss was now insistent. I felt an electrical sensation quite different from the comfort I was receiving. Hungrily, I kissed him again testing if I had accurately sensed a change in his kiss. He instantly confirmed my impression. I answered him. He sensed my own ardor and one of his hands rested on my thigh. I put a hand to the back of his neck as a quiet 'yes' to our growing intensity.

Marion slid us face to face on our sides on the big couch one hand keeping me from falling to the floor. I giggled at my precarious position. I loosened his tie, removing it from around his neck throwing it away wildly. I started on the buttons on his dress shirt while he unbuttoned my blouse.

Both of us had a hand on naked skin, our breathing becoming noisy.

Marion slid the hand securing me to the couch to my bottom holding our hips together, a silent wish about where he wanted us to be.

I responded with a French kiss to let him know where my mind was.

This moment had been suppressed for some time stoked by a lot of open dreaming of a marriage.

I broke free from him and stood, walking toward the kitchen. "Don't you dare get up," I commanded. His alarm transitioned into a smile. I noticed how disheveled I had become and how exposed my torso was. When I returned, I threw a dish towel at him and removed my blouse and bra kneeling by him.

I enjoyed his eyes feasting on my partial nakedness as he slid his trousers over his hips. As soon as he was flat on his back again, I grabbed him and worked him over. After a couple of moments, he was done. I covered him with the towel and lay on him our naked chests nestled.

"I adore you," he whispered.

"You are my baby," I responded.

"Yes, I am," he confessed. "I realize I need to propose to you," he punctuated with new kisses.

"Not tonight," I counseled, "as much as I would love to hear you ask.

We kissed again relishing the intimacy.

The next couple of weeks got us an agreement among the Negro law firms on the Wills and Successions project with young lawyers speaking in almost twenty churches.

Mr. O. John Rogge planned to visit our offices to discuss defending Edward in his federal contempt of Congress indictment. The Department of Justice hadn't issued an order yet but with the red scare movement running riot, we had to begin to prepare.

"Attorney Rogge will be in D.C. later this week and in our offices," Mr. Cedric told me from the doorway of our office. "I left a book open in the library with his work history for everyone to read."

"Thank you, sir."

"By the way, the crew in this office continues to shine. Keep up the good work," he asserted with a smile.

"Thank yous," rang out from our foursome and he walked away.

"Rogge?" one of the typists asked.

"He has federal experience. Edward will be tried in a federal court."

"Aren't Mr. Cedric or Mr. Brown experienced enough?"

"Yes," I replied, "but we need a higher profile attorney. I'll read his biography and we'll all know better why he's the choice."

"Thanks."

I had to stay at my desk because the flow of wills and succession work had risen as the response from D.C.'s Negro community increased. The partners took me off municipal defense cases permanently and they were promising me a recent law school graduate any day.

Many clients had resonated with the goal of safely and legally passing legacies to the next generation of young Negroes.

Only the rustling of my office mates grabbing lunch stirred me from my files in front of me. As they sampled sandwiches and fresh cups of coffee sweetening the atmosphere in the room, I walked up the circular staircase to read Attorney Rogge's vitae.

I sat scanning the book Mr. Cedric had left for us. He graduated from the University of Illinois in 1922 Phi Beta Kappa. He earned a law degree at Harvard where he was on the law review. After working in private practice, he returned to Harvard earning his Doctor of Juristic Science Degree.

He entered government service in 1934 working for the Reconstruction Finance Corporation, the Treasury Department, and two years as assistant general counsel at the Securities and Exchange Commission.

He investigated the alleged graft and fraud of Huey Long and his machine in Louisiana. In May 1939, he became the Assistant Attorney General. It was quite the resume and in 1947 he was still a young man.

Back in the office to eat lunch, I filled in everyone else.

~*~

A busy day with wills progressed into a busy week. I was booked with work including clients in the office to be interviewed, final documents to deliver and filings at the courthouse.

A couple days a week, Marion would break this happy grind of serving one after another Negro families by picking me up and taking me to McCrory's or the Crab Shack, or a hotdog cart at the National Zoo.

"Hello, Marion. How was your day?"

"I did well. Anything new for you?" he asked as he drove away from the curb.

"I could get bored with wills but every family's story keeps it interesting for me."

"Happy to hear it, since you will be the queen of wills in our firm."

"A marriage is plenty but our name the same and a law firm, too?"

"Good thing we like each other." We laughed. "Say, it's a nice clear night, let's take in the night sky and the view from the steps of the Supreme Court."

"I'm hungry."

"It'll only take a few minutes. Walking the steps will be good for us."

"You better get me to a hot dog stand in a hurry."

"I promise."

"I haven't done this walk up to the court since law school."

"You won't get walked off by the Capitol Police this time."

"Maybe our beer bottles are still up here."

"Ha, ha. No beer for you tonight."

I got to the top, in the glow of the court's façade lighting and faced the night lights of the District. I took it all in and was reminded how beautiful our city was. "Pretty, right?" There was no answer from Marion. I longed to get his reaction and he wasn't where I thought he would be. When I tilted my eyes down a bit his face was at my elbow. "What are you doing…?" my voice trailing off as his physical position holding open a jewelry box flashed my brain. "Ooooth," I reacted, as I adjusted a bit to face him. I lifted my hands to my mouth.

"Ella, my Sweetheart…"

"Marion…" I reacted realizing what he was doing. As the last syllable of his name escaped my lips, I felt a jab of hysteria drive a laugh out of me, and I hopped like an eight-year-old.

"Ella, make me the happiest man in the world and marry me."

He lifted the ring and it caught a shaft of light. The court's illumination bounced off the stone and made it dazzle madly.

I swiveled from the ring to his face. I wanted this moment but I couldn't say a word in the happiest instant of my life so far.

"Ella…"

"I…, I…," Marion started to smile, relieved my initial disorientation was starting to clear. He stayed on one knee his smile now at 1,000 watts.

"You… I will marry you, Marion," I finally managed to say. He knelt a little closer, took the ring out of the box and took my left hand and slipped it on my ring finger. I inspected my hand as he got up on his feet. "The ring is terrific on me."

He laughed and wrapped me up for a hug and a ton of kisses.

"How about a hamburger and a milk shake?"

"Now I only want to stand here on the court steps for an hour."

He laughed and hugged me as I studied my hand adjusting to how radically different I felt. I loved Marion. We had talked hours and hours about what married life would be like, how our marriage would support our plans. It was a foregone conclusion. But the ring...the ring...seeing it on my hand...it seemed to propel me into a new era of my life.

"Your reaction makes me happy," he murmured quietly.

I put my hands on the sides of his face and guided him to my mouth for a punctuation kiss.

An electrically charged idea seized me.

"Family. Let's go tell your parents and Auntie and Unc. C'mon," I yelled, grabbing his hand.

"Let's get a burger first. It's only six o'clock. We have plenty of time to get to Aunt Flora before she goes to work."

"You're right. Supper first."

Marion drove us into the DuPont Circle neighborhood to a corner restaurant we had been to many times. The waitress knew him and immediately noticed the ring.

"Marion, what did you do? Girls come see this," she called to the other servers. Heads swiveled from the other tables. The waitresses were in their forties and fifties but they feigned annoyance at him for getting engaged to me after supposedly offering them the world since high school. Laughter bubbled in the dining room as they gave him the business. Eventually, they returned to their jobs and the diners closest to us wished us well.

We ate, tried to pay, but our waitress wouldn't let us. We thanked her and left to make the quick drive to his parents' place. He parked in the family car spot in front of the shop. He opened my door. I greeted him with my biggest smile. We barely approached the workshop and Marion's father walked up to me wide-eyed. I held up my left hand stifling a laugh.

"All right," he bellowed and wrapped us up in a bear hug. The three of us were laughing like he had told us a funny story. He grabbed my hand and led me into the house to talk to Marion's mother leaving his mechanic to mind the store.

As we approached her working on dinner, she shut off the heat on the pots steaming in front of her. She focused on me expectantly.

"I agreed to marry Marion."

"I can stop praying now," as she gathered me into a hug.

As I received the hug, I replied, "I'm thrilled."

"I only have to worry about Veronica."

"Oh, please. Don't stop praying for us. You know we are going to need it."

"Did he talk you into going to the Supreme Court?"

"It took a little coaxing since I was famished, but once we got there, the lights and the special location made me feel at home."

"Did he ask you correctly?"

"He was patient as I acted crazy."

"So, you're happy?"

"Beyond words."

"We don't want to hold you up. You're Aunt and Uncle and calls to your parents need to happen."

"All true, but I promise to come back tomorrow and tell you a minute-by-minute retelling of Marion's proposal.

"Wonderful, Ella."

We returned to his car and he started to drive me home.

"How did you know to promise my mom to come back tomorrow?"

"I cherish the opportunity to become her daughter. It is a large gift you have given me."

"It's good you feel gifted because she's going to be folding you into our family."

"I wouldn't want it any other way."

"How do you think Auntie and Unc will take it?"

"I think they'll be happy for me. After the wedding, they'll expect us at Sunday dinner often, but I'm a niece after all."

"They never had kids?"

"No. They don't talk about why. They enjoy having me in the apartment but they will easily go back to their old rhythms."

"What they've done for you since you enrolled in Howard for law school is big."

"Because they have, I want to take good care of them when they get older."

We walked into my apartment building and up to their place.

"Hi, Aunt Flora and Unc," I called out as we stepped into the kitchen.

"You're home early…and Marion is here."

Unc got out of his easy chair. "It's good to see you again, Son," my uncle rumbled warmly. I was emotional about Unc's warm greeting to Marion.

"Just a minute, girl." Aunt Flora reacted instantly excited. "Ray, Honey, look at her hand."

"Her hand is just fine."

"Show your uncle your left hand," she responded barely under control.

"Son, did you ask Ella to marry you?" the mighty brick layer asked with a catch in his voice and a smile slowly spreading over his face.

"I did, sir," Marion replied using his courtroom demeanor, straight-faced.

"Wonderful," Auntie shouted coming around the table to hug me. "The best news ever."

"Congratulations, Marion," Unc announced. "I'm incredibly happy for you both."

"When did this happen?" Aunt Flora asked.

"About an hour ago," I shared.

"Sit down. I have peach cobbler and coffee."

We sat, nibbled, and told our story. They were charmed and promised to help us with the wedding.

More public than usual, Marion wrapped me up in a big hug and gave me a kiss carrying everything about our new status.

Chapter 14

When Attorney O. John Rogge visited Cedric, Brown, and Jacobs, Mr. Cedric asked if Attorney Rogge would address all the attorneys in the firm at once. I had only seen all ten of us in the conference room at the same time for birthday celebrations for one of the partners. These were joyful, fun, but brief as everyone took a piece of cake and hustled back to their desks.

This day, Attorney Rogge intended to bring remarks to the firm which the attorneys would hear first-hand, the transcript of which would be distributed to every secretary, investigator, and custodian.

I'd had such experiences at Howard Law. Some major figure would visit our school and a lecture to the student body would be a part of his or her visit.

We were all standing around the conference table catching up when Attorney Rogge walked into the room with the partners following him in.

"Good morning, everyone," Rogge called out in a jolly way.

"Good morning, sir," everyone replied answering his energy.

He sat down at the end of the table and we all sat.

"It's very good to be back in the district having lived and worked here in various positions in government service for more than twenty years. While I was here, your firm always distinguished itself in service to Negro men and women who come before Municipal Court benches and your work to help establish Negro businesses and organizations. You made this community more livable and influential long before the federal government put investments into the Constitution for minorities. You made the 14th and 15th amendments actualized in ways most haven't.

"Even before I knew I would visit you, the collaboration of Negro law firms here to do a wills and succession project was known at home. We instantly decided to copy you in New York City.

"But copying you wasn't enough. I called Ben to ask if I could join your team to help with Dr. Barsky's defense. So, I'm here to add Cedric, Brown & Jacobs to my resume."

A chuckle ran through the room.

"Seriously, this law firm has a history of making this country a more perfect union. Frederick Douglass' incredible article "What to a slave is the 4th of July," is well known to you. I'm part of a constitutional vein of understanding committed to undoing the original, unfortunate constitutional compromises of the 18th Century and amending the ugly disenfranchisement of America's original sin."

The room erupted with noisy applause.

"See, I knew I was right to come here."

We laughed.

"You've been battling and taking chips out of the wall of our awful compromises. It's about time more of us walked alongside you."

Applause warmly greeted him.

"Now, I want to hear from each of you. Please tell me your name and the nature of your daily work, newest add to the firm to the most senior."

He took almost an hour hearing each of us out, praising us, and suggesting growth opportunities including the partners which we enjoyed immensely. He told them they should be getting appointed to positions in federal government in D.C. "One of you should be an assistant attorney general."

We applauded as the three of them laughed with embarrassment.

"Thank you for your remarks, John. We don't often take the time to refuel and keep our daily work in perspective. Your personal attention to our whole team is greatly appreciated."

We gave Rogge another round of applause.

"Ben, Ella, John and I are going to take a fifteen-minute break. Afterward, we'll discuss Dr. Barsky's defense. Thanks, everyone."

Attorney Rogge walked off with the partners while I followed everyone else to Julia's desk to get our phone messages. I had a couple but nothing urgent.

I walked into the conference room reflecting how good it was to get positive support from someone outside of the firm. Our heads were always down, turning out the work, caring for clients. Of course, Dr. Barsky's case had been quite special for lifting me out of municipal court work. Now I was a regular at the Probate Division on 5th St., even defending beneficiaries whose will was contested. I was a member of the District's Probate Fiduciary Panel.

More legal work lined up as beneficiaries put their legacies to work starting or expanding businesses, building investment accounts for their children's college education, or re-writing their wills to pass on a legacy to their children.

Since Marion and I were engaged, I was making mental notes about the start of our firm.

I studied buildings on my way home on the bus with new eyes. I wondered if our firm should be embedded in a Negro neighborhood to be easily accessible. Walking the sidewalks shopping, I would inspect who had offices in the ever-present four or five story buildings anchoring a block.

The partners and Attorney Rogge returned. We sat down again.

"Ella, I want to catch you up on the interest developed by Dr. Barsky's case. A group of well-to-do donors, many Democrats but some Republicans too, have donated to a defense fund for him. My hours and yours, since you will be my second chair…"

My eyes opened a bit wider causing Ben and Mr. Cedric to smile.

"…will be paid by this defense fund. A former assistant attorney general is on this case because important people are watching. This group includes two prominent Negro millionaires."

"It's terrific to know people care enough."

"It's a good sign," Rogge agreed. "Some case law you can get familiar with is Kilbourn v Thompson, Re Chapman, and Sinclair v U.S. These cases tested the limits of Congress' power against individuals. Congress' interest in a person's conduct must relate to pending legislation said the court. An investigation of a witness must be conducted within Congress' oversight authority. We also want to use the Bill of Rights. We might want to defend Edward with those basic rights. Study all this thoroughly and send me notes. Remember to bill our interested parties."

"I'll be certain to send my thoughts, Attorney Rogge."

"Please call me, John, going forward."

"Yes, sir."

"Questions anyone?" We were silent. "Okay, Ella, I'm going to chat with the partners. Julia has my contact information."

"Thank you, John." I got up and went back to my office among my friends. I managed my messages, set up my desk for the afternoon, and took John's notes up to the law library. I couldn't sit there too long. I had wills to give to clients the next morning.

Kilbourn v Thompson was from 1880 and I got the relevance of the case immediately. I took notes, cross-referenced other issues, and set up my next visit to the library.

Returning to my desk, I prepped two will signings and finished a proposal to do the second will owner's business succession. He had already agreed it was an important idea but I wanted to hand him a plan in writing to think about.

Janice was about to leave the office when the phone rang.

"It's Marion. He's leaving work to pick you up."

"Thanks, Janice." I sat back. "Are you ready to bring Valerie over to Marion's for dinner?"

"I think both of us are ready."

"Wonderful. Marion and I will come up with some dates in the next week."

"Love it."

"Have you figured out how to live together without drawing too much scrutiny?"

"We're going to put the money together and have my brother buy us a place."

"Don't the bankers worry about where the money comes from?"

"We're going to set it up as a real estate transaction with all three of us as partners in an investment company."

"They won't care who lives in the house?"

"It needs fixing up and the bank knows it. Our story is we're rehabbing it while we live there."

"Well, if you need a lawyer…" I teased.

She laughed.

"I'd need O. John Rogge."

We laughed.

"Hey, we know the guy."

"Good night, Ella, my dear."

I finished up a few things and headed out to the street. Marion was waiting. I got in and gave him a warm kiss with one hand on his right cheek.

"I've been waiting impatiently for this date," Marion insisted.

"You've been missing McCrory's?"

"I always enjoy McCrory's."

After a few minutes his car arrived alongside my church. We walked into the church office and found Rev. Crossley sitting at his secretary's desk with a big book open on it.

"Reverend Crossley," Marion called out.

"Hello, Marion and Ella. Come see the Parish Register. I know you've gone to the courthouse to put your clients into one courthouse record or another. This book does the same for our church. I'm adding a couple of baptisms."

"…all those babies," I replied peering over his shoulder. "Take us to the wedding section. We aren't quite ready for a baptism."

Laughing, the burly cleric grabbed a tab and flipped the pages to his last wedding.

"You remember Gladys and Wilson Brown?"

"I attended that wedding," I responded.

"This is how it's recorded."

We inspected the register, noting the simple information listed there.

"So wonderful to become a part of a church's history." I observed.

"Truly. Your ancestors will be able to chronicle your history with a record like this. Of course, the two of you have made a big splash onto history with your college and law school graduations."

"I've never thought about our public record," Marion acknowledged.

"Your names are attached to cases you have taken to court. Your fingerprints are in a lot of places in this country." He got up and put the aging registry in its place on a shelf. "Come into my office, have a seat and let's talk about this happy thing you want to do," the preacher intoned.

We followed him and sat.

As he passed me to get to his desk, he paused to enjoy my ring. "It appears Marion is serious," he quipped laughing.

"I am, Pastor."

"Actually, Ella, from the first time you invited him to church, he seemed awe-struck."

We laughed.

"It's true." Marion agreed.

"Actually, Pastor, we could use your help scheduling this wedding. Our emotions are out ahead of our planning."

"I'm happy to help you with a date. Let me ask you a few questions. Ella, are you pregnant?" He wasn't smiling.

"No, sir." I responded quite embarrassed.

"Do you have a place to live?"

"We haven't talked about an apartment yet," Marion explained.

"Do you think a particular season in the year is better than another for a wedding?"

"No," we responded together.

"Have you thought about how many people you're going to invite? You have family but you also have law firms who might want to come. This is going to take money. Have you saved anything so far?"

"I'm so happy we started with you right away," I reacted.

The big man laughed a jolly belly laugh.

We talked through Pastor's questions adding more of our own along the way. We talked for more than an hour.

"I think we've made a good start," my pastor announced. "My suggestion is you make your tentative date a year from now. I'm putting a note to that effect in the back of this year's calendar."

"Sounds wise," I responded.

"Please start saving. Flora and Ray don't have a lot. Marion," he acknowledged, "you have a little sister who's going to want a nice wedding."

"All true," Marion answered.

"Come see me after Christmas."

"Thanks so much for getting us started," I replied.

"Bye bye, you two."

We walked hand in hand deep in thought. We couldn't wait for McCrory's for a burger and a soda. We ordered and sat there a bit overwhelmed by the event planning we had in front of us.

Finally, Marion said, "My parents would let us live rent free in my side of the house for a few years."

"Doesn't Veronica have two more years of high school to go?" I asked. "We could take a small apartment in Auntie and Unc's building."

"Small might be better."

"Let's count guests."

As we ate, our tally easily approached two hundred people among family, friends, and co-workers, if they each invited a spouse or friend.

"Have you ever worked a wedding?" I asked our waitress.

"I have an aunt who caters."

"Do you have any idea what she charges a person?"

"Anywhere from $8 to $15 a plate based on what you are serving," She walked away.

"$15 times 200 is $3,000," I computed.

We were silent.

I was thinking. Pastor was wise scheduling out our date a year. We vowed to make our personal savings accounts wedding accounts.

Chapter 15

"Mama? Hello."

"Ella, how are you doing, Darlin'?"

"I'm good, Mama."

"Busy at work?"

"Always, Mama."

"I love your letters. I loved getting the photo of Marion. He is so handsome."

"Yes, Mama. He's above average…"

She laughed.

"I bet he has to work hard to keep up with you."

"He got ahead of me the other day and proposed."

"Wonderful, El…I'm so happy for you."

"Thanks, Mama."

"Do you have a date?"

"Probably a year from now. We have good jobs but we haven't been at them long."

"I have a little nest egg for you and you can have it whenever it will help. It's not much but it will help."

"Thanks, Mama. It would be a great help."

"How are Flora and Ray?"

"Going strong."

"Tell Marion I like what I hear but I do own a pitchfork."

We laughed.

"I'll warn him."

"Thanks for the call."

"Talk to you soon, Mama."

She sounded good, I thought. *I knew her farm days were long and exhausting.*

My dad was harder to get ahold of. I would write him and a week to ten days later he would call. The long-distance call to D.C. was pricy so we talked fast and shared as much as we could in three minutes. Every now and then he would tell me he had a good night at blackjack and the call would be longer.

I hadn't seen him since freshman year of college. He had come home to Holly Springs to plan his mother's funeral and to settle her affairs. I was home for the funeral but couldn't afford to stay long. Our only long conversation was at grandma's place as he sorted through her belongings.

He spent the time reminiscing. I heard stories new to me. My grandmother, one generation out of slavery, had gone through a lot, but managed to own a successful pork barbeque business in the Negro section of Holly Springs. He promised me he would send me her secret recipe which he had among her belongs.

"You're going to get married? Is this guy worthy of you?"

"Of course, Daddy. He's a lawyer, too. He will be able to take care of me."

"He's lucky to be with you. You have an amazing mind. You have made our family proud."

"Thank you, Daddy."

"When is this going to happen?"

"We haven't set a date. We need to save up for it. Probably next spring."

"As soon as you set the date, let me know and I'll come in for it."

"It will be great to see you, Daddy. I can't wait for you to meet my young man."

"Send me a snapshot of the two of you together."

"I'll do that, Daddy."

"Got to go."

"Thanks for calling."

"Bye bye."

Later, I shared with Marion how the calls worked out.

"They couldn't have gone better. You and I should try to get to our reunions this year."

"What a great idea."

"We should take time off from work to make the trip to Holly Springs, but my reunion is in the District."

"Can we take a week off to be alone at the beach," I asked smiling.

"The beach is mandatory," he replied.

I laughed and fell into his arms. "I've never had mandatory be so happy." He kissed me with a soft mouth asking for closeness in return. I gave it.

~*~

As weeks passed, Marion and I concentrated on making the relationships among our contacts across the Negro law firms more substantial. We invited our collaborators to 'The Crab Shack.' I reserved the back room one Wednesday night.

Terrance, Adam, Carl, Shawn and Marion and I had ordered. We were waiting for Spencer when he burst into the room.

"Wait 'til you hear what the clerk at the courthouse told me."

"You're excited," Terrance replied.

"It's good news. The Clerk of Courts and the chief judge want to give us an award."

"What?" Adam reacted.

"We've barely started with this project," Carl observed with surprise.

"They've seen decided upticks in wills and business succession plans filed with the court. The clerk said we've caused a nineteen percent increase."

"What great news."

"How often do you get awards for pro bono work?" Shawn asked.

"Make sure your partners hear about this," I suggested.

"Will there be some sort of ceremony?" Adam wondered.

"Yes," Spencer confirmed. "They want all seven of us there. I asked if the Washington Tribune could cover it. They said, 'Of course.'"

"Terrance, are we getting on Eric Von's show on WLMS?" I asked.

"This news will make it easier, I think."

"Do you want to close the arrangements for the award ceremony with the court, Ella?"

"No, Spencer. You work the details out with the clerk," I replied.

"This award could help us with our concern about Negroes getting legal services from white firms," Carl asserted.

"We didn't want to cast a negative light on white firms. The award is from the court. Negroes served by white law firms will feel freer to write wills," Marion suggested.

"We'll get the wealth transfer to the next generation either way," I asserted.

"Indeed..."

The food arrived and dinner conversation devolved into the social lives of the assembled attorneys. They knew about Marion and me.

"I'm not going to be influenced by your engagement," Spencer said with a smile. "And, yes, I haven't shared your happy news with my girlfriend."

"Why not?" I teased.

"Me either," Carl chimed in. "We're not there yet."

"You mean, you aren't ready to pop the question," Marion teased.

Laughter erupted at the table.

"Can you keep your engagement notice out of the Tribune for a while," Shawn comically pleaded.

"It'll be in the paper Sunday," I joyfully announced.

"Oh, no," Shawn whined. "Corrine's mother reads the engagements religiously."

We laughed loudly, turning a few heads outside our meeting room.

"I'm going to keep working on you, Adam, since you refuse to tell us who you're seeing," I needled.

"Top secret," he reacted, as the other men laughed.

"It's easy to keep it a secret when there really isn't anyone."

"Maybe he's dating his cousin."

"I bet she's white."

"A good reason to keep it a secret."

"Prominent young Negro attorney indicted for becoming engaged to Kappa Alpha Theta sister."

We roared.

"Okay. I admit it. Bunny McNamara, a Kappa at the University of Maryland is my squeeze."

We laughed again.

"She's introducing me to Mummy and Daddee this weekend."

"Pack the smelling salts," Marion teased.

It was a great meeting, revealing the commitment we had to our community. The award was gravy and simply helped to publicize our project. News stories followed in The Washington Tribune and the Post. I was allowed to hang a photo over my desk of the seven of us with the Clerk of Courts and the Chief Judge of the Probate Court.

I would always get the question about the photo, "Which one is Marion?"

~*~

"I finished my trial file for Edward's Contempt of Congress," I informed Marion.

"I'm going to go see our travel agent and reserve a place for us at the beach."

"I won't be able to relax if it's too close to Edward's court date."

"And I guess it's important to go tomorrow."

"Thank you." I relaxed with an audible exhale.

"Assistant A. G. Rogge loved your court brief."

"I'm pessimistic about the mood in D.C. right now with the red scare talk shouting down Bill of Rights protections."

"No matter how Edward's trial works out with the mood in D.C., Rogge says he has the money to go to the Supreme Court with the case."

"There's some hope in an appeal."

"As I already told you those three cases checking Congress' power against individuals are potent."

"On this case, I'm trying to take the long view."

"I think it's wise."

"But you can feel my anxiety about wanting to do right for Edward."

"I think your feelings about this makes me love you even more. Edward's situation is so important on so many levels. For me it's a civil rights case."

"I think so, too."

"But there's a more personal question to consider." My eyes left the frying pan I had been watching. He seemed uncomfortable. "How will your family and friends react when we go off on vacation alone?"

The question suggested another. "Will the travel agent be put off? Will the resort rent to unmarried people?"

"Both questions are interesting. I won't know until tomorrow. Assuming the resort accepts our status, what about family and friends?"

"It helps we're engaged."

"I wondered how you would take to the idea of a vacation. You seem happy for the trip."

"I want to be alone with you for a week to see if we can stand each other more than a day."

Marion laughed.

We put the food on the table and sat down.

"Seriously, I want to be alone with you because I can't wait to make you my closest friend. I want to know if it will be as terrific as I think it could be."

"Imagine if, after a week together, we found out we are amazing together and we end up building a life even better than we imagined," he reacted catching my excitement.

"What if we surprise ourselves and become a scary capable couple much stronger together than we ever imagined we could be."

"Maybe we should slow down, Baby," Marion cautioned. "We might not be as special as we imagine."

I laughed. His careful braking of my runaway fantasies, slowing my hopes, didn't bother me. "I bet you'll be saying 'wow' by the end of our vacation."

"We're going to the beach not to some magical kingdom," he teased.

"We'll see if we end up being the magical element of our vacation."

We ate and the conversation veered quickly to normal day to day updates and reactions to the news of the day.

Law school had changed me from a person who loved to learn to a lawyer with the role of counselor. It was quite a shift from packing knowledge away in my head and making 'A's on tests. My professors had a radical community bent. They focused us outward, beyond the books, the memorized cases, or precedents, but to the hardships of our community and what we were going to do about them. Our teachers were not shy about letting us know it would get rough when the people who controlled Congress, cities, and towns were adamantly opposed to Negro lawyers trying to better their clients' lives.

Now, I was facing my next transition, building a family with Marion, and making both our families even stronger timbers holding up the mansion of our Negro community.

Marion had a keen sense of what I wanted because his family had an essential business the neighbors relied on. We wouldn't be fixing cars, but we would fit right into his Dad's ethic for leaving people better off.

Dishes done, we took iced tea to the living room and I lay in his arms listening to the radio and receiving the comfort of his embrace.

~*~

Later in the week, Marion reported the travel agent wasn't squeamish about our marital status and found us a room with a kitchenette and one bedroom a block from the beach with a property owner who only had a restriction about pets.

Our families gave us the green light, although Unc gave me a lecture. I obediently heard him out as I caught Aunt Flora snickering out of his sight line in the kitchen. After his tirade was over, I got up and helped Auntie cleanup dinner dishes. She whispered, "I'm sure everything Uncle Ray said will come to mind when you are alone with Marion."

"Poor Marion," I replied.

Auntie almost fell to the floor in paroxysms of laughter.

"I want to hear that joke," Unc called out.

We couldn't stop laughing.

~*~

The next day at work, a big, brown envelope arrived at my desk from Attorney Rogge. His top note read: "Your pre-trial files were excellent, Ella. Some of the best I've ever read.

"What you'll find included is my witness list and an outline of my approach to each witness. Share it with Ben and Walker and send me any suggestions they have."

I took a quick read and routed the material to Mr. Cedric and Mr. Jacobs. It was satisfying HUAC's counsel and one of the congressmen on the committee would be called to testify.

My days were filled with creating wills for a host of families and taking signed documents up to the Clerk of Courts. Whenever I filed wills at the courthouse, one of our friends was there, too.

"Carl, you're registering wills, too?"

"Yes, Ella. Our working group is making the clerk as busy as ever."

"It's a good feeling our community is doing better."

"This work doesn't come with immediate rewards. A lot of the people making wills won't pass on their wealth until after I'm gone," he lamented.

"Yes. There's a downside. For every ten I register here, we are only probating one. It's a delayed impact," I explained.

"Our gift to the future community."

"Exactly," I replied.

When I got back, I had an appointment to discuss the business of a renowned seamstress named Renate Templeton who had grown her business into a dozen custom dressmakers in her business on my bus line. I happily owned two of her daily wear dresses.

"Miss Templeton, it's wonderful to meet you in person."

"Ella, thank you. I probably should have come in sooner."

"Let's go into the conference room. Can I get you a cup of tea?"

"A glass of water is enough."

"Coming right up." I filled two glasses in the kitchenette and put them on the table. "Explain what you'd like to do."

"Ella, I don't know. My children have their own careers, my age is starting to slow me down, but I don't want my business to suffer because I haven't planned."

"Any stars among your employees?"

"Many but they're all stars in designing and turning out garments. It's the accounting and overall management person I haven't been able to find."

"Someone straight out of school wouldn't do?"

"No. I can't get ahead fast enough training someone into management."

"Would someone who's managed in another type of company work? Could they adapt to your company?"

"I'm sure. Do you know anyone?"

I sat for a moment thinking through the people I knew. After a moment, I offered, "I have a girlfriend who is the business manager for a medical clinic over on Anacostia Street."

"The White Clinic?"

"The very one."

"It's large."

"Yes, and she's running the place financially."

"Would she consider talking to me?"

I picked up the extension in the conference room and called Vi.

"Hi, Violet Baker, please…Violet, it's Ella."

"Ella, what a nice surprise."

"Do you have a couple of minutes?"

"Always, for you."

"I'm at work in a meeting with Renate Templeton."

"The Renate Templeton who's a dress designer and clothier?"

"Yes, the one and the only Renate Templeton."

Ms. Templeton laughed.

"She needs to add a financial officer to her management team and we'd like to schedule a meeting for you two to meet."

Renate shook her head yes.

"Me?"

"Yes, you."

"I would love to but…"

"Ms. Templeton, Violet is willing to meet."

"'Smokie's' at six tomorrow?"

"Do you know 'Smokie's' over by Templeton's Clothing Store?"

"Yes."

"6p.m. tomorrow."

"I'd like you to be there, Ella."

"It'll be the three of us."

"I'm floored, excited…, and I'll be there."

"Thanks, Vi,'" I replied hanging up. "Whether or not Violet works out, you'd be searching for a financial leader, a production manager, a store manager to be added to your staff?"

"And a buyer who could take over our relationships with fabric suppliers."

"Excellent. Let me put a plan together so you can choose from one of your lieutenants to become president of the company someday."

"I can't tell you how relieved I am to create this plan."

"It will give you the help you need to enjoy this part of your work life and take a lot of the worry about continuing what you've built."

"This meeting has been very satisfying."

"It's extremely important to us to help you prepare for the future."

Walker Cedric entered the conference room.

"I heard you were here, Renate."

I smiled.

"Walker…"

She stood and they hugged.

"Anything wrong?" he asked with concern.

"Not anymore. Ella and I have the outline for my business succession."

"Excellent."

As we made dinner, I told Marion about the meeting.

"Renate Templeton."

"Templeton, the dress maker?"

"The one and only."

"Ben's letting you have bigger clients now?"

"We have such a stream of wills clients now, our new attorneys from Howard have to help."

"You're keeping your eye on them, though?"

"Of course, but I had a new opportunity today. Renate, we're on a first-name basis now…,"

Marion laughed.

"…needed a financial manager and had no one to promote from within. I called Violet Baker."

"She works for the White Clinic. I met her at the Crab Shack, I think."

"You did. I notice you remember the gorgeous ones," I teased.

"Is she pretty?" he asked straight-faced.

I gave him a shove.

"Renate is interviewing her over dinner tomorrow night."

"Nice work. At the next Wills Team meeting we should share contacts to advance our up and comers into higher ranks."

"Terrific idea. I'm going to talk to my typists tomorrow if they are up to calling the other firms when we're needing someone with skills."

"Calling is a good way to get the word out fast. Do they like being on the phone?"

"They fight over a ringing telephone and they love to hear your voice."

"I won't let it go to my head."

"Better not," I warned him with a smile.

"Your schedule still good for our beach week?"

"Yes. I must get as many wills to the typists as I can before we go and the Monday after, I'll go crazy catching up."

"First vacation as a professional."

"It'll be doubly sweet," I smiled batting my eyelashes.

Marion shook his head taking plates to the kitchen table. I delivered the salad and the bread. He collected our drinks and sat down. We fell into the happy conversation of two committed people who knew each other well.

~*~

"Over here, Ella," Mrs. Templeton called out. As I approached the table, Vi and Renate were already sitting together with menus. I sat down. "Violet's been telling me stories about you."

"Uh, oh. She knows too much."

They both laughed.

"She tells me your fiancé is above average."

I gave Vi a smile and opened my purse for the photo I carried of Marion. I handed it to Renate.

She gave it a good assessment. "It's clear Violet will give me the straight story." We laughed and she handed the photo to my friend before it got back to me.

"Do you know what I can get you?" the waitress asked.

"You two start," I urged as I picked up the menu in earnest. When the waitress nodded her readiness for my choice, I told her, "Barbeque, Georgia style…Iced tea."

"Baked beans, macaroni and cheese, and cornbread are our normal sides."

"Perfect." She took my menu.

I refused to take the lead. The interview resumed.

"I told you the major aspects of my business. Besides the books, I need you to catch whatever is going on while I'm managing other issues. I used to be able to juggle it all, but not anymore."

"I can back you up as you are asking."

"In the beginning, bring me notes about what's going on and I'll walk you through how I'd handle it. After a while, you can go ahead and guide the staff yourself."

"I like your plan," Violet responded sounding a little worried. "I'll be nervous at first."

"Once you've been with us a while, our operation will be easier to manage. You have many more issues facing you at the clinic."

"I'll try to get the hang of things quickly, but I'll have to lean on you."

"Do, but in the beginning simply gather information and we'll make decisions together. Sound good, Ella?"

"I'm a simple country lawyer. What do I know about business?"

They laughed. Vi asked questions about her building. Renate took out a pad and drew illustrations of her departments, shipping and receiving, sewing room, offices, and the retail store Vi and I had already visited.

The food arrived and the conversation slanted personal. Renate's husband had died some years before. Her children were teachers and tradesmen. Vi had one son, age four and a husband who helped run his family's hardware store.

We were finishing up and Renate handed me an offer she had prepared for Violet. It was clearly a manager's salary. I wondered how it compared to what she was already making but there was a 1.5% bonus based on sales sweetening the salary figure.

I handed it back to Renate without giving away my feelings. She passed it on to Violet. Her eyes darted across the letter. She took the time to read it twice.

"Take it home and consider it with your husband," Renate suggested.

"I will. I don't need to sleep on it, though, because it is an attractive offer, giving me a chance to broaden my skills. Thank you for this opportunity."

"You're welcome, my Dear. I think you'll be a great help to me."

"Thank you, Ella, for getting us together," Vi added.

"I was happy to bring two important people together," I responded with a smile.

The two of them made plans and I left them heading home to Auntie and Unc's.

Chapter 16

Marion drove east out of Washington, a direction I hardly ever had traveled. We were quickly into Maryland, the suburbs of D.C. giving way to larger homes on an acre of land each. The expansive lawns sheltered with a mix of pine and maple, gradually yielded to poplar and weeping willow. Flowers accented front yard garden beds.

The towns gave way to farms, open land, and tiny commerce on crossroads, the countryside standing between suburbia and coastal wilderness.

Auntie had made sandwiches, Marion's mother, cobbler, and mason jars full of lemonade and tea. We stopped at a wayside with two picnic tables under some trees. We were alone, receiving a sunny breeze easing hot, summery temperatures.

I wore a skirt, bobby sox, loafers, and a sleeveless blouse. Marion wore slacks, a short-sleeved dress shirt and brown wingtips.

"We're almost there. I'm in the mood to savor this lunch," Marion suggested to me.

"I agree. I'm on a vacation. All I need is to be with you. What a wonderful luxury."

"Considering how hard we've worked, law school and taxing jobs for over a year, it's wonderful to exhale."

"Being on the bottom rung of a career ladder is exhausting. You try to do your best, taking every opportunity offered and giving it your all," I replied wearily.

"We have met every challenge. We are rising," Marion celebrated.

"Will vacations put us back together?" I wondered.

"Being on the beach together has gotta help, don't you think?"

"You put me back together every evening we're together. A week has got to be transforming."

We dug into the cobbler.

An old sedan roared into the wayside skidding to a stop. Three young white guys piled out of their wreck and walked over to us. They were barefoot, their trousers were torn and full of holes, old A-shirts were worn to the point of disintegration.

"You're sitting at my table, Pretty Boy."

"A lot of names are carved into this table," Marion replied matter-of-factly.

"Listen to the mouth on this boy, Mickey."

"I noticed that Erv," he replied sitting down next to me, his leg up against mine. The overwhelming sensation was the scent of a body that hadn't bathed in several days.

When I looked up, Marion was as coiled to act as I had ever seen. He was staring angrily at the closeness of the boy next to me. I was immediately alarmed he might leap across the table.

"We need to collect some rent from these two darkies for using our table."

"Right you are," the chunky third boy sounded off angrily.

"It doesn't have to be money," Mickey suggested, his face coming close to mine, his tongue lolling outside his mouth as I stared at Marion trying to keep him from reacting. "This one smells mighty nice," Erv informed his friend.

"Big man, let's have your woman draipse herself on our table for us."

Marion flexed his body in rage.

Two more cars sped into the wayside hopping the curb and stopping a few feet from the table, engines racing.

"Highway patrol…" I managed to shout out for Marion's benefit who was sitting with his back to the road. The three hoodlums scrambled from the table running into the trees and undergrowth away from the road.

The patrolmen called out, "You, okay?"

"Yeah," Marion called out as the two officers, pistols drawn disappeared into the woods.

I hurried around the picnic table and sat next to Marion shivering with anxiety. He held me. We could not see what might be going on out in the brush. We could hear angry voices. A shot was fired making us jump.

The shouting stopped.

A few minutes later, the patrolmen led the young men past us handcuffed and Marion got up and opened his attaché in our car. I followed at a distance. He approached the patrol cruiser with some of his business cards. He leaned into the back seats and made sure each boy had one.

"Could I have one?" one patrolman asked.

"Of course," Marion replied.

The officers read his card. "Thank you, Counselor."

"You two, okay?" the other officer asked.

"Yes. I think we'll finish our cobbler and be on our way."

"We apologize for not getting here faster."

"I hope your wife is okay."

"She's a little rattled but your timing was perfect." I managed a little smile and a wave.

They got into their squad cars and were gone leaving our tormentors' rusting hulk behind. I walked up behind Marion and put my arms around him as I recovered my emotions.

"We're used to moving around a city prepared for danger. Being on vacation took all the worry right out of my mind," Marion observed exhaling in relief.

"Don't you want to get back in the car and drive on?" I asked trying to read his face.

"I don't want the cobbler to spoil." I shook my head in surprise. "I want to ease us back into vacation attitude before I drive again."

"Good idea," letting Marion lead me out of a harrowing moment which could have ended badly for both of us.

We sat back down finding our drinks remained cold and the cobbler even sweeter. I paced myself on Marion's leisurely enjoyment of the food. Somehow, he seemed calm. I wasn't going to ask him anything about how he really felt.

"Mmm, this is good."

"There's more under the ice in the bucket."

"It should keep until we get into our room. I'll have some as my midnight snack," Marion decided.

"You're going to be awake at midnight?" I teased.

"I don't plan on wasting any time sleeping."

"I won't watch you eat. I'll be asleep."

"I'll be memorizing you in your pajamas."

"I didn't bring any."

He almost choked on his cobbler. "Aunt Flora wouldn't let you go without…"

"I packed my bag," interrupting him with a smirk. "You'll have to memorize something besides pajamas."

He laughed nervously. It was great to see him off balance again having bravely gotten through the ambush.

We packed up the remains of lunch and drove on.

After a good half hour, I asked him quietly, "What was your plan before the state police arrived?"

He didn't say anything for a moment. His jaw line tensed and he gazed down the road rather than give me a glance. "…to jump over the table and get between Erv and you."

"There were three of them…" I replied quietly.

"I noticed," he answered.

The forest gave way to scrubby pines and sandy ground. The breeze picked up and we noticed a light salty scent surrounding us. Road signs began to hawk the restaurants and bars in Highland Beach, Maryland, daily beach shower houses, and attractions catering to people on day trips. Billboards featured Negroes cooking, happy Negro patrons, and down home named truck stops.

"A police car is driving behind us. We must be close to the resort."

"Oh?" I wondered

"The police officer is a Negro."

As we rolled through the town, whites were a minority. I watched for Sixth Avenue. Our directions told us to turn left on Sixth and right on Oceanview until we got to Second Avenue.

"Here's second."

Ocean Rest Motel was on our right. Marion found an empty parking spot. We walked into the motel's office.

"Hello, welcome to the Ocean Rest."

"I'm Marion Forman and this is Ella Moses."

"Yes. I have your reservation right here. You're staying with us for a week. Wonderful. Could you fill out this card and sign it?"

"Of course."

"Thank you. I'll give Miss Moses your keys. You're in room 212 at the end of the hallway facing the ocean."

"Thanks," Marion replied. We walked up the stairs with our bags. Marion opened the door. As promised, there were windows facing the ocean and being on the second floor, we could see people were on the beach and in the water. Windows in the back of the room looked over a flower garden.

"Nice place," I observed. "I need to hang a few things from my case."

"Me, too."

After a moment, Marion suggested, "Let's change into sandals and check out this town."

"You get a hug first." We eased into each other's arms savoring the full joy of being a couple on our own. We kissed. "Vacations are a wonderful thing."

"Yes, they are," Marion replied. "Before we go, let's crack the windows so we get a breeze."

"Great idea."

Down in the lobby, "See you later," I called out.

Our host replied, "Have fun."

While we waited for the traffic to clear at the corner, we inventoried our neighborhood: a small grocery, a seafood shop, and a tavern. When we got up on the boardwalk, out plan had been to find a place for supper. But the ocean interrupted our dinner plans. We walked down a flight of steps onto the sand moving toward the surf. Families and couples were distributed around the lifeguard stand and I noticed one lifeguard on his feet staring intently at about twenty people in the breakers. To tease Marion, I kept my eyes trained on the lifeguard's lovely muscles as we walked past him.

"Hey…." he complained re-focusing my eyes on the water. I laughed happily.

We got to the wet sand kicking off our sandals. The power of the ocean sucked at our toes, even more powerfully as we got to the ebbing surf.

A flock of happy Negro children bubbled and flowed by us as the surf curled around our ankles. Benign cumulus clouds decorated the horizon and occasionally gave us a break from the summer sun.

Marion knelt to pick up a small conch shell handing it to me. It snuggled in the palm of my hand beginning a small collection I put in a mason jar on my desk of shells and rocks collected until I retired.

We sauntered up the beach holding hands with no destination in mind. I assessed his face seeing a relaxed satisfaction new to me.

"You seem as pleased as I feel," I gently observed.

"I don't remember feeling this mellow. I didn't know I had it in me," he confessed. "It's good to give yourself a glimpse of heaven now and then."

"This is heaven," I replied.

"As close as I ever felt. You're mostly responsible for the feeling," he added quietly breaking his reverie enough to sweettalk me.

"A beach doesn't hurt."

"We should try mountains sometime."

"The Great Smokies," aren't too far."

"True."

We were driven silent as we retraced our steps to our lifeguard stand.

We stepped into our sandals again trying to pick out the offerings on the board walk. A gift shop's windows were jammed with treasures. An open-air restaurant, great panels of walls hoisted and hanging on hooks allowed the cooling breeze to welcome diners. Fudge and taffy shops, barkers inviting us to entertainment within, an ice cream emporium, a sea food only restaurant causing Marion to ask, "Have you eaten fresh oysters?"

He promised me the experience, making me wonder if the growing extravagance of our vacation would make our wedding date slide out six months.

Looming ahead was a Ferris wheel. Before we got to it, bumping cars, a shooting gallery, ring toss, pins to knock down, a merry-go-round, all delights I'd never experienced presented themselves. Surprisingly, the Ferris Wheel had a more frightening sister called 'The Wild Mouse.' Screaming teenagers reacted to the drop, catapulting them through curve after curve until they were breathless at the bottom.

"Never ever…" I reflexively prayed.

"Oh, at least once," Marion replied staring at the ride.

"Something even more nervy than being alone with you for a week."

He gave me a shove and I roared with laughter.

"You know, with all this sea air, I could use a nap before supper," Marion suggested with a straight face.

"I am feeling a pillow calling, too. I wasn't going to say anything not wanting to be a spoil sport."

"After our exciting day, a nap will help us get through an evening of boardwalk fun," Marion suggested.

"Without a nap I would need to be asleep by eight," I teased.

"I'm open to either plan," Marion replied trying not to confess how much he yearned to be tucked into one of the twin beds with me.

"You'll have your fun either way, I suppose," I asserted acting as virginal as I could.

He laughed knowing I was as ready to get to him as he was longing for me.

We walked back to our room, shed a layer of clothing, and hid under a sheet, the sea breeze keeping us cool despite bodies aching for touch.

~*~

Back on the boardwalk, we rode 'The Wild Mouse' for the first time and felt completely jolted, laughing uncontrollably.

"Again," I begged as I caught my breath.

We got back in line.

"Who knew danger could be fun, too," Marion observed ironically.

"Danger's what we need to add to this boardwalk someday. A horror ride with groups of back woods crackers threatening mayhem at every turn," I visualized.

Marion shook his head. "It's good to learn about this macabre side to you," he observed straight-faced.

"People love horror movies. How about a scary ride?"

"It's tricky making average southern white boys the menace," he reacted laughing cynically.

"You don't think the white boy's scenario would have broad appeal?"

"Did you ever see 'The Oxbow Incident?'"

"Yes, but all those guys were white."

"I know what you were thinking about when you saw it," I asserted.

"Of course. But no white audience will consider our take."

"But a horror ride could make things very clear. People in Minnesota and Wisconsin might appreciate being 'enlightened.'"

"I'd put your idea on a back burner for fifty years," Marion cautioned.

We rode the roller coaster again surprising ourselves two times was not enough. We stopped to buy some fudge.

"Have you ever faced a situation like today?" I asked as the first bite of fudge melted in my mouth.

"Half a dozen beatings by the toughs in my hometown…" he replied calmly. "Nothing since I grew to six feet with these muscles."

"Mmm," I mused, "You mean the muscles which caught my eye the first time?"

"You didn't see my muscles for months."

"Even suits don't hide what you have going," I responded enjoying the verbal as well as the physical intimacy.

"Thank you very much, Honey." He kissed me. "What about you in Holly Springs?"

"I regularly got felt up by a pair or more of white guys."

"Regularly?"

"They'd wait for a situation where I was walking alone down the street. I'd get pushed into a corner and violated."

"Did those childhood moments come to mind at the roadside table this morning?" he asked softly.

"I was wishing we were in a town setting. I had never been cornered as far from help before."

"Despite my size, I felt outnumbered."

"Thank goodness the cops were already after them."

"Thank goodness they weren't smart enough to pass us by."

"Their stupidity was an asset we didn't know we had," I observed.

"The arrival of the highway patrol didn't settle my nerves so much," Marion admitted.

"Walking those three boys by us in handcuffs allowed me to exhale. What was that business about your business card?"

"It was a lesson in not assuming."

We walked on playing a couple games of chance and stopping for dinner. We had a hot dog with fries and a soft drink. As the sun began to set, we rode the Ferris Wheel and the lights came on. It was much easier to enjoy the predictable and slow-moving height changes on this ride. The bright man-made light from the boardwalk continued to illuminate the white froth of the breakers.

"Let's go to the water's edge tomorrow before breakfast. I want to find more cool shells," Marion suggested.

"You need to get some sleep," I teased with a tiny, sarcastic smile.

"Afternoon naps work, too."

I giggled like a schoolgirl.

We walked around a little more, got an ice cream cone and called it a day. It had been marvelous but the roadside scare had taken a lot out of us.

Back in our room, we showered together taking a coating of sweat and sand off us. Toweled down, we lay naked letting the breeze chill us until I couldn't leave him alone any longer. I rolled on top of Marion rubbing his shoulders and arms kissing him lovingly.

His arms gently but firmly held me, letting me know I was going nowhere. I was ecstatic to be alone with him. He seemed to be savoring our first night of vacation. We could hear cars moving through the intersection below us, voices of people walking by, and a distant rumble of music, voices, and other noises from the boardwalk. He laughed quietly.

"With our lights out, no one would know," he observed.

"Are you asking me to stay quiet up here? I don't think it's possible."

"You are noisy."

I tried to pound a fist on his shoulder, but he squeezed me tightly. "I…can't…breath…" He loosened his grip and I giggled.

"When we buy a house, we'll have to soundproof our bedroom."

"No. I want everyone to be jealous."

"'Famous jurist ticketed for excessive noise during sex.'"

"No one will care who we are."

"You already received an award from the Chief Judge."

"True," I reacted soberly.

"We'll simply have to be crazy while we're young," as his hands slipped from my back to cup my cheeks. I was thinking what to do about his hands when his tongue filled my mouth. He had my attention. Marion had enough room to roll me on my side without pushing me out of bed. His free hand played with my breasts and started my breathing. His hand explored my stomach. I didn't protest. I was too busy managing increasing feelings of excitement. By this point I was aching for every kind of contact. His intimate touching soon had me arching my back involuntarily trying to escape being known but, in my brain, fireworks were going off. Weeks before he proved he knew my anatomy and pleasure was the result. I tried to grab his penis but he wouldn't let me, insisting on forcing me to give into my body. I didn't disappoint and he wasn't satisfied until I was a helpless wreck. While I managed my ongoing overwhelmed nerve endings' pulsations, he walked away for a moment to return sheathed.

He grabbed one leg laying me flat on my back unceremoniously slipping into me to give me a moment I can't put into words, except the word ultimate. I wrapped my arms around him, turning my head so I could breathe and held on emotionally, happy, taken, thrilled, unnerved, off-balance, and certain he was everything to me. As easily as I was overcome, he was the opposite. I began to worry I couldn't take everything he was giving. I resolved to try when it was his turn to succumb.

We were panting, praising God, swearing our love for each other, and hearing the traffic and conversation, one floor below. Embarrassment swept over me until I realized the world had gone on without us.

The next day we explored the town finding more shops and restaurants to explore. I bought a skirt and a blouse in one shop and a copy of 'Rebecca' in a used bookstore. Marion bought a used toolbox full of old tools to add to his carving chisels.

"Your father has every tool in the world down the stairs from your apartment."

"True, but I'm not going to live there forever."

"You and I may live there for years," I teased.

"This used toolbox was such a deal and I'll have us out of there in six months."

"I believe you mean it. I don't know how we'll do it but I believe in you."

"Especially with our champagne tastes."

I shook my head.

"I plead guilty," I replied sheepishly. "How are we going to afford to be married?"

"We'll have two salaries and we'll both ride the bus everywhere."

"I think you're right."

We were trying to enjoy our vacation but I kept spending money.

"Baby, we've spent our budget," Marion warned. "The rest of the week we do the cheap activities…sun, sand, waves, and sex."

"Such a good list."

We laughed.

As the week continued, we got closer, like we hoped. Closeness and a lot of time worked wonders. A quiet certainty developed in each of us. We decided we were exactly what each other wanted. We adopted the song, "Darling, You Know I Love You," especially the B.B. King's soulful instrumental.

Driving back to Washington, we reflected on the work we both faced. We had gotten some recommendations from the desk staff at our hotel about lunch stops.

'Mabel's Grill' was the first one we found. We settled into a booth noticing the dining room had almost as many whites as Negroes. Everyone seemed at ease with each other. Our waitress was our age.

"On the way to Highland Beach or going home?" our waitress asked.

"Going home," I replied, smiling.

"Why are you happy about it?" she teased. I smiled at Marion. "Oh, you two are an item, I guess."

"Yes," I replied smiling even more broadly, revealing my ring.

"Well, good," she observed with a little laugh. "Drinks?"

"Two cokes," Marion replied.

"I'll be right back."

"It's nice nothing is in doubt about us," I observed.

"Perfect strangers can tell. Will our friends notice how finished we appear?"

"I don't know. We've told them about the engagement. Do we show it somehow?"

"We'll notice everyone's reaction. When we get home, we'll have to be more disciplined," Marion cautioned sadly.

"Vacation is a special time. I know we'll get back in our normal discipline. Simple fun will get us through.

"You're right, Ella. All we really need is each other."

"I'm certain of us," I replied grabbing his hand across the table.

The waitress put our drinks in front of us.

"What'll you have?"

"I'd like a cheeseburger and fries," Marion told her.

"You?" she asked smiling at me.

"A bacon, lettuce, and tomato sandwich?"

"Cole slaw or fries?"

"Cole slaw."

"Coming right up."

"Our friends will notice," Marion suggested.

"Of course, they will," I agreed. "We'll have to invite them over to your apartment now and then when we choose not to spend money to go out."

"We'll call them, 'Wedding Savings Parties,' so they get it."

"They'll love to come to those house parties. They'll have fun and it'll be a cheap evening for them, too. We can have a stone soup pot and invite them to contribute an ingredient."

"My mom has a perfect soup pot. Filled, it could serve a dozen."

"Sounds perfect," I replied

Our food arrived.

We took first bites and everything tasted great.

"Mmm, didn't realize how hungry I was."

"Me, either. Feeling happy makes me want to eat." He got a third into our lunch and Marion returned to our conversation. "The young lawyers at Watkins & Hopkins were spit balling about starting our own firms. One guy had an idea I liked. You buy a mixed-use property and live above your office."

"What's mixed-use?" I wondered.

"Like the three-story buildings on 'B' Street. You know? It's got a shop on the street with two nice-sized apartments stacked above."

I sat there for a minute trying to picture it. "Oh, like the building the cobbler shop is in near my work?"

"Exactly."

"But we'd only have one paying tenant."

"I know but by the time we leave our firms we'll have money saved and the new law firm would draw work from our name recognition."

"Here's hoping…" as I took another bite of my BLT.

"How would you feel living above your office?"

"I think it has possibilities if we can help client's find us," I teased.

"Bring your legal issues to 'Forman and Forman' right next door to 'Manny's Jewish Deli and Kosher Bodega."

I laughed almost spitting out a mouthful of sandwich. "We'll have to give Manny free legal services for a year."

"A reasonable trade off. Ads in Negro and white newspapers, a mailed announcement to every Negro law firm in town, and a mailing to every Negro business in south Washington," Marion replied.

"We'll have figured out how I pay for outfitting the office and paying the salaries of typists and a receptionist?" I asked.

"The scariest loan you've ever seen."

"How are you two doing here? Ready for some Rhubarb – Strawberry Pie a la mode?"

"Yes," we agreed in unison.

~*~

Not too long after the pie moment, Marion was parking in front of my apartment building. William was sitting on the stoop.

"Where have you been?" he asked in horror.

"On vacation with Marion…"

"Oh, okay… I thought someone offed you."

"Bull Dog, you know she's safe with me," as a memory flashed in my head of the three crackers.

"I know she is, Bullet. But I couldn't think of any place she might be."

"William, I'll be back down in a minute and we'll get some Italian Ice."

"Okay, okay."

We climbed the stairs and gave Auntie Flora and Unc a brief report on our week but they saw our oversized smiles and got the drift. I filled them in completely when I got back from my Italian ice treat with Bull Dog. I gave Marion a lingering kiss and a big smile. He drove off.

"Did you need me for something, Bull Dog?" I asked as we walked to the shop.

"Nothing special," he replied with a sullen tone.

"I'm sorry I didn't let you know where I was."

"I know I'm not your boy, but…"

"It was inconsiderate of me not to fill you in. Believe me, I won't keep you in the dark again."

"Thank you. I worry, you know."

"I know. I appreciate it." We walked up to their window, made our selection, and sat at a picnic table surrounded by neighborhood children Bull Dog knew well.

"We drove to the ocean in Maryland, rested, had fun, ate too much, and drove home."

"Sounds great," he responded brightening a bit.

"Marion and I are going to marry…"

"I knew you would."

"We want you to be an usher at the wedding…"

"What does an usher do?"

"You help everyone find a seat."

"They need help?"

"On formal occasions. You'll seat my friends on one side of the church, Marion's on the other."

"They don't like each other?"

"It's a custom. At the reception everyone will be mixed up together."

"A reception?"

"It's supper for everyone who comes including you."

"I like to eat."

"Eventually, Marion and I are going to open our own law firm and I want you to work there."

"Really? What would be my job?"

"When people come in, there'll be a young woman who answers the phone and she will greet anyone who comes in and find out if they have an appointment. If they do, you'll take them where they belong."

"I'll be an usher every day?"

"Yes – exactly and if anyone gets out of line…"

"I'll flatten them…" he replied laughing getting Italian ice on his shirt.

Chapter 17

A week later, I was sitting with Attorney Rogge and Edward at the defense table in the Federal Courthouse in D.C. I had Rogge's files and notes in the order he requested, ready to feed him documents as the case proceeded.

"Edward, have you had any time to get away with Vita and Angela?" I asked him, waiting for the judge to enter and start the proceedings.

"We spent most of our time in the last month in the Catskills. It didn't do much for Angela's schooling this year," he added laughing.

"I'm sure she won't be hurt too badly."

"We drove her into the local library and she worked on some projects which she mailed into several of her teachers."

"Mailed assignments are something."

"Mostly, we hiked, canoed, swam, cooked together and had a great time."

"Sounds perfect."

"Ben told me you and Marion got away."

"We were in Highland Beach on the Maryland shore."

"A good time?"

"The best."

"I'm happy to hear it."

"All rise. The Honorable Patrick Murray presiding," the bailiff intoned.

"You may be seated. Who's for the prosecution?" asked Judge Murray.

"Bertram Ryan, Department of Justice prosecutor.

"Oh, yes, Mr. Ryan."

"O. John Rogge, for the defense.

"Good to see you again, Attorney Rogge."

"Thank you, your Honor."

"Are we ready for jury selection?"

Both attorneys responded, yes. "Bailiff, please escort the prospective jurors into the jury box area. I never had to defend a jury trial in municipal court. I took personal notes as John and Mr. Ryan went through voir dire.

The process pushed into lunch. The jury and the rest of us were told to take a lunch break and John led us to an upscale restaurant nearby.

We ordered drinks.

"It's hard to pick jurors in this political climate, John," Edward suggested.

"You noticed," John replied with a sarcastic tone. "I don't get to ask direct questions to a juror, but an answer to a leading question will tip me off."

"It seemed like more than half of the jury has an open mind."

"I think so, too. I don't know how long things will go today. Food was a good idea."

The waiter brought our drinks and took the food order.

A friend of John's walked up to us. "Larry, I haven't seen you in an age. Dr. Barsky, Attorney Moses, this is Larry Smalley. He's the legislative aide for Senator Hubert Humphrey."

"Hello, everyone," Larry replied. We knew who Humphrey was so we welcomed our visitor. "I know what kind of day you're having so you should know about Margaret Chase Smith's comments in the Senate this morning."

"We're all ears, Larry."

"She complained, 'Freedom of speech is not what it used to be in America. It has been abused by some and it is not exercised by others.' She asked her fellow Republicans not to ride to political victory on the 'four horsemen of Calumny – Fear, Ignorance, Bigotry, and Smear.'"

"Really?" I reacted.

"Word for Word," Larry responded.

"Courageous..." I responded.

"A devastating speech coming from another Republican," Rogge reacted.

"She's the first member of congress, woman or man, to break the code of complicity of the McCarthy gang," Dr. Barsky noted.

"I thought it wouldn't hurt your day to know," Larry commented smiling. As he left us, we were staring at each other.

Dr. Barsky broke our hesitancy to celebrate with the question, "How many more people will need to speak out before the demagogue is silenced?"

"Even after he is gone from the scene, will the red scare be behind us?"

We sat silently. The waiter brought our lunch. My BLT was perfect. "I had a wonderful week on the beach," I announced breaking the dark mood at the table.

"Excellent," Edward reacted cheerily.

"Where did you go?" John asked.

I dominated the conversation through lunch and all the way back to the court room.

Each attorney made opening statements after we were gaveled back in.

Mr. Ryan called to the stand Attorney Frank Tavener, counsel to the House Un-American Activities Committee.

"Mr. Tavener, did the Committee issue a subpoena to Dr. Edward Barsky to appear?"

"Yes."

"Did he appear in person?"

"There were negotiations between the committee and Dr. Barsky but he finally did appear."

"Did he sit for a lengthy interview over a series of days?"

"No."

"Why not?"

"Despite our detailed subpoena, Dr. Barsky appeared without the tranche of information requested in our document."

"What was his rationalization for appearing empty handed?"

"He asserted his Board of Directors had voted to keep him from releasing the documents we requested."

"Dr. Barsky didn't reveal until under oath he had failed to obey the subpoena?"

"Correct."

"Did Dr. Barsky promise to get the documents you requested?"

"He did. But time has passed and there was no movement."

"You still have not received the documents in question?"

"No."

"What was your reaction to this failure to act by the plaintiffs?"

"We've referred the whole board for prosecution to the Department of Justice."

"No further questions, Your Honor."

"Attorney Rogge, do you want to cross?"

"Yes, Your Honor."

"Attorney Tavener, what pending legislation is being written which will be informed by the committee's subpoena?"

"My role is outside the actual writing of legislation."

"I understand, Mr. Tavener, but your role includes alerting the committee when their actions are unconstitutional."

"The committee is exercising its oversight responsibilities under the Constitution."

"There are at least three precedents in Supreme Court history which have found against Congress for belaboring individual citizens, which is what you've been doing, correct?"

"Those are minor rulings which have failed to protect us in 1952."

"You acknowledge the cases I'm referencing?"

"Yes, but…"

"In this case those three Supreme Court decisions have been ignored by the House Un-American Activities Committee because you have admitted no pending legislation undergirds your work, correct?"

"I disagree with your reading of the law."

"Happily, we have a jury for this trial. No further questions, Your Honor."

"Do you wish to re-direct, Mr. Ryan?"

"No, Your Honor," Attorney Ryan responded with a sarcastic laugh."

"What a great job, John did," I thought.

"You may step down, Mr. Tavener. Next witness, Mr. Ryan."

"The State calls Congressman J. Parnell Thomas to the stand," the attorney announced. Thomas was sworn in. "Congressman Thomas, when Dr. Barsky appeared before the Committee, the cause was a subpoena?"

"Yes."

"Why did the committee issue the subpoena?"

"Dr. Barsky's organization was supporting communists with money and goods known to sustain them in the United States."

"Where did these people come from?"

"They were immigrants from the Spanish Civil War who backed the sitting government in Madrid which the Communist Soviet Union propped up with military advisors, munitions, and logistical support."

"These people Dr. Barsky's organization supports were fellow travelers with the communist backed government of Moscow?"

"Absolutely."

"Why did you refer Dr. Barsky to the Department of Justice?"

"He failed to give us the documents from his organization we requested."

"He still refuses today?"

"He does."

"No further questions, Your Honor."

"Mr. Rogge?"

"Thank you, Your Honor."

"Mr. Thomas, did the Immigration Service of the United States admit, after review, the immigrants from Spain needed asylum resulting from their Civil War?"

"I do not agree asylum was a correct decision by the Immigration Service."

"Does the Congress, of which you are a part, write and approve the laws governing the Immigration and Naturalization Service?"

"Yes. But I don't agree allowing communists to immigrate is a healthy policy."

"Why hasn't Congress voted to prevent the Immigration Service from allowing Communists to enter?"

"There aren't enough intelligent members to pass an anti-communist vote."

"People of your mindset are a minority?"

"For now."

"In his testimony, did Dr. Barsky explain his organization's contributions to Spanish refugees were given to the President's War Relief Control Board for distribution?"

"Yes."

"The contributions from his organization were not made directly to the refugees, correct?"

"Correct. But we're also trying to find out who approved those payments in the government. They have some questions to answer."

"Why was the Immigration Service willing to approve the payments?"

"We'd like to know why."

"Could it be the Spanish refugees only had the clothes on their back and needed the help?"

"We're not interested in providing support and solace to Communist sympathizers."

"Doesn't the First Amendment's clauses regarding 'free speech' and 'peaceably to assemble' protect refugees as well?"

"Objection. The Committee is not on trial today."

"Mr. Ryan, I was waiting for you to comment on Mr. Rogge's line of questioning but since you waited until now, the objection is denied. Mr. Thomas, please answer the question."

"By giving these particular refugees financial support, we are increasing the risk they will take actions to overthrow our government."

"Do we prosecute people for their thoughts, Mr. Thomas?"

"When they're thinking of corrupting our Democracy, I think we should."

"But is thought policing lawful?"

"Emergencies require extraordinary measures."

"No more questions, Your Honor."

"Mr. Ryan, care to re-direct?"

"No, Your Honor."

"Do you have another witness?"

"I call to the stand, Dr. Edward K. Barsky."

The bailiff asked, "Do you swear to tell the whole truth and nothing but the truth, so help you God?"

"I do."

"Dr. Barsky, have you complied fully with the subpoena the Committee sent you?"

"No. Not yet."

"Will you?"

"The list the committee has requested is so extensive, I can't predict when copies of all of the materials will get shipped to the Committee."

"No further questions, Your Honor."

"Mr. Rogge?"

"Dr. Barsky, does the Joint Anti-Fascist Refugee Committee hold meetings to discuss the advantages of Communism?"

"No."

"Does your refugee committee require the refugees to become card carrying members of the Communist Party?"

"No."

"Has the American Communist Party even made contributions to the Refugee organization or paid the salaries of any staff members of the organization?"

"No."

"How do the refugees from the Spanish Civil War identify themselves then?"

"Most identify as Catholics."

"Why?"

"Spain was a monarchy with ties to the Vatican."

"Why did Spanish Loyalists accept help from the Soviet Union?"

"The United States had a foreign policy of neutrality in the 30's despite Great Britain's declaration of war against Germany after they sank the S.S. Athena."

"They would have accepted help from other nations?"

"Objection: conjecture."

"I'll allow, Mr. Ryan. The witness spent three years in Spain unlike the rest of us."

"The Soviet Union's offer of help was their last resort."

"Thank you. No more questions, Your Honor."

"Re-direct, Mr. Ryan?"

"No, Your Honor."

"In an effort to get this case to the jury this afternoon, let's begin attorney summations. Mr. Ryan."

"Thank you, Your Honor. This is a simple verdict to deliberate. The Committee subpoenaed Dr. Barski, he appeared before the Committee without fully complying, and then presented the Committee with the ruse his Board of Directors prevented him from presenting the documents the Committee requested. In essence Dr. Barski defied the subpoena. You must find him guilty."

"Mr. Rogge…"

"We've established the Committee's subpoena was created in falsehoods about the refugees which put the House Un-American Activities Committee in conflict with the First Amendment and three Supreme Court cases. Those cases checked Congress' use of its standing against individuals when legislation was not being created on an aligned issue.

For all these reasons, we ask you to find Dr. Barsky innocent. Thank you."

"Members of the jury, I'm going to release you to the jury room to choose a foreman and to go over the rules for your deliberation. Take a vote to see where you are on this case and if you don't agree, tell the Bailiff, and consider yourself in recess until 8a.m. tomorrow. Bailiff…"

The jury exited. When they were gone, Judge Murray shared, "Ladies and Gentlemen, thank you for your earnest work today. Our courts bring the public intimately in touch with our system of laws. Defendants get a fair hearing and the prosecutor representing the community tries to sanction lawbreakers. This courtroom is the heart of Democracy. Because I asked the jury to take an initial vote, please go no further than the hallway outside this courtroom in case the jury brings a verdict tonight. We'll let you know as soon as we know. We are in recess."

The three of us stood up, took a deep breath, and Edward asked, "Rest room?"

John led us to a backstage area. After personal time, nearby comfy leather chairs collected us.

"Where can I drop you tonight, Ella," John asked.

"DuPont Circle is closer than the office. Drop me at the garage."

"The garage?" Edward asked with a smile.

"Her boyfriend's parents own a car repair shop."

"Terrific. I wish it was in New York. Vita has been pestering me to get our car a tune-up."

We smiled.

"Where are you taking me for dinner tonight, John?" Edward asked assuming a conviction was delayed.

"Ben recommended a place which has great brisket."

"Lovely. Are the Washington Senators in town?"

"I think they're in Cleveland," I reacted. I grabbed a thoroughly read 'Washington Post' from a nearby table and checked the sports section. "Yes, they're in Cleveland," I reported.

"Bad timing," Edward reacted sarcastically.

We laughed.

A Bailiff walked in. "No verdict tonight. See you tomorrow."

We gathered our belongings and our box of files and John drove me to Marion's apartment.

Chapter 18

I waved to Marion's dad and his mechanic, stopped to pass the time of day with his mother, and caught up with him as he was about to put dinner on the table.

"Hello, Honey…" I intoned as our eyes met. I passed on a hug to avoid the spill-stained apron he was wearing.

"How far did Edward's trial get?"

"The judge managed to charge the jury before calling a recess. He asked the jury to poll before they left for home but there was no verdict."

"How was Edward?"

"Stoic. He was more interested in how life was proceeding for everyone else."

"Mr. O. John Rogge?"

"He's remarkable. His questions were sewing reasonable doubt in the jury's mind and appeal possibilities for the appellate division upon review."

"It's a tough hill to climb. They never responded to the subpoena." Marion paused to pour me a glass of wine. The food steamed on the plate in front of me. I had nothing about which to be positive regarding case. Marion sat down and put a forkful of chipped beef on toast in his mouth.

"When are you scheduled to visit Edward in prison?"

"Day three."

"Who's going to drive you to his penitentiary?"

"Columbia Private Investigators, who helped us at the House Un-American Activities Committee hearing."

"I like a security officer taking you there. What materials can you get accepted by a prison inspection?"

"Letters, messages, commissary money, photos, books, magazines, and newspapers. I'll have a nice box for him. Vita will come down for a visit soon after."

They ate and cleaned up the dishes.

Ella had a little corner in Marion's closet where she kept a couple of work shirts and a dress. In one half of a drawer in a chest, she had lingerie so she could stay over and go to work from his place. It was one of those nights.

"There's a little less anxiety for you here, closer to the office, and with me," he suggested as I snuggled in next to him. To be cooler, he was in boxers and an 'A' shirt. An oscillating fan collected slightly cooler air from outside. "You've lost in court before and you knew this one would be an uphill climb."

"Yes, but like every case, someone's thumb is on the scale."

"I know the feeling."

"Rogge's line of questioning could get a better reception someday at the Supreme Court."

"Replace a justice and the pendulum starts to swing back."

"I plan on being a sore loser, always working for a day when life is better. I can afford to be feisty because we found each other," I observed quietly.

"Goes double for me," he murmured lifting my body up from his side, cradling me across his body, lifting my face to his. We kissed. The conversation was over.

Tomorrow would be stark for us, but time alone like the current moment transcended the evil in the world.

~*~

"Thank you for being prompt this morning," Judge Murray greeted us. "I believe we are properly gathered, so we're going to send the jury off to deliberate. Members of the jury, you will be given an envelope with the choices you have for a verdict. You will discuss how you see this case. Your foreman will fill out the appropriate verdict form and alert the Bailiff. Bailiff, you may take the jury out."

They filed out.

"Mr. Rogge and Mr. Ryan, please remain within the courthouse letting the officers of the court know how to find you. We are in recess."

Rogge led us to the building's basement cafeteria. It was all but empty at 9:30 in the morning. We got coffee and settled into a booth.

"Your practice is in New York City, John?" Edward asked.

"Yes, I'm mostly doing real estate law these days but I'm always willing to take cases like yours until we counter America's populism."

"It's a pretty deep vein in the culture," Edward countered.

"There are leaders who know how to call out our better angels."

"Stevenson?"

"There's a younger generation coming up the ranks who are much more charismatic and fluent in a new language of politics filled with idealism."

"Someone to appeal to Ella?"

"Ella will hold office someday. She's the type we see rising; young, educated, quick to express a vision of governing co-equal Black and white."

"Is elected office what you're dreaming about, Ella?"

"Couldn't have said it better myself," I replied, smiling.

"Tell him about your wills and successions project," John coaxed.

"What's this…?"

"Seven Negro law firms in D.C. are collaborating to encourage our community to transfer our wealth to the next generation through wills and business succession plans."

John smiled.

"A spectacular idea."

"Think of the building up of the community which would result, Edward. Ella's community would instantly identify with a political candidate who communicates optimism. As well, they'll be able to contribute to his campaign."

"Who is this superman?" Edward asked.

"I don't have a clue, but he'll come out of the generation of men and women who fought in Spain and later around the world for FDR."

"I hope you're correct."

"I think Adlai will have a tough time with General Eisenhower and who knows how long the Republicans will prevail but there's a voice for a new, positive non-populism approach to governing who will emerge."

The dialogue between Edward and John was scintillating, two heavyweight thinkers of their own generation. I think I filled their coffee cups twice while they mapped out the future of the American presidency.

A Bailiff stepped into the cafeteria.

"Mr. Rogge?"

"Yes, sir."

"We have a verdict."

We proceeded toward the courtroom. There was no conversation now.

Within ten minutes we were at the defense table when the prosecutor walked in. The Bailiff announced the judge and he and the rest of us settled into our seats.

The jury returned and was seated.

"Mr. Foreman, do you have a verdict for me."

"We do, Your Honor."

The verdict paperwork was passed to Judge Murray and after he read it, he handed it back to be read by the Foreman.

"We find Dr. Edward K. Barsky guilty of one count of Contempt of Congress."

There was a murmured reaction to the verdict, the three of us stepped closer to each other but were interrupted by the judge.

"Order, please. The court thanks our jury for their focused deliberations. Their work is now completed. Bailiff, please escort the jury out."

Once the jury was gone, the judge announced, "Dr. Barsky, I sentence you to six months at the Federal Penitentiary at Petersburg, Virginia, your sentence to begin immediately. Bailiff, remove the prisoner."

Edward quickly took charge. "Thank you for everything you've done for me. You've both been superb but this is the best way to protect the people my organization serves," Edward explained as the handcuffs were snapped around his wrists behind his back.

"I'll be down to see you, Monday. I'll have a care package," I reminded him.

"Thanks," he replied with a smile.

"Goodbye, Edward. We're going to appeal," but they walked him off before another word could be spoken."

"Noel, this trip is a haul," I called up from the back seat.

"We should have you home by supper."

"They're not going to let me talk to Edward for long anyway, are they?"

"No. He's a convicted prisoner, after all."

"At least I can tell him it was you who drove me over."

"Thanks."

The countryside rolled by as I reflected on everything I'd been through in my short career as an attorney and the momentous changes in my immediate future.

The hard part going forward would be the grind of slowly building toward our goals as a couple.

After a little over two hours, we arrived at the Petersburg penitentiary. Noel carried the box with Edward's materials into the processing area.

"Good morning, how can I help you," an older man in a guard uniform asked me.

"I'm Ella Moses. I'm the attorney of Dr. Edward K. Barsky who is a new inmate. This is a letter from one of my partners vouching for my identity along with my Bar Association ID."

"Thank you. This box of materials are for Mr. Barsky?"

"Yes."

"Okay. We'll start the inspection and we'll try to get it done before your session is over."

"Thank you."

He walked away. Noel and I sat on a nearby bench. Although we were in an entrance area, a variety of noises filtered toward us. We were silenced by the realities of where we were. I took a quick glimpse at my watch when the officer returned. It had been thirty minutes.

"You can come back now. Please wear this name tag. Your visit is only twenty minutes once it begins. Expect Ms. Moses back in an hour," he advised Noel.

"Thanks, Noel," I remarked thankful for his protection and driving help.

"Happy to help."

The guard passed me off to someone on the other side of a door and we walked a good distance where I was passed off again and escorted into a waiting area with a window where I could see one other inmate seated at a small table speaking to a visitor. About another dozen tables waited empty.

As Edward was led into the room, I was allowed to enter, too. His guard gave us the rules. "No touching, you have twenty minutes. If the prisoner becomes agitated, the interview will end." He walked away to stand against a wall near us.

"Thanks for the box of reading material. I feel like a rich man."

"How is it here?"

"Not fun but livable." There aren't many Jews, so I'm a bit of an oddity."

"I hope they won't be intimidating."

"I've already promised to help a few well-known characters to take advantage of the library and the news has gotten around."

I laughed.

"Has Vita scheduled a visit?"

"I haven't been here long enough for a message to filter to me."

"Do they know you're a physician?"

"The guards know and they asked me if I would spend time in the infirmary and I agreed."

"It sounds like you're okay."

"The books and the writing material will be a big lift until Vita can make it."

"I'm going to stay in touch with your wife to coordinate her stay with Ben and to stagger my visits with hers."

"Thanks. Can I write you with a list of things you can bring me?"

"Anytime." I called out to his guard, "Can I give him my business card?" The guard walked over, inspected the card, and handed it back to me. "Yes, you can give your card to him."

"I especially appreciate the stash of stamps and the steno pads should I feel like writing a novel, like 'My Hard Time in the Federal Pen.'"

I laughed.

"I hope you don't have too many moments begging to be retold."

"Me either," he chuckled. "I'm hoping these few months will protect all our refugees. More members of my board may be jailed, but in the end the financial support they received will not be in jeopardy."

"It's a pretty stiff cost…" I ventured.

"In comparison to their displacement, pain of war, and probably never seeing their home country again, these months are nothing."

"As time goes on, we hope you'll stay in touch with Ben. We want to back you up anyway we can."

"You are exceedingly kind. Tell me more about your wills project."

"In recent history, families without wills tended to be victimized by unscrupulous agents promising to guide them through probate but bilking them of their funds instead. With the protection of a will this is less likely and any funds available lift the next generation."

"To some of us, this is something our families have taught us but this is not the case for all."

"We already have a robust business community in D.C. but passing wealth to the next generation can only make our Negro community stronger."

"I agree…"

"Dr. Barsky."

"Yes, Carl?"

"Your visiting time is up."

"Thank you, Carl."

"He called you doctor," I whispered.

"I wrote a prescription for his gout."

"Please take care of yourself, Edward."

"You too, Ella."

The guard walked him out and I found my exit and was walked out of the prison. Noel was right there to meet me as I emotionally exhaled.

"Tough visit?" Noel asked gently.

"It hurts to see such a principled man have to go through this."

"He didn't leave us in our time of need in Spain and he's still protecting the refugees struggling here," Noel observed.

"Were you wounded in Spain?"

"His hospital staff patched me up a couple times. Nothing major but his doctors and nurses didn't have to be there. He doesn't have to be here."

"You've got it right."

Noel opened the backseat door for me. I climbed in.

"Ella, my office researched a couple of restaurants where we'll be welcome."

"Good. Strangely, I'm hungry."

He started the drive home and I couldn't help but imagine what Edward's living situation was like with so much metal and brick in the construction of a prison. I had a hard time getting my first prison experience out of my head. Noel was using his road map to start our return trip. He was going back a slightly different way to find the restaurant recommended to him.

He passed me a mason jar of water, as he had in the morning, so I could quench my thirst.

Finally, I removed a notebook from my bag so I could write a summary of the visit for Ben, Mr. Cedric, and John Rogge. It took me a while to get started but the details began to flow. As I was finishing, Noel reported, "Our restaurant is coming up."

"Oh, good. I'm so hungry."

He navigated into a gravel parking lot. The eatery had once been a classic diner with a chromed front but sometime along the way an addition had been built behind it to double the seating area and create a larger kitchen.

Noel led me in, ever vigilant.

"Table or booth?" an older woman asked.

"A booth," Noel replied. He sat facing the door.

A waitress quickly approached after we were seated. "Something to drink?"

"Black coffee," Noel replied.

"An RC."

Inspecting the menu, I found an odd combination plate which sounded perfect; two fried eggs over hard, bacon, grits with a home-made sticky bun. Noel ordered a hamburger, fries, and Cole slaw.

"Tell me about your family," I asked my hard as nails driver.

"I married a Spanish girl I met when I was serving in the civil war. I helped her, her parents, and a brother and sister to immigrate. My wife and I live in D.C. Her family settled in New York. We have a girl and a boy."

"Lovely."

"Is your family experiencing harassment from the red-scare folks?"

He laughed.

"We're taught to be invisible," he advised smiling cynically.

"My mouth runs loose. I'd be in trouble all the time."

He laughed again.

The waitress brought the food.

Noel made me take a taste of his Cole slaw. I offered him a corner of my sticky bun. We both bought sticky buns to go.

We were back in the car, spoiled by the cooking and focused on getting home. I was able to think about my wedding to do list. There were some items which needed my attention soon.

Chapter 19

Six months later…

Unc and Auntie Flora helped me down the staircase of our apartment house in my wedding dress. Well-wishers stood in their doorways calling out congratulations, some of the older women with tears in their eyes. My exit onto the stoop caused more reactions, collecting praise and jeers. Some men thought I could have done better with them. William glared at them as he held the door open for me. Tucked inside the car, he joined me in the back seat.

Janice Fellows, Veronica Forman, and Violet Baker stood up for me.

As we walked into the back of the church, Marion and Wills Project lawyers Spencer and Adam were standing up front with Pastor Crossley.

The congregational choir sang an arrangement of 'Oh Happy Day.'

Finally, the pianist played the wedding march and my two ladies lead me, Owen, and Unc down the aisle. I improvised with two important men escorting me. My father had not come in from Vegas. My mom was sitting on the aisle in the front pew tears streaming down her face.

In the excitement of what Marion and I were doing, I only remembered one paragraph from Pastor's sermon.

"Ella and Marion have so much love for each other it spills over onto whomever they encounter. They work hard to lift everyone to new heights."

The pressure was really on us now.

The choir sang "God is My Strong Salvation."

Pastor invited us to exchange our vows. We both were crying as we did and a lot of people in the pews were crying as well. We managed to get the words out and Pastor pronounced us. He gave us permission to kiss. We did with tears staining each other's cheeks.

Pastor prayed over us and the congregation and we were totally swept up in our happiness.

The last hymn was "'My Life Flows On in Endless Song' above earth's lamentation, I catch the sweet, though far off hymn that hails a new creation. No storm can shake my inmost calm while to that Rock I'm clinging, Since Christ is Lord of heaven and earth, how can I keep from singing."

We picked up a nearby hymnal and sang it with our family and friends.

The organist played a very jazzy rendition of "Soon and Very Soon" and we greeted everyone as we proceeded down the aisle. Our wedding party joined us and we created a receiving line which guided everyone down into the church basement for a meal.

The celebration continued until we said goodbye to our last guests.

Ten years later…

Edward Barsky had lost a Supreme Court Case, his license to practice medicine, eventually regained his license, and was a physician for several union healthcare systems in New York City.

Men and women from the Joint Anti-Fascist Refugee Committee's board also served relatively short prison terms in federal prison for failing to respond to the House Committee on Un-American Activities' subpoena.

Watkins v U.S. redefined the freedom to associate and the limit on Congress to summon citizens as witnesses where pending legislation was not aligned.

Joseph McCarthy had been dead for three years.

Marion and I had added a daughter to our family and another baby was on the way.

We lived above our law firm not far from DuPont Circle where we, two recent Howard Law graduates, two typists, a receptionist, and William worked.

Unc and Aunt Flora lived in the flat above us on the third floor caring for Hattie, getting her to kindergarten, and preparing her to be a big sister.

One of the candidates for president for the Democratic Party was a young, handsome fellow from Massachusetts named Kennedy. He made me think of O. John Rogge's prediction years ago.

The civil rights era had blossomed into a movement, Dr. King was very active, and we referred to ourselves as African Americans.

Marion focused on Real Estate law, I had become a probate attorney who also did a ton of wills and business succession work. One of the new attorneys worked with me. The second work with Marion.

William, as I had promised him, was our security guy and master of ceremonies guiding clients to the appropriate attorney in the firm. He couldn't stand a tie, but he liked a vest worn over a white business shirt. He had also started to date a young woman who worked at The Crab Shack.

We were on good terms with our former firms and sometimes picked up work from them. Cedric, Brown & Jacobs' name hadn't changed but Mr. Brown had died, Mr. Cedric was retired, coming into the office some days, and Ben was the managing partner. He had brought in some new talent hoping to keep the firm going.

"Ella, this is Betts."

"Yes, Honey?"

"I've got a call for you from Senator Edward Brooke. Can you take it?"

"By all means." Marion and I had met Senator Brooke at a fund raiser for D.C.'s Special Needs Adoption agency. He had been told of our wills project and wanted to meet us.

"Senator Brooke, how delightful to get your call."

"No, Ella, I'm lucky to get through to you, busy as you are."

"My time is your time, Senator."

"I'm happy to hear you say so. Can I crash your schedule this morning? I've got a meeting at the White House and the Senate's in session later today."

"Of course."

"See you in an hour."

I couldn't even talk this development through with Marion. He was helping a client get through the local zoning maze to build a new office building on Pennsylvania Avenue. I walked out to Betty and William.

"Senator Brooke is stopping in this morning."

"Wow, he's handsome," Betty reacted.

"He certainly is. He may be accompanied by a couple of people. William, this man is a Senator, so make him welcome and make sure I have enough chairs in my office for this meeting."

"I understand, Ella. We've had famous guests here before."

"Okay. Betts, please let the rest of the office know what's up."

"Yes, indeed."

Luckily, I usually didn't have court dates or will postings on Tuesdays. I was in the office. I worked on some files I needed to get to the Clerk of Courts. I got lost in my work and my desk ended up like a movie set dresser had prepped my office for a scene from "Adam's Rib." Of course, my desk remained disheveled when William rapped on my open door with Senator Brooke and two aides.

"Ella, Senator Brooke and his assistants are here for their appointment."

"Thank you, William. Welcome Senator, gentlemen."

"Hi, Ella. This is Steve Bertram and Mike Ewing, two of my staff members."

"Nice to have you here, Coffee? Glass of ice water?" I asked.

"Water would be great."

"William?"

"Coming right up," William replied.

"How can I help you, Senator?"

"I have a former colleague from the Senate, Vice-president Richard Nixon who wants to help President Eisenhower pick some people for open judicial seats which would help get votes if Nixon was the Republican nominee for President."

"There are a number of lawyers who are registered Republicans I could suggest," I offered.

"But Nixon wants to seem moderate so he's recruiting for progressives."

"I could offer you some names of a liberal persuasion as well," I suggested smiling.

"Actually, Ella, I'm here to recruit you."

I sat back and replayed his last statement. After a pause, I replied, "Vice president Nixon doesn't want a Black, female probate judge…" I reacted with a laugh.

"I think it's a masterstroke appointment which could help get Nixon elected by outmaneuvering a Democratic opponent."

"But Senator, what happens to you if the Democrat wins? Your party will be tough on you."

"Nixon will win. Besides, I only want good people in D.C. courts. If Dick has overthought this appointment to your advantage, I'll be happy I helped you either way. You will be a judge much longer than Nixon could be president and your record will make me appear brilliant," he commented smiling.

"Unimpeachable logic but I'm only 35."

"I don't think your youth disqualifies you. I've got to leave for the White House, right now. Tell me you're leaning strongly to let Eisenhower appoint you."

"I'm leaning, hesitantly."

All three men laughed.

"I can go to the White House with your name?"

"Yes. People will think you've lost your mind."

"We'll see who official Washington thinks is daft, you, Nixon, or me." We all laughed. "Thanks, Ella. I'll let you know how it goes."

"Thank you," I replied shaking my head as I walked them out."

It was my night to pick up Hattie from Unc and Aunt Flora. We passed the time of day with my wonderful surrogate parents. They were thrilled to have our daughter under their care.

Hattie and I sat and talked for a while as we often did. She sang a made-up song up against my belly to her new sibling and later sat at the kitchen table with a coloring book and some crayons.

I prepped some barbeque we had purchased from a restaurant we liked who had a take-out window. I broke some lettuce, chopped some onions, carrots, and tomatoes throwing a salad dressing together in a bowl. Hattie chose the canned vegetable side. Everything was simmering on the stove when I could hear someone running up the stairs to the apartment. He used a key to enter. Hattie yelled in pure joy. It was Marion, out of breath and wide-eyed.

"What did Edward Brooke want?"

~*~

It was a bit of a wait for the White House. In the meantime, our son, Franklin, was born. Franklin Owen Forman joined his adoring sister and gob smacked parents in the middle of election season.

As if on cue, President Eisenhower appointed me a judge in the Probate Court of the D.C. circuit. There was an after-hours party in our law office. William played bartender, my staff managed the food catering, and about three hundred of our 'closest' friends stopped by to celebrate. Our children slept blissfully in the third-floor apartment and we sent Unc and Aunt Flora plates of food and sherry.

By election day, we were forced to rent the store next door, creating a hallway between the existing office and the addition. Our staff increased including an old friend from our wills, coalition, Adam.

"We boasted quietly to each other we would make this life happen," Marion reminded me as Hattie slept nearby and my husband cuddled our newborn. "I didn't know I'd ever feel this feeling," he admitted.

"What feeling, Honey?"

"I thought loving you was the greatest love," he confessed.

"There's something bigger than us?" I quietly replied playing his fool.

"With these two in my arms, I am overcome with a love huger than us."

"But it's us plus the two babes, isn't it, that makes a love too big to calculate."

"That's it exactly. We've acted out our goal by turning the gifts of our ancestors into a new business, but we also gave our community these two new heroes."

"Think how proud we'll be when this young woman and young man take their places as adults," Marion imagined.

"I'll hardly be able to stand it."

Epilogue

On the sixteenth of May 2012, I was sitting on the dais at the Howard University Law School Commencement dutifully listening to the speakers ahead of me. At eighty-four years old, I had been invited by my Alma Mater to address the graduating class. Reminiscing was inevitable and I held in one hand the figure Marion had carved of himself before we were married. I needed him to be with me to give me courage to get up and speak not having the strength I once had. Bull Dog, his hands resting on a cane was sitting next to my granddaughter, Gloria, to the right of the stage. His white hair, beard, and dark blue suit reminded me of Owen Townsend, my friend at the McCarthy hearings.

I had two speeches on my lap. One was scholarly. The other was emotional. I wrote two of them not knowing which Ella would win the dementia tug of war.

The President of the Law school approached the lectern.

"Class of 2012, it is with great pride I introduce to you a treasured alumna of our school. Judge Forman has a distinguished career as a Circuit Court jurist in the District of Columbia. Many

Howard Law students have benefited greatly in her classroom as an adjunct member of our faculty. She lived the law during turbulent times and her wisdom is sought out by many. Please help me welcome, your 2012 commencement speaker, Judge Ella Forman."

A warm round of applause greeted me as I stood to speak to these graduating third years, their family, friends, and their faculty.

"Thank you, President Wilson for your invitation and your introduction. Class of 2012, I am indeed honored to have this opportunity to speak to you at your commencement. You and your families should be exceedingly proud of the major accomplishment you have attained. I congratulate you."

Appreciative applause responded to my opening.

"I must apologize to you ahead of time and warn you at eighty-four years of age, a great deal of my early experiences in Holly Springs, North Carolina has flooded my brain lately. I have been able to remember the advice of my grands and great grands from when I was a toddler. One message resonates today and I wanted to share it with you."

I paused for dramatic effect. "Don't be a horse's ass."

A reaction of surprise, laughter and discomfort emanated from the crowd.

"From the reactions of the faculty behind me, there now may be some regret about inviting me here today."

Laughter broke out.

"There may have been too many Sloe gin fizzes imbibed those first few years at Cedric, Brown, and Jacobs."

There was some tittering from the women among the graduates.

"I saw what you just did ladies. I have some specific advice for you after the ceremony." More general laughter from the women in the hall.

"We've all had instances of horse's assery in our careers. My era of blind fool arrogance lasted almost ten years. You don't need to confess yours. You may be too idealistic to have had an egotistical disease. Yet. I'm still knocking around so when I see horse's assery coming from you, expect the irate email."

They laughed.

"I'm serious. Before too long you could be on the staff of a member of the House. Ten years from now guiding a member of the Senate. If I find you advising them to pull some horse's assery stuff, you will hear my raggedy, death-rattly voice on your phone."

"Strange political behaviors continue to impact our community. We must remember President Obama is not going to be in office forever. You may be advising cabinet staff, governors, or even one of the next presidents and if you are part of some horse's assery stunt, you will read me bitching about you from the op ed page of the Washington Post."

There was laughter and a variety of other positive reactions from the graduating lawyers and their families.

"Worst of all, if I come to know you have damaged The Constitution through some horse's ass stunt or obstruction or suspect legislation or other nefarious sedition, I will claw my way out of my frosty grave, go to your house, and deliver a night visitation on you which would make any British writer of Christmas theater cringe."

The room erupted.

As the room almost settled down, I added, "Dickens never had to deal with this North Carolina zombie." The room blew up again.

I stood back and let the pandemonium return to almost quiet.

"African Americans built this country, helped to save it time and time again, have led it once as President and will lead it again as President, but you know…," I paused so they were all ready for the punch line… "the leaders for and the protectors of the rule of law for the next sixty years are in this room. There is no greater role to have in this country than to defend The Constitution."

Applause rolled.

"2012 class," I announced softly, "of the Howard University Law School," I paused again… "congratulations."

I carefully eased myself from the podium to sit back down, taking in the eyes of mostly stunned faculty faces although the youngest faculty members were on their feet. I sat down and the students and many family members were standing. Some were calling for me to say more. I remained seated. Class leaders were upset the President was not reacting to my speech. One young man emerged out of the crowd and invited me to join the graduating lawyers on the floor of the hall. I did. He gave me his chair and knelt beside me as the lawyers received their JD. I was busy giving high fives as third years exited around me.

After the benediction, I faced the throng around me and was surrounded by third years and their parents. I signed autographs and traded stories. Eventually, my granddaughter and Bull Dog joined the well-wishers suggesting I should take my leave. Gently, she guided me to the appropriate exit on Bull Dog's arm. I left Howard University, never again to return.

Historical Notes

The Burl Ives interview before the House Un-American Activities Committee was scheduled after Dr. Edward Barsky was referred to the Justice Department. I reversed the order to enhance my story.

While I depict Ella Moses operating as a full, fledged lawyer in 1952 and even though Howard University Law School matriculated attorneys since the late 19th Century, African Americans were not admitted to the

Bar Association in the District of Columbia until 1959. The fictional Ella was admitted immediately after graduating from Howard Law into the African American created National Bar Association, established in 1925.

The term Negro was used as an omnibus designation for African Americans in 1952. It is used in this book until the Civil Rights movement is in full swing.

"In 1950, after three years of unsuccessful legal appeals, the [Joint Anti-Fascist Refugee] Committee's entire Executive Board was jailed. Barsky received the most severe sentence. It was the biggest single incarceration of political prisoners in America during the early Cold War. Upon release, Barsky lost his right to practise medicine." *A Blot Upon Liberty,* Phillip Deery

Kevin Phillips, in his 1991 book "The Politics of Rich and Poor," reports that there were 27,000 African American millionaires in 1953. There were one and a half million millionaires in the United States in 1991 and even more today.

Eric Von was a radio personality and call-in host in Milwaukee, Wisconsin for many years who one of his biographers described as an extremely welcoming host. He had a skill for interviewing guests with wide perspectives on life, often different than his African American listening audience. He died in 2016 at the age of 58.

In 1852, Frederick Douglass wrote an essay, "What to the slave is the Fourth of July," which was a thorough critique of the compromises hammered out in the U.S. Constitution in 1787. It was a must-read document for any African American attorney as soon as Black law schools began to open after the Civil War. I think it's a must read for any anti-racist of any ethnic derivation.

The made-up word 'draipse' used in Chapter 16 is an homage to Ken Curtis' portrayal of character, Festus Haggen, on Gunsmoke whose broken Texas Hill Country English always astonished the rest of the cast.

Acknowledgements

Angela Dennis' articled '6 Historically Black Beaches to Visit This Summer' was helpful in researching summer destinations for African Americans in 1952. Highland Beach, Maryland was the vacation destination for my main characters.

'A 28-Recipe Virtual Potluck to Celebrate Black History Month' by Meiko and the Dish, provided recipes for my characters to enjoy when growing closer over a meal.

The images on the covers of this book were provided by Spotmatik / Dreamstime.com, File IDs 25454744 and 25454808. "The persons in the images are models and there is no connection between the models and the characters in the book."

Isabell Felix, editor, reader, and consultant did an initial sensitivity reading of the original 20,000 words of this book and made significant comments and guidance. As a result, this book was heavily rewritten. Ms. Felix did not review the finished book. Any failures to follow her guidance that are found are mine alone.

Zo Trembley and Heidi Surprenant, members of OnWords, a writers' group I am a part of served as beta readers and offered many helpful suggestions as the book was written. I am beholden to them for their help. However, flaws in the final version of this book are mine alone.

The Congressional Record provided the verbatim interviews of Burl Ives and Dr. Edward Barsky, although Dr. Barsky's interview was edited by the committee before it went into the Congressional Record. Since the interviews are conversations from mid-century, some language and spellings are not the quality of an edited document. These anomalies were not corrected or edited but appear as they were originally submitted to the Congressional Record.

The sources for Adlai Stevenson's speech in Richmond during the 1952 election and the Civil Rights plank of the 1952 Democratic Party were referenced in the text of the story.

The dialogue from Dr. Barsky's criminal proceedings for Contempt of Congress was created by the author.

Author Biography

Many of my early books were historical romances set in the Hudson Valley of New York State during WWII. It was fun to return to another historical romance set in Washington, D.C. in 1952. I don't know if it's even legal to call a book set in 1952 a 'historical.' I don't know who to contact to get permission. It was a challenge to write African American characters but it's beyond time for white writers to immerse themselves in the Black experience and make the attempt to write that reality.

My characters are inspired by my four children, their significant others, and friends who continue to amaze me by their courage, intellect, and love. My personal understanding of love continues to be informed by my over thirty-year relationship with my wife, Shari.

I retired in October of 2016 and live in Southeastern Wisconsin. I work a part-time job as an early morning stocker for a large home store retailer, which I call my anti-dementia job. I freelance as a writer beyond novels and enjoy having much more time to write these days.

Visit Bob's webpage at: bobyoungauthor.com.

The following is the first chapter of the third mystery in the Ishraat Sarabhai Murder Mystery Series, "Ishraat's Doll Collection." This book is scheduled to be published in the first half of 2023.

Ishraat's Doll Collection

By Bob Young

Chapter 1

"Hi, Isaac."

"It's good to see you, Gopal."

"Did you have any problem finding this spot?"

"No. Your directions were terrific. This is a quiet location. Are we on the far northwest corner of the Cherokee Marsh Conservation Park?"

"You would think so, but my client found this parcel available to buy outside the marsh conservation area."

"A lovely find backed up against a wilderness area so close to town."

"That's why she pursued it," Gopal explained.

The ChemLighthouse investigator and the attorney from McCartney, Tormé, and Krall stood there for a while noticing the waterfowl, natural grasses, and nearby prairie soaking up the sunny, peacefulness.

"How's the new gig at Ishraat's firm going for you? Missing your gun belt and cruiser," Gopal teased.

The former cop laughed.

"I have a twitchy moment now and then when I go days on end with quiet. Don't get me wrong, her ability to run into trouble keeps me on my toes."

Gopal smiled.

"I'm happy she was able to add your experience to her team."

"It's a little bit of a luxury to have me on staff but I like the part of my job description that gets me out surveying sites. What was it you wanted me to look at?"

"It's down this deer path. What Sheila Goodwin wants to do on this property is to spread out groupings of houses and have a naturalist create trails to enjoy this edge of the marsh."

"Wow. Sounds lovely. Living right on the nature area."

"It's the global warming era alternative to living on the golf course," Gopal quipped.

"Right." They laughed.

"As Sheila walked the property, she found this location where something weird was seeping to the surface."

"Seeping?" Isaac questioned.

"I'll show you."

They walked along the edge of some marshy ground surrounded by a small grove of weeping willows beyond which a group of birches stood.

"This is an amazing natural site," Isaac noted.

"You can see why my client went crazy for the place but this has her jumpy." Gopal walked Ishraat's security chief away from the marsh to a dark colored, mucky puddle under a willow.

"Awful. Someone junked up this lovely, pristine area with their oil changes," Isaac complained.

"I don't know what it is," Gopal replied perplexed. "It could be a marshy addendum to Cherokee Marsh. It needs to be tested.

"I'll take some samples but it looks like there's garbage in this pit, too. Look at that smooth plastic in there."

"Yeah. I see that. Sad," Gopal reacted.

"Let me get my field kit out of the truck. I'd like to collect some of the crap put in this marshy ground."

"Looks like childish mischief," Gopal suggested.

"How close is the nearest neighborhood? What kind of a trek on a bike would it take to get here?"

"I'll research that."

It only took Isaac a couple minutes to pull the equipment he needed and return to Gopal.

"I'll start with the liquid samples and I'll retrieve debris from the dump site with this handy pickup and reach tool."

"Good thinking. I see the genius of having you on staff."

"I love evidence collection." He labeled the liquid samples and put them in his kit. "Okay. Time for the reach tool. A cheap beer can. Two cheap beer cans. Crushed water bottle, a piece of rope, and an empty shampoo bottle. Junk."

"Can you reach that smooth plastic?" Gopal asked.

"I'm going to use this branch to pull it closer. There's probably more junk in this pit. We'll see if it's worth it to do a full tilt excavation. It may take some heavy equipment to remediate this mess." Isaac used his reach tool to pull the plastic out of the muck.

"It's not a small piece of plastic," Gopal reacted.

As Isaac retrieved the object, it looked like a doll with a plastic bag around its neck.

"What the heck?" Isaac uttered under his breath.

"There's something in that bag, Copper."

Isaac struggled in Nitrile gloved hands to untie the knotted bag opening. After a minute, he managed it. He allowed the object in to drop onto the grass next to him. It was an envelope. The front of the envelope was face down. Out of habit, he turned it over. It was addressed to Ishraat Sarabhai at her personal address.

"Shit," the big ex-cop reacted.

Gopal jumped to stand over the unexpected artifact lying there. "I don't know what to do with such a bizarre find?"

"I'm calling Ish. She's got to tell me what my next move is." He called her office phone.

"Hi, Isaac," Ishraat greet her field investigator cheerily. "How's the site Gopal wanted us to see?"

"It appears we have an illegal dumping site within twenty-five yards of the marsh."

"Can't wait to test your samples."

"There's also debris in the muck that included a surprise."

"I don't need any surprises, Isaac," Ish teased.

"I'm sending you a photo," the ex-cop explained.

"I'm opening the photo…is that a doll…and a letter addressed to me?"

"Yes, Boss. The letter was inside a drug store bag tied around the doll's neck almost totally submerged in the muck."

"You two have to be kidding me. This is a joke, right?"

"It may be a joke. Give me permission to open your mail."

"Yes, of course, Isaac."

Still gloved he managed to pull up the envelope flap and ease out a single sheet of paper folded once. He saw the message and photographed it. "I'm sending a photo of the message."

"Okay…" Ishraat saw the photo arrive and opened it. In severe block print it read, 'We're watching…' In the next line was the word 'Not.'

That was it. "This is weird stuff. It's not the first interesting mail I've received working for ChemLighthouse."

"That's for sure," Isaac replied. Gopal laughed.

"The delivery method is unconventional. Call in the local police, show them the dump site, the debris, and the letter and come back with the samples."

"Right."

"Gopal can decide if the law firm or his client are going to file a complaint about someone creating a toxic waste site so close to a pristine habitat."

"We're on it."

"Thanks."

Ishraat texted Roberta Worthington and Sierra Doktor to join her at her pod in the middle of ChemLighthouse's chemical assay work room. Robbie was a close friend who stood up at Ish's wedding and Sierra was her CFO. She showed them the photos and gave them Isaac's report. Ish wanted help deciding if this discovery was worth any worry.

In the meantime, Gopal called his paralegal, Angelique, to help him figure out which police department served his client's property.

"I think Ms. Goodwin's lot is in the city of Madison but I'll look at the copy of her deed to make sure."

"Perfect. Call me back. I'm holding up ChemLighthouse staff here until we know who to call."

"I understand. I'll get back to you soon."

~*~

"It sounds like a crackpot who is mimicking a TV show they saw once," Sierra suggested.

"I agree. You've had a ton of visibility in the press this past year but let's see what Isaac wants to do."

"We have been careful. The local police will be involved chasing the polluters. I want to shrug off the hate mail as a gag. Let's not get derailed," Ishraat asserted.

"Sounds good," Sierra replied.

"Ishraat, Ms. Barnhart has arrived."

"Thanks, Caroline." She turned to her two confidents. "See you two later."

Ishraat got up to greet the manager of the second ChemLighthouse location soon to open in Beloit. The UW Chemistry Department had been going crazy with assay requests from the business community there and hired Carol Barnhart to lead a new site.

"Hi, Carol."

"Hello, Ishraat."

"We're so happy you decided to join us. You are such a talent."

"You're very kind to say so."

"Between your resume and your involvement in the LGBTQ community in Beloit, you are the total package."

"Ishraat, I appreciate your warm welcome but your fame has spread to Beloit, too. I don't have any sleuthing skills," she shared laughing.

"Good thing. Dr. Wagner and Dr. Benner can only handle one of me."

"I'm thrilled how much support you've committed to the new location. It makes our start up much less daunting."

"How's the contractor doing?"

"Thanks to the great work the city did converting the former factory to a business incubator, the contractor has been able to install power and data lines easily. They are a week away from starting the pod installation."

"That sounds great. How are interviews going?"

"We made an offer to a CFO candidate and a Production Manager. We're hoping they can start in a month."

"How's April?" Ish asked smiling.

"She's fabulous," Carol responded beaming.

"I was happy I got to meet her when I visited you last. Between her curator job at the Hendricks Center and her own art creations, she is a marvel."

"She's one of those people who can communicate so well through her art."

"She was amazingly generous to show me her studio at your place when you had me over for dinner."

"April's sometimes secretive about a work in progress but extremely open with her process. She loves to teach."

"I was blown away with her talent."

"Thanks. She enjoyed meeting you."

"You're going to plan today with Robbie and the two other team members who are going to put in a week with you later this month?"

"Yes. Ready to go."

Ish texted Robbie.

"Here's your crew," Ish noted.

"Great."

"Hi, Carol. Shall we meet in the breakroom?"

"Near the snacks? Sounds perfect," Carol quipped. All the women laughed.

~*~

Isaac backed the university police vehicle into Ish and Raj's garage after work. It was his job to protect her as she moved around the area.

Raj and Ishraat had recently married in Mumbai. Their wedding night had been marred by an attempt on her life. Isaac had thwarted that attempt.

She watched Isaac leave and the garage door closed securely. She stepped through the garage man door into the mudroom and set down her briefcase. She looked up to see Raj cooking something that smelled terrific.

"Have I told you lately that I love you?" she asked with a smile.

"Are you hungry?" Raj asked in response.

"Famished."

"Something to drink?"

"Yes. Today had bizarre moments."

"Uh oh."

Other books by Bob Young

Ishraat's Interrupted Wedding Night, murder mystery 2021

Ishraat's Long Night, murder mystery 2020

The Diamond Shaman, romance 2019

Evanescent Death, romance 2018

Mason's Taxi of Love, romance 2018

Kiki and Connor Are Both from Mars, romance 2017

Julia's Bombardier, romance 2017

The Last of Mrs. Workman, adult romance 2016

Escaping Jeremy, romance 2016

Crushed Love, Well Shaken, romance 2014

When Love Shaped Us, romance 2013

Made in the USA
Middletown, DE
24 September 2022